THE FIRST SERVANT

Alexander Jacobs

Prologue

A relentless heat wave smothered the river in a blanket of scalding sand, so the water that now trickled into Shallow Canyon drew all five hundred residents to gawk with joyous disbelief. Dirt cracked off faces unaccustomed to smiling while children splashed and adults prayed. The working canal promised to lift Shallow Canyon from the margins of the Defiant Empire after decades of obscurity.

As the day wore on, most miners wandered back to the fields, eager to resume their hunt. The older children retreated to the shade to complete their daily chores, leaving only the youngest to sit at the canal's edge and swing their legs over the growing current. By midday, all fled the heat aside from one child, Grey, who stayed even as the persistent warmth radiated into his legs and baked his covered head.

"Dinner's ready, boy," Isa said as evening approached. She hunched above her stewing pot and stirred the suspect liquid with a ladle that dwarfed Grey's bony arm. He sniffed and plugged his nose, a rude gesture that prompted Isa to laugh. "You're free to eat elsewhere. And sleep, too." When Grey didn't respond, she chuckled again and offered him a heaping pile of fish jerky.

As he gnawed at the strips of tough flesh, his thoughts turned to Madsen—his father. Dark-skinned and bald, the man had taken care of him well enough during the years they lived in Shallow Canyon. Did that mean Grey should love him? He searched for a hint of sadness, recalling the day he'd identified his father's lifeless body. Nothing arose. Isa blamed his absent grief on the trauma surrounding Madsen's death, yet Grey wasn't sure. He couldn't recall a moment of sadness, happiness, anger, or any other sentiment that Isa insisted were fundamental realities of being human.

A roaring swoosh startled Grey from his thoughts and sent him rushing outside, where he spotted boats barreling down the filled canal. Oars extended to scrape the canal walls, and soldiers leaped from the vessels, forming ranks at the outskirts of town. Grey counted over a thousand men, each boasting the First Servant's crest of twin fists shattering a coiled chain. To Grey, the men appeared glorious with their gleaming swords and stiff uniforms, but to Isa, they seemed tired and battle-worn. Many were unshaven and unwashed, and some wore blood-soaked bandages.

"You're from the Pillar," Isa said to the closest soldier.

The man nodded. "You should take your child and hide. We come for battle." He placed his calloused palm atop Grey's head and ruffled his soiled hair. "Our enemy surrounds the Defiant Empire, and the shifters descend from the north to capture our most vulnerable towns. Hide if you can, for the shifters do not take prisoners."

"Then the canal wasn't a good omen."

"No. Our engineers flooded the channel early to send soldiers. If we cannot hold Shallow Canyon, Arndak and Harkk itself may come under direct attack."

A whistle sounded, and the soldiers turned towards the dak fields and marched. "Pray that we return victorious," the soldier said over his shoulder, and Grey nodded, trying to remember any of the First Servant's prayers.

"Aren't you going to hide?" Grey asked Isa, who had

returned to her stew.

"No," she said with food in her mouth. "The shifters will discover us in any hiding spot. Let's eat and pray."

Grey shook his head and stood in the cooling evening air for a moment before deciding to join the Pillar soldiers out in the dak field. The tiniest spark of excitement ignited within his chest, and without knowing why, he wanted to kindle it into a roaring fire.

Shallow Canyon lay before him like a giant dust bowl, its edges hidden in the shimmering heat. Way across the dak fields, where his father had perished, the horizon darkened behind the Pillar soldiers. Grey picked a spot to watch the coming battle from atop a gentle slope, and he squinted to make out the incoming shifters.

The creatures separated from the horizon and streamed over the sand, stopping amidst a cloud of debris a hundred yards from the nearest soldier. Six spiked legs supported their flat, circular bodies, which matched the color and texture of sand with such accuracy that Grey struggled to guess their numbers. Echore, a mirrored sphere that passed overhead each night, rose above the shifter army, capturing their image with perfect clarity on its reflective surface.

The pending battle did nothing to shake Grey's calm. He understood the danger, but his inability to access emotions meant fear of death held no meaning in his unusual mind. The Pillar soldiers were not so lucky, for they quaked before their enemy in obvious fear, shaken by memories of past battles. Still, the shifters didn't attack until three Pillar soldiers leaped into the air to soar above the field in defiance of gravity. When they neared the enemy line, the shifters pounced, pushing off all six legs to scurry faster than Grey had seen any man sprint.

Brutish soldiers carrying wide shields strapped to each arm stepped forward to meet the shifters, while sword fighters struck between the shields, severing limbs and retreating behind their defenders. Overhead, the floating men lobbed rocks, which exploded when they neared the ground. Shrapnel tore through shifter flesh as the swordsmen and shieldmen continued to slice their way through their foes.

Although the Pillar deployed superior tactics, sheer numbers overwhelmed their shield-bearers. Soon, shifters breached the Pillar's defense and tore into vulnerable swordsmen with relentless precision. The battle turned, and Pillar soldiers retreated towards the canal to prevent the enemy from encircling their position. Shield-men grouped to the front, keeping the shifters back by pushing their shields out with impressive strength, sending shifter bodies flying. Soldiers with the metal balls strapped to their chests tossed them high into the air. When they crested, the soldiers made elaborate motions with their hands, and the metal balls shot off in unexpected directions, puncturing shifter flesh.

Grey admired the Pillar's confidence, for their organized retreat allowed them to protect their own while continuing to destroy the enemy. Then the ground lifted beneath the soldiers' feet, and a shifter rose underfoot. It dwarfed the others, towering above the battlefield and sending soldiers tumbling in every direction. In seconds, the Pillar's retreat devolved into a panicked sprint to the canal.

Idiots, Grey thought. Didn't they realize that running wouldn't save them? From his perch outside the battle, he judged the soldiers with emotionless clarity without realizing that years of war had already driven most of those men to their breaking point. A man can only watch so many friends die before his fear overcomes discipline.

Grey edged towards his village, but the sand beneath his bare feet exploded in a plume of dak, the blue aerostatic gas that his town's miners sought day and night. As he choked in mouthfuls of the deadly poison, he hoped with detached interest that Isa would emerge from the battle unscathed. But Grey didn't die. His vision cleared, and he stood in the scorched patch of sand.

The massive shifter loomed ahead, and a nervous energy ignited in Grey's neck, spreading into his back and moving forward until it consumed his chest. When he jumped, he soared above the giant shifter, landing on its back. He heard a soldier cry, "Look!" Grey slammed his tiny fist into the shifter's back, and the creature grunted under the blow. Grey's hand had punctured its armored flesh, letting loose a torrent of blood as red as any human's. Joy rushed through Grey's mind, and he reeled from the unfamiliar emotion. He wanted to experience more.

He dug his hand into the shifter's flesh, grabbing a strip of it and running along the length of its back. Its flesh peeled off like skin from a boiled tomato, and Grey dropped from its back with the meat in his hand. Blood soaked him from head to toe, infusing his nostrils with its intoxicating odor as the shifter collapsed in a pool of its own steaming guts.

Many soldiers cheered, and the other shifters halted their attack to watch their massive brother fall. The sight of Grey, a ten-year-old boy, killing such an enormous beast brought new courage to the Pillar men. They regrouped near the village and charged. The sword-men fought better, and the shield-men bashed and bullied the shifters. The fight was long, but their renewed efforts eventually repelled the shifter invasion.

Through all this, Grey stood amidst the ruin of the massive shifter. His heart beat with excitement, and an array of emotions too complex for him to understand played through his mind. The world had been colorless, but now it surged with vibrant hues that transformed his surroundings into a fresh nirvana of possibilities.

The same soldier who'd spoken to him earlier approached

Grey and said, "That was quite a performance." A deep gash ran the length of the soldier's arm, but he'd tied a bandage tight around his shoulder to slow the flow of blood. Grey allowed the soldier to lead him back to the canal, where he stripped and plunged into the cool stream. A minute of harsh scrubbing cleaned most of the blood, and since his only outfit washed down the canal, the soldier fetched him a spare uniform.

"He's a remarkable boy," the soldier said to Isa when Grey approached. Isa shrugged. "He must have inhaled a diluted bit of dak, which he used to defeat a shifter giant all by himself. I've lived through dozens of battles, but I've never encountered a boy more naturally gifted than Grey." Isa offered the soldier a disinterested glance before returning to re-light the flame beneath her stew pot. The soldier followed her and said, "We'd like to recruit him into the Pillar."

"It's up to the boy," Isa said, shrugging again. "He just stays with me."

"Wonderful!" The soldier capped his hands. "Grey, what do you think?"

Grey didn't respond, for a man descended from Echore as if walking down invisible stairs from the sphere's flawless surface. The First Servant's teachings explained that Echore held the banished gods of their past, but this man appeared human. His suit resembled a nobleman's attire, with a black waistcoat and a long tail that dragged across the ground. His skin, though, was as pale as lifeless flesh, and his cheeks were strikingly gaunt.

"You should kill her," the strange man said, motioning towards Isa. Grey looked at him, confused. "There's a poisonous root you could slip into her stew. It grows in the shade behind her pathetic hut. Slip it into her pot when she isn't looking."

"Grey," the soldier said, ignoring the odd nobleman. "Do

you want to come with me? We need soldiers like you to win the war."

"Murder him, too," the gentleman said. "He presumes to teach you? You could kill him now with your bare hands."

"Do you see…" Grey trailed off.

"See what?" the soldier asked, puzzled. He tried to follow Grey's unfocused gaze, but he saw only empty air. "You're exhausted. We'll discuss this later, after you've rested."

Grey nodded, turning to leave while Isa stayed to speak further with the man. Instead of returning to the canal as he'd intended, Grey circled Isa's hut. A handful of brown leaves protruded from the sand, and Grey pulled them into his hand. He touched their wicked purple roots, and without deciding to move, he snuck into Isa's hut while she was too busy conversing to notice.

The gentleman was sitting on the ground, his legs crossed. "Now drop them in," he said. "She won't catch them amidst all those rotten fish."

Grey's hand hovered above the pot. He realized that poisoning Isa was wrong, but his fingers quivered, then flexed open, allowing the roots to fall into the stew.

"Good," the gentleman said, and a rush of intense pleasure flooded Grey's senses. Pure joy mixed with utter relaxation to form an intoxicating cocktail of delight unlike anything Grey had ever experienced. He would do anything to hold on to the addictive sensation, which soon subsided, leaving him chilled to his core.

"You'll go with the soldier tomorrow," the gentleman said. Grey nodded.

By the time Isa died, crumpled in pain from an unknown ailment, Grey had already traveled with the remaining Pillar soldiers many miles from Shallow Canyon.

Chapter 1

Blue sky morning shone through a slatted window, the silence of dawn broken only by an occasional grinding of wheels from delivery carriages speeding past the tavern. Unwashed clothing covered the floor, while the only piece of furniture, a bed frame in a corner, held the room's longtime occupant—a boy, snoring through his fifteenth hour of sleep. Grey fought an unconscious battle to stay asleep, grasping with a weakening will at the dream keeping him in a state of blessed unreality. A nightmare by another man's standards, the dream soothed Grey, for even as he slept, he feared the absolute nightmare to which he'd awaken.

A gentle knocking at the window grew louder and louder until, with a great crack of splitting wood, the window swung inwards, glass panes shattering as they slammed into the brick wall. Another boy, holding a sledgehammer as large as his torso, vaulted into the room. Still, Grey slept, so the boy reached through the broken window, grasped a bucket of water mixed with acetone, and dumped its contents onto Grey's face.

The result was disappointingly mild. Grey rolled onto his side before swinging his legs off the bed and groaning into a sitting position. Though Grey looked like an average fifteen-year-old, his intruder was proud he'd uncovered the truth. At six feet, Grey's thin face bore freckles that stretched across the bridge of his nose, and his red hair hung in an unruly tangle above his creased forehead. But it was his eyes, large and filled with subtle shifts of color that varied depending upon the light, that hinted at his abnormality.

"Did you put paint thinner in that water, Marion?" Grey asked the boy.

"Water wouldn't have woken you," he said. At that awkward age of budding adolescence in which he was neither boy nor man, Marion's long limbs stuck out at odd angles from his still childlike torso, and his wide nose seemed determined to outgrow the rest of his face.

"I told you, never wake me—"

"Yes, yes, I know. But it's an emergency," Marion said. Before Grey could reply, he continued, "I rose early to fetch water for my ma's wash, and I walked by Lino's metalworking shed. Before you scold me, I realize it's not on the way… but I had to peek at the new swords before Lino ships them all to Harkk. Anyway, right before I opened the door, I heard a noise, and I snuck to the window. Guess what I saw?"

Marion paused, clearly waiting for Grey to ask a question. When he kept quiet, Marion released an exaggerated sigh. "Fine. I saw two bandits attacking Lino. So… you have to help!"

Marion looked with anxious expectation at Grey, who was struggling to distinguish the dream he'd been having from the boy in front of him. Ghostlike images drifted through the room, a persistent surge of subconscious imagery being pushed into his conscious mind. The amount of napthal he'd taken the day before made it difficult to grasp reality, though that was the entire purpose of drinking the stuff.

But now Marion had created a dilemma. The insular village tolerated Grey's presence because the bar owner

Reyes had promised to watch over him. Refusing to help Lino, a man of central importance to the entire village's economy, would wipe out all the goodwill he'd built over the past year. Besides, the other villagers would surely hear about it from Marion if he refused.

Damn my carelessness, Grey thought, recalling the vorster attack a couple of months ago. When a pack of the cunning creatures had attempted to sneak into the town under cover of darkness to raid food supplies for their colony, Grey had been gathering ingredients for Arlo's signature whiskey in the hay fields. He relied on the old medic's liquor recipes to satisfy the thirsty workers, but the ingredients weren't available in a small town like Faycliff. Marion had been playing in the field when Grey had disposed of the vorsters. There'll be no making him forget that incident, he thought.

"I'll come," Grey said finally.

"Great," Marion yipped, jumping into the air. "I'll get your sword." Before Marion moved his hand halfway to the nearby sheath, Grey had grabbed the boy's wrist, twisting just hard enough to cause the boy to cry but not hard enough to inflict any lasting damage.

Grey growled. "Don't."

Marion whimpered as several tears escaped his eyes before he blinked them away. Grey released Marion's thin wrist and pretended not to notice the tears. Though Marion was only two years younger than Grey, Faycliff's isolation left him innocent and protected from the shifter War.

"Shall we use the door?" Grey asked.

"What? Oh, yeah. No one was in the tavern at this hour, so I had to climb in through your window."

Grey shrugged, exiting the room and descending the solid oak stairwell into the dusty tavern hall. The owner, a thick stump of a man called Reyes, wouldn't arrive for many hours to serve thirsty workers from chilled barrels containing

Grey's brews. The glowworm bondmen dangling from the ceiling also awaited the opening hour before they'd light the space, so Grey tripped over toppled chairs and barstools on his way to the door. That damn Reyes never cleans up, he thought, but he chuckled at his anger. Who was he to judge, given his own lack of hygiene?

Outside, Grey broke into a jog, his stiff legs not quite in sync as the napthal worked its way out of his system. Marion ran alongside him, and Grey almost told the boy to return home before deciding it'd be no use. Better to keep the boy in sight than have him sneaking around. The smithy's shop stood near the tavern, since the town's planners built both buildings near the outskirts because of their occupants' propensity for generating noise.

Shops, houses, and other buildings huddled around the base of a silver cliff, which shielded the residents from the sun's hot rays. Barren desert surrounded the ridge, save for a single road bisecting the town and, of course, the still-dry aqueduct construction project. Grey surveyed the land for any unusual activity, but the morning's peace lay undisturbed, and he soon reached the doors of the metalworking shop.

The stone structure stood crooked against the sandy bluff, resulting from a faulty repair following a quake a few years back. The steel door, which was required by law to stay locked at all times, stood ajar. Grey motioned for Marion to stay, but the boy shook his head and continued to follow. Grey frowned, but he didn't stop him. If the boy wants to watch, then let him.

Grey pushed the door inwards and stepped into the dark. The noxious odor of metal mixed with blood struck his nostrils, and he soon found the source. The master metalworker Lino stood, shaking, near a rack of sparkling new weaponry facing the two bandits. He was bleeding from many nicks and cuts, some deep, though Grey noted with appreciation that the portly man still clung to his sword.

The creaking door drew the men's attention, and they spun to face Grey, who paused to assess the threat. Both were much larger than the average citizen, tall and bristling with tensed muscle. Their clothes hung like rags from their shoulders, much like Grey's own garb, and they each gripped one of Lino's longswords with a steady hand and evident expertise.

"Stay out of our way, boy," said the man to Grey's left. Just past his prime, the man's balding head and leathery skin suggested years of labor in the sun. Perhaps on the battlefield, Grey thought. He's old enough to have served many years in the Pillar. The other man was much younger, in his mid-twenties, and he raised his weapon, pointing the glinting steel at Grey's chest.

Ignoring the weapon, Grey said, "Return the weapons to Lino's rack and leave."

"What are you, the sheriff? You can't be thirteen. Now scram."

"I'm fifteen." Grey blinked, forcing himself to focus through the napthal. "And I'm not the sheriff."

"Well, neither are we. But we served our time in the Pillar, and look where it got us. We'll take a few of these fine swords as payment and be on our way."

"Go to another town. Steal their weapons. I don't care what you do elsewhere. Just don't do it here."

"Slit their throats," said a voice to Grey's right, and he groaned. As adrenaline forced napthal to drain from his system, the Gentleman appeared like clockwork. The razor-thin man leaned against an empty weapons rack, his stiff black suit without sign of dirt or wear, as usual. "I'll sit here and watch you murder them," he continued, crossing his legs.

"Be quiet!" Grey shouted at the invisible man. The older bandit frowned, wondering if Grey was crazy, but the younger man to Grey's right, filled with the confidence of an inexperienced brawler, thrust forward the sword he'd been pointing at Grey. He'd aimed for Grey's gut, and had the blade connected, the wound would have been fatal.

Grey sidestepped the blow and knocked aside the blade's flat edge with his hand. The man's eyes shot wide with surprise as the sword swung in a circle, and instead of releasing his grip, the man allowed the momentum to turn his entire body. Grey stepped on the man's calf. Bone crunched, and the man fell to the ground, squealing with pain.

Instead of turning to run, the older man adopted the standard combat stance drilled into every soldier in the First Servant's army. Oh, so you were part of the Pillar, Grey thought, eyeing him. With his sword raised in preparation to parry an incoming blow, the ex-soldier edged his way towards Grey. Grey lacked the patience to wait, so he grabbed the older man's hands around the sword's hilt and said, "I'll give you one more chance, man. Go. Take your injured friend." But battle rage already consumed the soldier's eyes, and Grey understood only violence would end the confrontation. So Grey pushed the man's sword up through his jaw. He kept going until the blade penetrated his brain.

The Gentleman cheered. "Let his blood stain the ground around his unworthy body."

Both men now lay at Grey's feet, one unconscious and the other dead. Grey looked at them with despair. Violence. I fled the Pillar to find peace, yet violence follows. He sensed Marion's eyes on him, appreciating the mixture of fear and wonder emanating from the teen's mind like a turbulent wind. He wondered how this moment would shape the boy, how seeing what pain one person could inflict upon another would change him. At least Lino had the good sense to pass out before the violence began.

"Kill the boy, too. He's not a worthy witness of your glory."

"Marion, tell the healers they're needed," Grey said, ignoring the Gentleman.

"What about the sheriff?"

"Yes, I suppose you'd better fetch him as well." Marion shot Grey a nervous glance before scurrying down the gentle slope towards town. Grey walked over to Lino, reaching to take his pulse. Strong, good. He's not seriously injured. Most of the wounds were shallow, though they'd need binding.

Grey contemplated dropping his new life and leaving Faycliff. After gathering his sword, no one would prevent him from hiking to another village on the outskirts of the Empire. He hung his head. With one bandit dead, even Faycliff's sheriff might consider it his duty to track Grey for answers or at least report Grey to the Pillar. So he leaned against the weapons rack next to the Gentleman and waited for Marion.

Since he'd stopped moving, the napthal screamed back in full force, and Grey was dozing when Marion returned with a healer and the sheriff, Calum. Years in the dust weathered the practiced lawman, and from the way he surveyed the bloody scene with a cool eye, Grey wondered at his experience in the shifter War. The town hadn't seen violence in years, but Grey suspected Calum had seen his fair share when the wilds still stretched within a hundred miles of Harkk.

"Tend to Lino first," Calum said. "Now, what happened here?"

"Grey fought them off," Marion said with price. "These men were here to take our weapons, and Grey stopped them."

"Your father was an herbalist, you say?" Calum asked, eying Grey with suspicion.

"No, my friend Arlo was an herbalist. My father was a dak miner."

"These bandits look like soldiers. Maybe even ex-Pillar." Grey nodded. "Yet somehow, though you claim to have followed in your friend Arlo's footsteps, you disarmed two veterans, all without a weapon of your own?"

"They weren't expecting a fight."

"Lino seems to have put up quite a struggle before you arrived. It's fair to say these men were on guard."

"They were hostile."

"You're not a stupid boy, Grey. And despite your assumptions based on our distance from Harkk, I'm not a naive man. Faycliff thrives because its residents live with purpose. We work to expand the Defiant Empire in the First Servant's name, and everyone must adhere to that mission. I allowed you sanctuary because of your skill with wines and spirits and also because Reyes promised he'd monitor you. This crime scene tells the story of a warrior child living in our midst. Please don't mistake my words for lack of gratitude, but trouble begets more trouble. And this is more trouble than our town has seen since the shifter War ended."

Grey grasped at the slipping fiction of his life, and though napthal had all but killed memories of the shifter War, he still clung to his pathetic position in Faycliff. "I'm not a warrior," Grey said. "Marion saw danger and ran to the nearest building in town. He woke me, so I acted like any good citizen."

"Since your actions seem to have benefitted the township, I'll take you at your word for the time being. But I'd pay a passel for an Array mind reader…"

"This peasant questions you?" the Gentleman asked, standing and leaning in so close that his nose grazed Calum's weathered cheek. The Gentleman sniffed, though, of course, Calum didn't perceive his wicked presence. "Cut his legs off at the knees. Do it. There's plenty of steel here."

"I promise, Sheriff," Grey said through gritted teeth, "I am no threat to you or any of the people under your protection."

"Very well," Calum said, mulling over the implications of hosting a young warrior in their small town. Then he turned to the healer and asked, "How is Lino?"

"He will be back on his feet in a matter of days. His wounds are minor."

"And the injured man?"

"He'll not walk again, and internal infection may claim his life."

"Do what you can. We'll bury his companion in our cemetery, away from our honored dead, for even criminals must seek passage to the Circle. Grey, you may return to the tavern while I ponder this incident."

Grey nodded, leaving the bloody scene and the Gentleman, though, of course, the evil man appeared on the hill ahead, laughing at Grey's discomfort.

Marion jogged behind Grey, asking, "You're not going back to sleep after that, are you?"

"I am."

"Won't you attend the celebration tomorrow? The bandit attack won't stop the aqueduct's opening, will it?" Flashes of Grey's battle near Shallow Canyon sent him reeling, and it took him a five long seconds to regain his composure.

"Go home," Grey said, struggling to think. Marion opened his mouth but reconsidered when he noticed Grey's stern face. He turned and trotted off, still excited by the brief skirmish.

Grey paid Marion's departure no attention as panic built in his mind until it roared in his ears like the screams of men slaughtered in battles fought long ago. He stumbled back to his room, shut the door, and took several deep breaths. The Gentleman's dry laugh filled the small space, but Grey blocked it out until his chest loosened, and his shaking limbs became still. He reached down, rummaging amidst the clothing-strewn floor, until his hand knocked into a bottle. Only a few sips left, but it should be enough, he thought in relief as he chugged the napthal. The Gentleman faded as the drug sent Grey back into unconsciousness.

Chapter 2

Agony's Joy. The blade severed flesh and bone with the ease of a machete cutting dry grass. Grotesque, fleshy shapes split under its power, showering cascades of blood over Grey's soaked uniform. Archers fired arrows into the endless shifter horde, but Grey paid the falling missiles no mind. The entire shifter army would fear him, fear Agony's glint as it twisted and slashed under the glowing sky. The blade knew where to cut, its owner wielding the cruel instrument with deadly speed.

Grey woke with Agony's curved hilt gripped so tightly in his hand that he'd lost sensation in the tips of his fingers. His chest shook from the bloody vision that still danced before his waking eyes, blending in with his uncleaned room. He shook his head, puzzled. Even a few sips of napthal should have kept him asleep until the following night. But here he sat, awake and gripping the blade he remembered using only during his worst nightmares.

Did his brief fight with the two bandits shake him that much? No, that's not it. Something else tugged at his mind, keeping him conscious despite the potent drug sitting in his veins. Forcing his grip to loosen, he slid Agony's Joy into its scabbard and tucked it under the mattress. He had to escape his cramped room, which activated his intense claustrophobia, so he clawed himself through the window and onto the roof. For a minute, he lay back against the shingles, drawing in deep breaths.

The roar of hundreds of people cheering floated through the still, humid air. The aqueduct opening ceremony is today, Grey remembered, glancing at Echore as it began its descent below the horizon. Its position showed it was just after dawn, and Grey squeezed his eyes shut, wishing himself back to sleep to escape from a day that reminded him of Shallow Canyon. Five years ago, the Gentleman first appeared, descending from Echore to whisper murderous words into Grey's ear.

The soldier who'd first recruited Grey into the Pillar dubbed him the Hero of Shallow Canyon, and his story spread throughout the Defiant Empire, inspiring the tens of thousands of weary Pillar fighters. The First Servant summoned Grey to Harkk, but after that, Grey's memory faltered.

Two years passed before he awoke with Agony's Joy at his side and the round-faced herbalist, Arlo, hovering above him with tender concern. Agony's Joy lay at his side, and since no one recognized him as the Hero of Shallow Canyon, Grey didn't bring it up. He spent much of the following two years working under Arlo to treat soldiers wounded in battle.

It was there that he'd discovered napthal. Arlo used the drug as an anesthetic for soldiers undergoing surgery, though Grey soon learned it served a more recreational purpose in lower doses. As soon as he'd ingested a sip of napthal, the Gentleman had vanished. Since then, Grey hadn't stopped drinking the stuff.

As he lay on the tavern roof, with these thoughts swirling through his head, Grey decided that he wouldn't be able to ignore Faycliff's celebration. He vaulted from the top of Reyes' tavern and jogged towards the center of Faycliff.

Despite the rising heat, a shiver ran the length of his spine. The still air held an ill scent that conflicted with the crowd's cheer, and he braced himself as if he stood near a storm's edge; at any moment, a terrible wind might sweep him from his feet. Grey gritted his teeth in frustration at his lack of control over his thoughts. The war ended a year ago with the Treaty of Limited Population, when the First Servant agreed to define his Empire's population growth, and the shifters agreed to stay in their lands. No one had seen a shifter since.

As the aqueduct came into view, even Grey was impressed. The canal itself wasn't innovative, but the mechanism that would produce water pressure for Faycliff's residents was intriguing. They called it a bondman, though it looked nothing like a man. It looked more like a two-story tall human heart, with one fleshy tube dipping into the empty aqueduct and another running up the cliff into an artificial basin. Fanciful stories claimed that everyone in Harkk used bondmen as servants, but such mindless creatures were for the wealthy. He'd never seen one in person unless you counted the glow worms that lit Reyes' tavern.

Grey had overheard Reyes bragging to a traveler that the Empire's elite aerostacy guild, the Array, crafted Faycliff's bondman. The Array's aerostatic artists wielded each of the four aerostatic gases to sculpt flesh into any shape—for a price. The only acceptable currency was the gases themselves, and the Array charged far more in gas than it used.

The entire town, around two thousand citizens, gathered around the fleshy bondman. With flowing water, Faycliff was well-positioned to expand its granite mining operation and population. Granite wasn't as valuable as an aerostatic gas, but it provided a decent storage solution for two of the four gases and was always in high demand. Grey figured that the miners hoped they'd someday strike marble, the only long-term aerostatic storage material. In the meantime, granite would sustain the town's economy.

Grey joined the crowd and craned his neck towards the platform, which held the sheriff, the mayor—a stern woman named Odette—and a boy around Grey's age. The teen's refined clothing would have marked him as a nobleman had his erect posture and combed blond hair not already given away his status.

"Thank you, everyone, for coming," Odette said. Her sharp voice carried across the crowd, and she waited until the dozens of conversations stopped and all grew silent.

"It has been a hard year," Odette continued. "I doubt there's one among you who has not lost a loved one or a friend during the shifter War." Many in the crowd murmured in agreement. "The First Servant asked much of you during your time of grief. When despair crushed your spirit, he asked you to help rebuild. When you wanted to reflect upon what we lost, he asked you to believe in what we would create together. He asked you to defy expectations by sacrificing your time, bodies, and wealth for the Defiant Empire."

Now Odette shouted so that her words rang in everyone's ears. "And we have been defiant! Today, we pause to remember our defiance of the shifter horde. Today, we celebrate our courage, which reminds the First Servant of his defiance of the gods when he banished them to Echore ten thousand years ago. By ignoring our limitations, we may accomplish marvelous deeds, and from what I've seen of your hard work these past two years… you all live without limit! You… are FREE!" The crowd roared, many raising their fists and breaking invisible chains towards Echore in imitation of the First Servant's crest.

"Let the water flow!" Odette shouted even louder. "Let us become rich with the First Servant's reward for our work."

The blond boy on the platform reached out to touch the

bondman, and it pulsed. Water streamed down the dry channel, flowed into the bondman's lower tube, and pumped to the basin. About a minute later, water fountains fed by hidden pipes ending in sprinklers showered water over everyone. The ground softened, and unhinged residents hugged and wrestled with gleeful abandon.

Grey wondered at Odette's ability to deliver cheer to Faycliff's stoic population. He shook his head, contenting himself to stand at the edge and watch the others dance and play.

After a minute, the goosebumps on Grey's neck drew attention to the boy on the platform. They locked eyes, and the boy smirked. He didn't understand why the boy was looking at him with such intensity, and he became uncomfortable. Then the boy's eyes flickered to the cliff. He pointed towards the basin, and Grey followed his arm to spot three shapes on the bluff a mile from the bondman. Then someone slapped his back, and he twisted away, ready to strike.

"What were you thinking to do, boy?" Reyes asked. "Punch me?"

The tavern master's red face and perpetual smile hid his bitter heart. Reyes was quick to anger and even quicker to hit, a propensity he'd demonstrated many times by beating Grey until his arms grew tired and his breathing ragged. Grey accepted the beatings with detached curiosity, though he'd always wondered at the disturbed man's motivations.

"We'll need plenty of wine to feed these thirsty mouths once the celebration is over," Reyes said. "Return to my tavern at once."

Grey wasn't paying Reyes any attention, though, because the shapes had reappeared almost directly above the platform. His stomach dropped. It just can't be, he thought. Shifters. Three of them. They weren't like the ones from

Shallow Canyon, though Arlo's wise words prepared him for nearly any form the foul creatures adopted. No two groups of shifters looked alike, and these beasts were shaped like giant men without heads.

"This can't be happening," Grey said.

"Boy, I'm done warning you," Reyes said, grabbing Grey by his worn shirt collar. Grey brought his hand over Reyes' stubby arm and twisted with most of his weight channeled into the man's wrist. Bone snapped. Reyes shouted, but no one heard, for others had also spotted the shifters.

The shifters dove from the cliff onto the platform where the blond boy had been standing a minute ago. No one was there now, but wherever the kid was, he'd soon be dead. Grey opened his mouth to shout a warning, but only a quiet gurgle emerged. This was worse than any nightmare.

A second later, the shifters tore into the crowd. Their razor-sharp limbs spun like the swiftest swords, sending flesh soaring dozens of feet in every direction. Faycliff's entire population would be slaughtered in minutes, yet Grey did nothing more than stare in disbelief.

Then Marion came running down the hill in a mad sprint, waving an object in his outstretched hand. He skidded to a halt, too breathless to speak, but he held out Agony's Joy. Grey gripped the slim handle and pulled the mirrored blade from its scabbard. Flawless metal gleamed as if it had just been polished, though, to Grey's knowledge, no one had ever cleaned it. Blood and dirt slid from the blade like butter against a searing pan, and even fingerprints faded from its mesmerizing surface. The bottom of the hilt held the blade's only flaw, a cracked and hollow cavity where someone had carved what Grey assumed to be its name: Agony's Joy.

Grey rushed into the chaos, approaching the shifter near the flowing aqueduct. He couldn't recall ever having used the blade except in his nightmares, but its blade nestled in his palms as if its metal surface extended from his flesh. For its strength, it weighed little, while its sharp edge allowed it to cut through almost any material with minimal force. He drew close enough to see that the shifter's arms were much broader and thicker than any human's, and its body was taller, too, towering at least two feet over Grey's six. Its skin wasn't flat, either, but a series of blades organized at angles around each of its limbs.

Grey crouched, preparing to leap. With his feet planted against a stone, he sprung towards the shifter. Agony's Joy neared the creature's back, eager to taste blood. The beast whipped around, knocking the blade aside and Grey with it. A razor arm came down, but Grey blocked it with Agony, which he still gripped in his left hand. He was on his feet instantly, already swinging the blade down towards the creature's legs. It hit, cutting through part of the limb before stopping as if striking rock.

Another swipe forced Grey to withdraw. This shifter was faster than any he remembered in the War. It was all Grey could manage to block its blows, stepping back towards the aqueduct in a reluctant retreat. Still, its limbs moved ever-faster, slicing through the air so quickly they blurred. Grey missed a crucial block, and the blunt end of the creature's limb landed against his chest.

The aqueduct lay ten feet behind Grey, and he landed in the channel. His vision closed in, narrowing from the edges until he looked through a dark tunnel at the shifter, which stepped towards him. Though it had no discernible head, Grey got the distinct impression it was examining him with intense curiosity.

"Grey, I'm coming," said Marion, who sprinted across the battlefield with the scabbard in his hands like a sword. No, Grey thought, but he lacked enough energy to shout. The napthal roared back into his blood, forcing him to sleep. Why now? Just before darkness descended, he watched the shifter whip around with deadly speed and sliced the boy clean in half. Marion's torso spun through the air, but Grey never saw where it landed.

When he awoke, a soldier was bending over him. Arlo, Grey thought. But it wasn't the medic who'd given him much of his knowledge of wines and spirits. This man's jaw was too firm, his shoulders too square. He grasped Grey's forearm and helped him to his feet.

"What happened here, boy?"

"Where am I?" Grey asked. He stood near a large basin filled with red water several feet from a cliff, and he stumbled over to the cliff's edge, sinking to his knees. The bondman had somehow sucked him in and spit him out above Faycliff. Below lay a scene of utter horror. Blood stained the entire town red, but the bodies were missing. The shifters must have taken the dead townspeople for their foul purpose.

The same soldier pulled Grey to his feet and said, "You'll be taken to Harkk, boy, where you'll no doubt be questioned." But Grey didn't listen, for the Gentleman appeared, splashing in the bloody water as his black coat turned a deep red.

Chapter 3

Grey had listened to a hundred Pillar soldiers describe Harkk's inhuman grandeur but had never appreciated the capital's scale. Every soldier he'd asked had tried to describe how Harkk's twin peaks rose from an ancient forest, dwarfing everything else in the land. Arlo had attempted to explain Harkk's size by telling Grey that all of Arndak—the city of a hundred thousand dak miners—could fit within Harkk's eastern peak. Only now, as he stood before the Defiant Empire's capital, did he appreciate the spectacle.

"No time to rest, boy," said Grey's escort, an older Pillar soldier who'd led him from Faycliff at breakneck speed. The man never offered his name, and Grey never inquired, so he nodded at the nameless man and continued following. Still, he kept his eyes fixed on Harkk.

The First Servant built Harkk into two mountains that rose from a barren stretch of dirt, as if the monarch had pulled giant rocks from the land. The western mountain, which held the Pillar, was split into three rings at different elevations. Small structures filled the lowest level, a few hundred feet above the ground. They comprised the housing and training facilities for the First Servant's army, the Pillar. The middle ring supported four towering fortresses, outposts from the cities responsible for mining the four aerostatic gases:

Arndak, Ventrahl, Devum, and Estril. The upper ring, which sat at the midway point between the ground and the peak, held the First Servant's palace, a series of four grand arches that circled the entire mountain. The arches were each larger than the fortresses below, but the most imposing piece of engineering had to be the fifth half-arch, which stretched towards the eastern mountain. Its tip hung at a dizzying height over the central point between the two peaks, and the notion of anyone walking to the end and peering down made Grey's head spin. It looked like it might collapse, plunging five thousand feet to the ground.

The Array hadn't built as many structures on the eastern mountain, choosing instead to burrow into the rock itself. In its own way, though, it equaled the Pillar in architectural accomplishment. Tens of thousands of illuminated tunnel entrances dotted the mountain. At night, the glowing holes created a wedge of stars, like a slice of heaven had fallen to the ground.

The Pillar soldier prodded Grey to jog, building up speed to a brutal pace to reach the forest surrounding Harkk's lower reaches by sunset. No canals led into Harkk, and roads were unnecessary because the soil was packed, so Grey and his escort jogged across miles of empty land until the forest surrounding Harkk's lower reaches blocked their progress.

The trees were ancient, grown together to build a towering wall the height of at least twenty tall men. A sheer wall around twice the size of the tallest tree greeted them when they emerged, rising to Harkk's lowest ring. A bondman stood near the base of the wall, a spider-like creature with curious hooks for feet and a broad, flat back. The soldier led Grey to stand on its back, and it climbed, using its hooks to latch onto short pegs in the wall. The smoothness with which the creature moved astonished Grey, for it hardly shifted under his feet. In less than a minute, they'd scaled the wall and stood at the edge of the lower ring, which housed two hundred thousand Pillar soldiers.

Perched atop the buildings were horrifying statues, identical and terrifying, with gaunt, muscled bodies and faces upon which terrible black eyes shone. Grey recognized them from across the Defiant Empire. From the Estril's westernmost coastline to Devum in the far east, the maramor statues watched over the Empire's citizens. One even stood atop Faycliff's town hall. In Harkk, though, the maramors were ubiquitous. Common knowledge dictated that any maramor might spring to life and enforce the First Servant's authority, no matter how far from Harkk you wandered. Though Grey had only seen them as motionless statues, he believed the tales.

Grey's silent companion from the past week descended atop the bondman to disappear below Harkk's wall, and the Gentleman materialized from behind the nearest building. Grey's breath caught in his throat, but as the figure approached, he sighed; the man wore the Gentleman's signature suit, but his youthful features differed from the Gentleman's drawn cheeks and sunken eyes.

"Follow me," the young man said. He didn't make eye contact with Grey, but he wrinkled his nose at Grey's unbathed scent. "You must bathe before your audience with the First Servant."

Grey allowed himself to be led a short distance to a bathhouse, a long structure nestled against the mountain. Inside, a trough of water flowed from a gap in the mountainside, winding across the ground before re-entering the mountain. No one else was bathing, so Grey shrugged off his clothes and plunged into the water.

"I'll set clean garments for you here," the man said, leaving Grey alone.

Grey hadn't realized how tense he'd been until he jumped

into the warm water. As dirt fell from his body, carried away by the gentle current, his muscles relaxed. The water smelled perfumed, pleasant but not overbearing, and he closed his eyes. He leaped from the water, though, when images of Marion's severed body appeared behind his closed eyelids. What right had he to experience even a moment of relaxation? If he hadn't taken so much napthal, then perhaps he would have been able to save Marion and some of the others. Then again, taking too little might have allowed the Gentleman to appear.

Grey pulled on the plain shirt and trousers and found the young nobleman waiting outside.

"Much better," the man said. "Now that I can stand to be within ten feet of you, let me introduce myself. I am Emerson, fourth son of the king of Devum and your assigned escort for your visit to the First Servant's palace."

"I'm Grey. My father is dead." He didn't know if Emerson expected him to announce his father or if that was a custom only among royalty.

"I… see. Sorry to hear that, Grey. Perhaps you should keep such morose information to yourself. In fact, I advise you only to answer the First Servant's questions. He has very little patience, after all." Grey nodded his understanding. "Now, come with me. We don't have time to take the gondola, and I'm afraid you're not important enough to call for a Flyer, so we'll be taking the faster but more unpleasant mode of transportation."

As they wound their way through the lower ring, the streets swelled with Pillar soldiers, leaving mess halls after their evening meals. Emerson pointed out training facilities, sleeping quarters, and entertainment centers. He didn't seem to need any response to continue talking, so Grey tuned out the young man's words and focused on the soldiers. These men weren't the gaunt and hopeless veterans he remembered from the shifter War. They were fed, rested, and filled with a festive happiness that bubbled into frequent laughter. They only grew silent as Emerson passed, bowing before returning to their conversations.

"Doesn't it make you wonder?" Emerson asked.

"Huh?"

"All these soldiers." Emerson gestured at the streets, which had now become so crowded that they had to push their way forward. "There's two hundred thousand warriors in Harkk alone, and who knows how many scattered across the Empire. That's an enormous army for a time of peace."

"The war only ended a year ago," Grey said.

"Yet the First Servant's forces have swelled during that year. Imagine the expense!"

"shifters attacked Faycliff two weeks ago by a group of shifters, so keeping a large defense force is wise."

"Oh, now that is interesting news. Interesting indeed. Now I don't regret accepting this menial task."

Grey just shrugged. "I'm sure the news would reach Harkk eventually."

"Information, Grey, is the most valuable currency these days—aside from the aerostatic gases, of course. Knowledge flows through the House of Ahl, but maybe it's Devum's turn this time! Come, let's board our coffins. I'm quite eager to return to Keep Devum."

"Coffins?" Grey asked.

"You'll see..."

Grey followed Emerson into a building that matched the bathhouse, save for a different color roof. It, too, contained a river flowing from the wall, though this river moved much more swiftly, bubbling and frothing as it gushed into a dark hole fifty feet away. Emerson pulled a lever, and a clank echoed from within the mountain, followed by a dark cylinder that shot out into the stream. The object sped along until a net near Grey's feet caught it, and when the top swung open along a single hinge, Grey understood why Emerson had called it a coffin. Its plush interior held a cushion upon which a single man might lay. Already, Grey's claustrophobia clamped around his ears, inviting sour bile to his throat.

"In you go," Emerson said. Grey looked at the contraption, his entire mind telling him not to allow himself to be trapped within, but he didn't see he had any alternative. So he took a deep breath and stepped into the coffin, laying down with his arms at his sides. Emerson adjusted the padding to mold around his hips, fitting a device against his nose and mouth. "Remember, inhale through your nose and exhale through your mouth. And don't vomit."

Emerson shut the lid, trapping Grey in utter darkness. His claustrophobia escalated to full-out panic, and he tried to cry out as the coffin shot down the river, entering the mountain and tilting to ascend. Grey understood the need for ample padding, for the entire capsule knocked around the tunnel. What if the capsule kept running through this mountain channel forever? What if the pod indeed became a coffin? How many minutes would the air last? But just when insanity threatened to send him into an animalistic rage, the coffin stopped.

The lid swung open, and a Pillar soldier pulled his limp body from the coffin and deposited him on a plush carpet. Emerson sprung out, no worse for the wear other than three unruly strands of hair, which he smoothed back against his scalp.

"Well," he said, clapping his hands, "that gets the blood pumping. I've always said these would be wonderful amusement rides for children." Grey swallowed with difficulty, squinting his eyes to stop the world from spinning. When Emerson noticed Grey's distress, he asked, "Did your pod leak? You're soaking wet."

"It's sweat," Grey answered.

"Sweaty or not, we've got to get running. Literally. There's only a few minutes left before your audience."

Emerson pulled Grey to his feet, and the two jogged into a hallway lit by so many glow worms that its steel-blue carpet became almost painfully bright. The chill air produced goosebumps on Grey's arms, though the air was warmer than he'd expected for the elevation. Perhaps a bondman heated the palace? Grey didn't recognize any fires or steam pipes.

The hallway ended at a circular door raised from the carpet by six inches. An attendant stood outside, a man around Emerson's age wearing a similar coat, save for an extra collar that stood up high around his neck.

"Hi, Owen," Emerson said, greeting the man.

"You're late."

"The audience doesn't begin for another five minutes yet," Emerson said.

"You're supposed to arrive an hour before the scheduled appointment. We don't have enough time to dress the boy."

"We had to stop for a bath. Trust me. You'd rather the boy go in naked and clean rather than well-dressed and smelling as he did."

"Very well," Owen said, frowning. He didn't seem to enjoy any of Emerson's cheer. "Put this jacket on over your clothing, boy." He offered Grey a coat, and Emerson helped him button it. There weren't any mirrors, but Grey imagined he looked absurd in the black jacket with its long coattails. "After entering, ascend the pedestal in the room's center. Emerson, you may stand on the ring below him."

The door slid open, and Emerson stepped inside. Grey followed, then stopped. He tried and failed to accept the space's sheer size, for he stood within the hollow interior of one of the four arches he'd first seen from miles away.

Marble, the most valuable substance in the Empire besides the four aerostatic gases, covered the floors, walls, and ceiling. Slabs of marble larger than houses merged with tiny chips of colored marble that formed intricate mosaics. Familiar scenes depicting the First Servant's imprisonment of the old gods in Echore were the size of buildings. The First Servant's marble face stretched higher than the cliff above Faycliff.

Grey had never paid much heed to legends about the First Servant's heroic past, but these murals caused something inside him to shift. Humans couldn't craft such wonders, so a higher power must have intervened. The very space stood as irrefutable evidence of the First Servant's feats.

Emerson nudged Grey towards a pedestal that rose from the ground near the center of the space, about halfway to the far wall. The pedestal appeared as a dark outline against the decorated wall, and it took several minutes of brisk walking to reach the multi-tiered structure. Grey climbed the narrow set of stairs winding around the pedestal until he reached the top.

The space stood empty, aside from Emerson, who balanced on a lower rung. Now that they'd stopped walking, the room grew silent, any ambient noise muffled by the structure's impenetrable walls. Grey's breath and heartbeat became the only sounds in his world.

Footsteps invited an unfamiliar nervousness into his chest. Aside from panic caused by claustrophobia, Grey never experienced the same level of fear he observed in others, but when he spotted a figure high atop the arched wall, his heart skipped a beat.

The figure dropped hundreds of feet to the marble floor in a dazzling fall that should kill any man, whether he had strengthened his body with the aerostatic gas dak or not. Then the figure leaped, closing the distance between the wall and the pedestal in a second. He landed in a crouch, long cloak draped about stooped shoulders.

The First Servant, the ageless ruler of humanity, stood below Grey. He'd expected a wrinkled, ancient whiff of man, but the First Servant appeared young, even younger than Emerson. His body was that of a man just out of his teenage years, though his shoulders were broad and his body strong. Covering his powerful form was the strangest cloak Grey had ever seen, its silvery material pulling up the color and texture of the marble floor wherever it touched the ground like a flexible mirror.

No scars or blemishes of any kind marred the First Servant's face, and his cheeks glowed a deep olive. Short, golden hair hugged the back of his smooth head, framing a face so symmetrical and handsome it would make any other person appear ugly in comparison. Grey's cheeks reddened, for he was ashamed of his unkempt hair, strange freckles, and scabby knees.

"You are Grey," said the First Servant. He paced around the pedestal, forcing Grey to turn. Based on the First Servant's demonstration of strength, he understood the tyrant could kill him without effort.

"You lived in Faycliff until the attack last week," the First Servant continued. His voice was deep and impossibly smooth. The minor inconsistencies and quivers in most people's voices didn't exist in his speech. He talked with absolute precision, no sound unsteady, and every syllable pronounced with inhuman accuracy. Grey opened his mouth to agree, but he closed it when he realized the First Servant had not asked him a question.

"How is it you withstood the shifter attack long enough to hide?" He stopped pacing and looked up, dark eyes boring into Grey's skull with ferocious intensity.

"A shifter knocked me into the aqueduct. The bondman

sucked me up and spat me out in the basin."

"The shifters would have torn you to shreds had you not blocked their attacks. Is this so?"

"Yes, I blocked several attacks with a sword brought to me by a boy named Marion, who lived nearby."

"Why did Marion assume you could wield a sword?" Grey sensed any delay in his responses would be unacceptable, for the First Servant's limbs tensed under his robes like those of an animal ready to pounce.

"Marion watched me fight off a couple of bandits, so he expected I could protect Faycliff from other threats."

"Was he correct?"

"No," Grey said, lowering his head. "He died."

"Did you fight in the shifter War?"

"Once."

"Where?"

"Shallow Canyon."

"You are the Hero of Shallow Canyon, then?"

"Yes," Grey said before he could stop himself. He cursed, unsure what effect his notoriety would have on the First Servant's disposition.

"I'd arranged to meet you years ago, but this audience took longer to materialize than I'd hoped. Where is the sword Marion brought to you in Faycliff, the one you used in your fight with the shifters? Do you still have it?"

"No," Grey answered. "It was gone when I awoke."

"You are a dak user?"

"I… I'm not sure. I inhaled dak once in Shallow Canyon."

"In the dak field there?"

"Yes."

"Grey, leave this chamber with Emerson."

Grey raised his eyebrows, puzzled, but the First Servant had already turned his back. He'd lost all interest in the conversation and Grey himself. Grey followed Emerson, and during their walk, he imagined the First Servant might leap from behind and rip him apart. Only once he'd stepped through the porthole and Owen had shut the door did he allow himself a deep breath. With a dense wall separating the First Servant from him, Grey's emotions stabilized into their usual pattern.

"Descend to the lower ring and find regiment eight for sleeping quarters and a meal," Owen said, handing Grey a slip of paper. "These are your directions. Follow the blue line."

"I take it I'm free to return to Keep Devum?" Emerson asked.

"You may do whatever pleases you, Emerson," Owen answered.

"Come on, Grey, I'll show you to the gondola."

"Hand over the jacket before you leave, boy." Owen stretched out his arm, and Grey struggled out of the now-sweaty coat Owen had lent him for his audience. He handed it over before once more following Emerson, this time to a gondola.

Every fifty feet, a bench hung from a metallic rope, strung between wheels spun by bondmen sitting atop long poles. Grey sat next to Emerson on the bench as it moved, his feet dangling over the edge. With the mountain spread out below him, he smiled. The ring holding the soldiers was far, far below, and one of the four keeps on the middle ring grew large as they approached.

Once they'd cleared the upper ring, Grey asked, "Is the First Servant always like that?"

"Like what?"

"So quick, so direct. He doesn't seem quite human in the way he talks."

"This is the third time I've heard our ruler speak."

"But you must have an impression of him."

"He doesn't like to waste any time," Emerson said, carefully picking his words. "It's ironic. You'd think everlasting life would allow one to waste more time on frivolous pursuits, but it's had the opposite effect on the First Servant. Each moment is precious to him, and every action he takes has a purpose. Or so everyone says. It's an attitude we should all strive to emulate."

Grey wondered how the knowledge of eternal life would change him. How would he fill his time?

"That's my stop," Emerson said as the gondola bench closed in on the surface of the middle ring. "Keep Devum, how I've missed you." Emerson beamed at the structure that towered overhead, a giant metal box with a few windows and various jagged ramparts protruding at odd angles. Grey had never been to Devum, the city that controlled mining of the aerostatic gas vum—the gas of destruction—and if this Keep represented its architecture, Grey didn't want to visit.

"It's been a pleasure meeting you, Grey," Emerson said, getting ready to hop off. "I rarely encounter anyone from the outer regions of the Empire. Perhaps our paths will cross again?"

"They might," Grey said, unsure how to respond. Emerson smiled, then jumped off the bench as they neared the ground, landing on his feet. He waved goodbye, then stuck his hands in his pockets and walked away, whistling to himself.

The gondola passed over the edge of the second ring, and Grey directed his attention downwards, readying himself for his landing. The last hundred feet passed quickly, with the gondola bench soon descending below the level of the tallest buildings. Something caught Grey's attention, and his eyes darted to see a glimpse of blond hair atop a face he recognized. Amidst the crowd of Pillar soldiers stood the boy from Faycliff who'd brought the bondman to life, the one who'd pointed the shifters out to Grey. A moment later, Grey passed a building and lost sight of the boy. He jumped from the gondola at the height of ten feet, landing with a small grunt and jogging around the corner where he'd spotted the boy. But he was gone, so Grey set off towards the eighth regiment.

Chapter 4

Grey spun Owen's map in his hands, trying to make sense of how the narrow, blue markings lined up with the streets. He'd wandered a few blocks from the gondola, but he couldn't figure out which way to turn next. Buildings all looked the same on the map, and the streets grew dim as Echore passed overhead, announcing midnight's approach. Grey saw all of Harkk reflected upon Echore's shining surface, a warped display of crisscrossed lines and angles that provided no help in finding his way.

"Excuse me," he said to a drunken soldier leaning against a nearby wall. Most soldiers had wandered back inside, leaving the streets emptier than when he'd waded through the lower ring with Emerson.

"You're young to be Pillar," the man said, slurring his sentence into a single word. Grey recognized drunkenness, having served men like him in Reyes' tavern for a year. The smell of his clothing was overpowering.

"I'm not Pillar. I need to find regiment eight."

"Regiment eight, eh?"

"Yes."

"I don't remember," the man said. Grey sighed and turned to continue his search, but the man grabbed his shoulder. He leaned in until his foul breath permeated Grey's nostrils.

"You should leave now, boy," the soldier whispered. "Flee and don't return. Once you catch the plague, a maramor will drag you down to rot below the deepest mountain."

"What plague?" Grey asked, but the man released him and slid to the ground. Grey had listened to many drunk men tell unbelievable tales, so he shrugged and set off to find someone less inebriated to question.

After receiving proper directions, Grey raced along the path laid out on the map. Wide streets grew increasingly narrow as the road transformed into an uneven jumble of shattered cobblestones. Glow-worm bondmen that lived in glass balls strung between buildings lost their charge, and inky shadows stretched across the ground. A rotten odor suffused the air as if the buildings had decayed like rotten fish.

A shape emerged from the shadows ahead. Stone walls stretched up on either side over a hundred feet, letting in very little light and making it impossible to see the figure. Grey approached until darkness peeled back to expose the Gentleman. His perfectly tailored suit clung to his skeletal form, its deep black color reminding Grey of the peek he'd gotten under the First Servant's silver cloak.

The Gentlemen raised his chin, and Grey ducked just as a sword whizzed passed his head and hammered the stone behind him. The large man who'd thrown it froze, for he'd expected the missile to hit its target. Grey had just a second to gather his senses before the stranger tried to grapple him, a clumsy move that Grey used to plant a kick against the sluggish man's kneecap.

When the man didn't flinch, Grey realized this shieldhand had inhaled dak, which strengthened his flesh to resist all but the sharpest blades. As the shieldhand turned, Grey noticed a shape above him. Flyers snorted ril to adjust their buoyancy to float through the sky like balloons, using pressurized air canisters to direct their flight.

The flyer threw a ball at Grey, and Grey's experience taught him that a blaster lurked nearby, ready to direct the ball's momentum with explosive vum, second of the four aerostatic gases. Tiny deposits of marble across the ball's surface would explode at the blaster's command, allowing the deadly ball to move in any direction the blaster pleased.

Grey dove headfirst through one of the few windows at ground level. Glass tore bloody streaks across his flesh, though his forearms took the brunt of the blow. I have to end this, he thought. He'd seen enough Pillar soldiers use these powers during the War to accept his slim chances of surviving a well-coordinated attack. Flyer, blaster, shieldhand, and swordhand worked together to outmaneuver their shifter enemies with ruthless efficiency. The shieldhand had thrown the sword, though, so this squad may have lacked a dedicated swordhand. Still, their joint powers presented a formidable threat.

Grey eyed the broken glass, grabbing shards and shoving them in his pockets. Then he picked two long and pointy fragments, which he gripped. The glass cut into his fingers, but he ignored the pain and dove from the window just as the flyer lobbed another grenade, which would soon explode into a thousand metal balls. Now that Grey stood outside, the flyer and blaster both hesitated, gifting Grey a precious moment to throw a glass shard at the blaster's exposed neck. The makeshift weapon found its mark, piercing flesh and causing the man to slump forward with a loud gurgle.

Grey threw the second shard of glass at the flyer, but the floating man used his maneuvering pack to swoop away, somersaulting off a wall to push himself at Grey. Grey readied himself, fishing another piece of glass from his pocket and squeezing it between his index and middle fingers. When the flyer soared within arm's reach, Grey swung out, but the man altered his trajectory to the right, and Grey's fist hit only air.

A distraction, Grey realized, but it was too late. The shieldhand had used the flyer's distraction to move close to Grey, and the giant man kicked out with incredible force. Grey jumped, but the shieldhand's foot caught his thigh. Bone shattered, and pain fired tiny points of light across his vision. The shieldhand stomped, and Grey pushed himself free with his working leg only to receive a fist to his chest.

"You little bastard," the shieldhand said, his deep voice echoing through the alley. "I's just gonna kill you's like I s'pposed, but seeing's as you's killed 'ol Pepper, I's gonna drag it out."

The shieldhand's blow had cracked several ribs, and Grey had trouble inhaling as his attacker's meaty hand reached out to crush his throat. But in that moment, Grey glimpsed a figure leap from the rooftop over the shieldhand's broad head. The newcomer landed atop the flyer, and a silver dagger flashed from the soldier's belly, sending him careening into the shieldhand with a terrible wail.

The boy who arose atop the flyer's body had blond hair and pale skin that glowed against the black night. It's the nobleman from Faycliff, Grey realized as his world stopped spinning. With a rage-filled cry, the shieldhand charged at the boy, who struggled to pull the sword from the flyer's back. He wasn't fast enough, and the shieldhand cuffed the thin boy across the cheek.

The shieldhand held his fist over the boy's head, but he stayed his hand. Grey was on his feet instantly, limping forward despite the pain. He fished another piece of glass from his pocket and rammed it between the shieldhand's shoulder blades. Even his hardened flesh didn't protect him from a direct strike, so the large man howled in frustration, swinging his wide shoulders around and flailing his arms.

Grey stepped under his arms and plunged another shard of glass into the shieldhand's biceps and yet another into his forearm. Grey held on to this last shard, letting it rip through the shieldhand's muscle as he tried to pull back.

Pure, unfiltered rage seethed from the man's eyes, but Grey recognized the battle had ended. The shieldhand tried to hit Grey again, throwing forward his uninjured arm. Grey dodged the blow and pushed another shard of glass into the shieldhand's abdomen. Blood poured from his several wounds, and though the dak may have prevented pain from reaching his brain, he no longer had the strength to stand. His knees quivered and then gave out.

Grey collapsed as pain consumed his mind. He held on to consciousness, though, and the blond boy raced to hover above Grey's narrowing vision. Up close, Grey noticed the boy's pale skin stretched across his bones, lending his features a delicacy that verged on feminine beauty. Hollow cheeks framed his narrow eyes and a long, thin nose, while his mouth formed a tight line. Blond hair so fair it was almost white clung to his sweaty brow, and a red mark developed where the brute had struck his cheek.

"Can you walk?" the boy asked in a soft, musical voice, offering his hand to Grey.

"I think so." Grey ignored the hand, pushing himself to his feet and putting weight on his injured thigh. Pain shot into his hip, but the bone held. "Yes, I can walk."

"Good. We'll have to hurry because it might be half an hour before these soldiers' superior officer becomes suspicious."

"Who are you?" Grey asked, ignoring the boy's apparent urgency.

"Trust now. Explain later."

"Why would I trust you?" Grey asked.

"Well," the boy said, surprised by Grey's response. "You

should. I pointed the shifters out to you in Faycliff, remember? And I saved you from that flyer just now. My name's Bow, I'm from the Array, and I came here tonight to rescue you. You can wallow in the street, where more assassins will arrive to finish their job, or you can follow me to an uncertain fate. Which do you prefer?"

"I prefer you tell me our destination."

"The Array, on Harkk's eastern mountain."

These injuries might prove fatal, Grey thought. From his work in Arlo's medical clinic, he'd learned that the force of the blow to his chest had almost certainly triggered internal bleeding. Plus, Bow made a good point; if more soldiers attacked, Grey lacked the strength to fight in his condition.

"Fine," Grey said. "Let's go."

"Great," Bow said. His broad smile introduced a youthful levity to his angular face, but he blushed and turned from the alley. Grey followed, allowing himself one last look at the three dead bodies. He shook his head, not trying to make sense of what had happened.

Ten minutes later, they arrived at the gondola platform, and as the carriage approached, Grey saw it was much larger than the small seat he had ridden with Emerson. This gondola, which swung from a thin cable stretched over a thousand feet to the eastern mountain, contained three rows of benches between a floor and a roof. Metal bars kept the structure rigid, though one might fall from between them, plunging to death on the jagged rocks.

The carriage paused for a while when it reached the platform, giving Bow and Grey plenty of time to climb aboard the middle row. A man already sat upon the front bench, though Bow didn't seem at all concerned about their fellow passenger. Then Grey realized why.

"I was wondering whether you'd lost your killer instinct," the Gentleman said from the front, turning to face Grey. The gondola lurched forward, clearing the Pillar's lowest tier to hang over open air.

"I killed those men because they attacked me," Grey said to the Gentleman.

"Hey, you don't have to explain yourself to me," Bow answered, thinking Grey's directed his comment towards him.

The Gentleman sneered. "Kill this unworthy peasant, too. You'll enjoy it as much as you enjoyed killing the soldiers."

"I didn't enjoy killing them," Grey said, but the Gentleman laughed, for they both knew it wasn't true. Grey relished the fight. The thrill of making split-second decisions, when a single miscalculation could lead to death, brought forth a happiness he lacked in all other aspects of his life. A veil dulled his world, but combat pierced the wall that barricaded his natural emotions into a distant corner of his mind, granting him rare access to addictive pain.

"No one said you did," Bow said gently in response to Grey's earlier comment. He stretched his hand to Grey's shoulder, but Grey recoiled slightly, so Bow grabbed the back of the seat in front of them instead.

"You said earlier that those men were assassins?" Grey asked, forcing himself to ignore the Gentleman.

"Yes, they were alerted as soon as you left the First Servant's palace. His attendant would have given you a map to lead you to an abandoned part of the lower ring, where an ambush wouldn't be noticed."

"But why? I'm from the edge of the Empire. I can't imagine why I'd be important enough to warrant an assassination squad from the Pillar—or, come to think of it, important enough for someone from the Array to save me."

"We have some idea."

"We? You mean the Array."

"No. Well... yes and no. You'll see soon enough. We're

nearing the other side."

The gondola landed, pausing long enough for Grey and Bow to disembark before swinging back out over the dark valley. Bow led Grey directly into one of the thousands of brightly lit tunnels dotting the mountainside, and Grey narrowed his eyes to slits until they had a chance to adjust. The walls glowed a warm, vibrant yellow that cast a shadowless light in the narrow tunnel while simultaneously radiating a pleasant heat. Every few feet, more tunnels branched off in various directions, and Grey lost track of where they were as Bow began to guide him through dozens of turns.

"It's a long walk," Bow apologized. Grey grunted in response, for the tightness around his chest had deepened to the point where he could barely breathe. He wasn't sure he'd be alive in another hour. Arlo himself wouldn't be able to save him if the internal bleeding turned out to be as severe as he now expected.

Eventually, Bow stopped at a seemingly unremarkable portion of the wall and placed his hand against the glowing surface. The solid material rippled like loose flesh, then split down the middle and peeled open. Grey followed him into a room the size of Lino's workshop in Faycliff, with racks of weapons lining the walls and a young woman floating on her back above a round table at the center of the space. She hovered a foot above the table's rough, wooden surface, laying on her back and bobbing as if floating on a gentle sea. She rotated towards them when they entered, her eyes widening in surprise.

"Westing told you to follow the boy, not bring him here." She tumbled neatly onto her feet, walking towards Bow with an accusatory finger pointed directly at his face.

"I know, Kip, but hush up and fetch Dilan. We need him right now."

"Yeah, I'll walk into the little boys' dormitory in the middle of the night and wake him up. That sounds like a great idea."

"Fine, I'll go. But watch over Grey while I'm away." Kip shrugged, and Bow said to Grey, "I'm sorry to leave you like this, but Dilan's the only one who can treat your wounds. I'll be back with him in a few minutes." Grey nodded weakly, sagging into one of the chairs at the table.

"So," Kip said, launching into the air as soon as Bow left, "you look like you're dying." Grey shrugged indifferently. "Bow's been talking about you for more than a month, you know."

"I only first saw him a week ago in Faycliff."

"Yeah, but he saw you before then. He drove a bunch of vorsters towards you and watched you kill them all."

"I guess Marion wasn't the only one there that day." Grey felt his vision narrowing. Something near his ribcage was bleeding, and it had worsened for two hours. When he passed out, he didn't imagine he'd be waking up.

"Westing had Bow and a couple of others running around the Defiant Empire looking for someone like you." Kip folded her legs underneath her body and continued to float about the room.

"What does that mean?"

"I'd better let Westing explain. He loves being the one to spill the secrets."

"And if I don't live long enough to see him?" Grey asked. He coughed, and blood sprayed onto the table.

"Oh, stop being so dramatic. Dilan will immediately fix you if Westing thinks you're worth the trouble. If not, then yeah, you'll probably die. Which will be annoying because I'll be the one to drop your body into a pit where no one will find you."

"Do you always float about like that?" Grey asked,

ignoring her morbid comment. He had to crane his neck to see her as she swam through the air.

"More fun than laying about on the ground, isn't it?"

"Ril is poisonous, though. It's killing you every time you inhale it."

"We all die, little boy. Sooner or later, we all rise to Echore, or sink to feed the demons in the earth, rot in the soil, or go wherever it is you believe people go when they die."

The door irised open before Grey could respond, and three people entered. A young boy who looked to be about the age Grey was when he fought in Shallow Canyon came through first, followed by Bow and a somewhat older, bald man. The man strode purposefully over to where Grey weakly lay in his chair. Every movement of the man's body was quick and precise, and though thin, his limbs seemed packed with sinewy muscle. Grey instinctively recognized the man as a practiced fighter.

"I'm Westing," the bald man said. "I'm rather pleased to meet you. I'd normally go about this sort of thing differently, but you don't look like you have much life left, so we'd better get on with it." Grey felt too weak to respond, so he just stared as Kip handed Westing two marble canisters.

"We could have Dilan heal him first," Bow suggested.

"You know we don't use Dilan's talents needlessly. We have to test him now, and if he's what you claim he is, Dilan will heal him." Bow nodded, but his cheeks were drawn, and he blinked away a few tears. Why does he care what happens to me? Grey wondered, thoroughly puzzled.

"You'll have to inhale these gases, Grey." Westing held a canister in each hand, placing them at Grey's mouth, his thumbs on the release valves. "I hold dak in my left hand and vum in my right hand. These are pure samples, enough to kill an ordinary man who has not built up a tolerance. So this may be my only chance to apologize for doing this, but one life is meaningless in the battle we're fighting." Westing depressed the valves, and blue and red aerostatic gases buffeted Grey's face. He took a deep breath, letting the gases fill his lungs.

A burning sensation, familiar from when he'd accidentally inhaled dak in Shallow Canyon, spread through his chest. This time, he felt a tingling crawl like electric ants across his skin, and his eyes flew open. The world brightened as the dak forced his pain to a tiny corner of his mind where he could safely ignore it. His injuries hadn't been healed, but he could hardly feel them anymore.

Sparks continued to travel through his limbs, eventually reaching his fingertips and jumping from his body. An explosion sounded from across the room, and a metal ball came flying towards them. In one smooth motion, Westing dropped the canisters of aerostatic gas, drew a blade from his belt, and deflected the ball with a casual flick of his wrist. The ball crashed into a weapons stand, knocking several swords to the ground.

By the time the swords finished clanging, Grey felt the power beginning to drain from his body, and he slouched back against the chair. The pain came back with a vengeance, roaring into his consciousness. He whimpered.

"I think that settles it," Westing said. "Dilan, you know I won't ask you to heal this boy, for his wounds are very grave."

"I know," Dilan agreed in a high-pitched voice. The ten-year-old stepped over to Grey, placing his tiny hand gently against Grey's cracked ribs. "Lift him onto the table, and remove his shirt," he ordered, and Westing scooped Grey up to deposit him at the edge of the table. Dilan stood beside him, tracing complex patterns over Grey's torso with his thin fingers.

Time passed, and Grey phased in and out of consciousness.

At one point, he heard the door open again, followed by at least two sets of footsteps. He felt Bow's hand on his brow, wiping the sweat from his eyes while Dilan worked. Grey thought that hours had passed, though, without external reference, he had no natural way to judge time. He only knew that, gradually, strength began to flow back into his limbs. Another hour or so later, Dilan removed his hands and stepped back.

"His body will take care of the rest," Dilan said in a shaky voice. Grey sat up, gingerly feeling his ribs. A sharp pain spiked across his torso, but he could tell the bleeding had stopped. Somehow, the young boy had sealed his wounds and set his ribs, all without making a single incision. Arlo would be astonished.

"Put this shirt on and sit with us," Westing said. His voice had gained a hard edge, and his eyes watched Grey closely. Grey took the offered shirt and carefully pulled it over his shoulders, buttoning the front and sitting in the same chair he'd occupied earlier. Westing, Dilan, Kip, and Bow were joined around the table by two others: a large, muscular man and a woman with long, light hair held up in a tight bun.

"Since you did survive," Westing said, "allow me to apologize again for that test. As much as I trust Bow's instincts, I had to be absolutely certain you are what he said you are."

"Which is what?" Grey asked quietly, still dizzy from the blood he'd lost.

"We'll get to that soon, but first, I'd like to introduce everyone properly. You've already met Bow, our user of the aerostatic gas ahl. He's a Seer, though his talents are underutilized at the moment."

"I'm so pleased you're alive," Bow injected, smiling brightly at Grey. Grey kept his expression impassive.

"Kip here fancies herself a bird," Westing continued.

"She's our flyer, which I'm sure you already guessed—just as you probably guessed that Dilan used ril to heal you, which makes him our Knitter." Grey had never heard of a Knitter before, and he glanced at Dilan, who shook terribly as if he were freezing. Grey imagined it was a side effect of the healing process because, as far as he knew, all of the aerostatic gases demanded a high price in exchange for their powers.

"You haven't met Callan yet. He's our shieldhand, albeit with much more academic focus than you'll find with most of his ilk." Grey examined the man, who had the typically large frame shared by most shieldhands. He wondered whether it resulted from using dak to strengthen one's body or if larger men tended to have an affinity for dak.

"Lastly, let me introduce you to Jeanne, a vum user who is a truly outstanding blaster."

"I'm glad you've arrived," Jeanne said. Her voice floated through the air melodically in stark contrast to her explosive abilities.

"And what about you?" Grey asked Westing.

"I'm a swordhand."

"Okay, so now that the introductions are out of the way, what in Echore do you want with me?"

"Well," Westing said, pausing dramatically and rising to his feet. "We need your help to save the world."

The Gentleman materialized in the corner of the room, and he said to Grey, "Don't kill this one yet. I'm eager to hear what he has to say." Grey allowed a smile to crease the corner of his lips, for he couldn't recall a time when the Gentleman hadn't immediately suggested murder.

Chapter 5

"The world isn't ending," Grey said.

"Oh, it certainly is," Westing retorted. He smiled, but the expression held no warmth, and Grey realized that he'd wandered into a den of insanity. Humans could pick up on the subtlest social cues, judging someone as crazy by walking past them on a crowded street. Minor details, like the oversized whites of Westing's eyes, painted him as a man who'd strayed beyond societal norms. He stared at Grey, his off-putting smile twitching near his cheeks.

"Whatever you're doing here is important, but I have no interest in becoming a part of it."

"If you're going to leave, at least murder them first," the Gentleman said.

Grey ignored him with a tremble and limped towards the door, pausing to say, "Thank you for healing me, especially you, Dilan."

"You're not going anywhere," Westing said in a near-whisper, and his five companions sat in awkward silence as Westing's smile melted into a dangerous frown. Grey recognized that crazy, near-mindless look he'd seen in many soldiers' eyes before a fight, so he flexed his torso, deciding whether he might triumph in a brawl. He almost choked from the pain that radiated outwards from his ribcage. Nope, not up for fighting.

"Grey, please don't leave," Bow said. "You're suspicious, and you don't have much reason to trust us… but Westing's words might interest you. Won't you come back and sit?"

"Yeah, you ungrateful prick," Kip said. "Dilan saved your life. The least you could do is sit on your ass and listen." Neither Kip's anger nor the dangerous look on Westing's face persuaded Grey. Oddly, it was Bow's eyebrows, lifting over his clear eyes, that convinced Grey to cooperate.

"Great," Westing said, clapping his hands. His foul expression lifted, cheer replacing the anger a bit too quickly. Everyone else relaxed, leaning back in their chairs. "Now then—Grey, have you learned about the Defiant Empire's beginnings?"

"Everyone knows that story," Grey answered, perplexed by the sudden change of topic.

"Humor me, then. Tell us the tale."

"It's pretty simple. Before the Empire, gods controlled humanity. Everyone was enslaved without free will. About ten thousand years ago, the First Servant escaped their control, imprisoned the gods inside Echore, and built the Defiant Empire to teach humans how to live without the gods."

"While a massive oversimplification of the First Servant's alleged heroics, you grasp the basics. But do you accept the story? Is that what happened all those generations ago?"

"I'm not sure," Grey said. "I never paid it much attention, but after visiting the First Servant's palace, I expect a superhuman power built it. And Echore is too round and reflective to be natural, which is more evidence in the First Servant's favor."

"Let's assume the First Servant created this fiction for his own purposes, and we will be left with a set of facts."

"Sure, whatever you say." Westing glowered at Grey's

disinterest, but he continued.

"First, the First Servant is more than a man. He possesses strength and longevity greater than that of any other human. Second, he has lent his power to the maramors, who are stronger and faster than the most skilled dak user. They create explosions more accurately and at greater distances than any Blaster, including Jeanne, and their utter lack of concern at taking a life is more pronounced than even the worst serial murderer."

"You've seen a maramor?"

"Oh, yes. Every fear their statues invoke is warranted—it's all true. But beyond the First Servant and his maramors, everything else is mere speculation. We don't understand Echore's purpose, nor can we prove events from ten thousand years ago. Today, we only observe that the First Servant kills his citizens at an alarming rate."

"You're suggesting the shifter War was a ruse?"

"No, the shifters pose a genuine threat."

"Then what? High casualties ended with the War."

"Did they? What do you call the massacre at Faycliff?"

"A shifter attack. You just told me the shifters are a genuine threat."

"Those weren't shifters," Bow said. "They were maramors, dressed up in costume. You probably suspected the creature you fought was faster and more powerful than any shifter you encountered during the War."

"Even if they were maramors, Faycliff was one incident. I met a nobleman earlier today who hadn't heard about other killings."

"Not yet," Westing agreed. "Faycliff escalated the First Servant's devious plan of murdering his citizens. More people have died in the year since the War ended than during any prior year."

"You can't believe that."

"The Array has evidence to support my claim. Our outposts in Arndak, Ventrahl, Devum, and Estril kept detailed records of the population during the War to recruit soldiers into the Pillar. We've continued to keep these records, and the death rate has only risen. The vast majority of these deaths are from unknown causes."

"I can explain that. Since more people used the aerostatic gases during the War, more people will die from their effects. The gases shorten lifespans in direct proportion to how much they're used."

"Very clever, Grey. A conclusion worthy of the First Servant's most skilled propagandists. But your theory has a fatal flaw: the Array's Knitters can identify aerostacy as the cause of death."

"Okay," Grey said, thinking. "If you can't find the cause of death, then you can't tie the deaths to the First Servant."

"You're right. We can't prove he's responsible, only that his maramors transport the heads of the dead to the First Servant's palace. After the massacre at Faycliff, Bow watched the maramors collect and prepared the bodies for transportation."

"They cut off the heads of the villagers," Bow said. "It took them hours, but they removed every head and placed them in marble tanks."

"The First Servant is slaughtering his population," Westing said, waiting for Grey's reaction. Even if Westing was correct, no one held the strength to stop the First Servant. His prowess in battle would topple an army, and the Pillar was the only true military force in the human world. No one held a position capable of challenging his rule. In fact, no one had even tried to test his power. Sure, the nobility would fight amongst themselves, but they would never question the First Servant's commands.

"Can't someone ask the First Servant about these deaths?"

Kip chortled. "He's gone to extraordinary lengths to keep all of this a secret. The Array's leading commanders haven't made the connection, so we're the only ones who've discovered this terrible truth. If the First Servant kills us, that'll be it. His plan will continue until all humans are dead."

"But why? Why kill everyone? He's led the Defiant Empire for ten thousand years, and his citizens never suffered."

"People have been suffering," Callan said. "Especially in recent years. Starvation is common, driving many to adopt a bastardized offshoot of ahl for relief. The nobles call them Fizzers, disgruntled citizens who drug themselves to death. We must discover the purpose behind these deaths because no one else will."

"Why risk telling me?"

"We need you," Bow said. "You can absorb undiluted doses of aerostatic gas with no ill effect, even multiple gases at one time—something that leads to immediate death in anyone besides the maramors. With enough of an aerostatic gas supply and the proper training, the eight of us will challenge the First Servant."

"You want to study me."

"Yes, but not only that," Westing said. "We want to train you. We need your help to take control of Arndak, Ventrahl, Devum, and Estril and wrestle the supply of each of their gases from the First Servant."

The Gentleman laughed, and Grey shot him a look. He'd never seen the invisible man show any other emotion than hate.

"Do you have any napthal in here?" Grey asked. The room wasn't small, but claustrophobia set in nonetheless. He would do anything to banish the cackling Gentleman from his mind.

"Why do you need it?" Jeanne asked.

"For the pain in my ribs," Grey said. She looked doubtful.

"I used it to numb the pain of many soldiers during the War. A man named Arlo taught me how to dose it. I know what I'm doing." Jeanne nodded, then brought the bottle. Grey accepted it with shaking hands and took a solid swig, enough to drive him into sleep.

Westing snatched the bottle with nimble fingers, then said, "Bow, keep him awake."

The Gentleman disappeared, but Grey didn't fall asleep. Bow's eyes were closed, and his fists trembled at his sides.

"You woke me up that morning in Faycliff," Grey said in realization. "I had wondered why the napthal didn't keep me unconscious the whole day."

"Keeping you alert was the only chance I had to save you from the fake shifter attack," Bow said, opening his eyes and nodding. "Ahl allows me to increase your wakefulness and offset the tranquilizing effect of napthal."

"If you teach me to use ahl myself, can I learn to take napthal, yet keep myself awake?"

"Napthal holds trace amounts of ahl, allowing it to gain absolute power over the human mind. If you can use ahl, you'd be able to replicate any of napthal's effects without the drowsiness—with proper training, of course."

"I see." Grey's mind spun with the possibilities. He'd be able to block the Gentleman at will. I bet they have plenty of the gas here, in the Array, he thought. "I'll help you in exchange for the training you offered."

Chapter 6

"Watch your mask," Callan said, his mild tone unaffected by whatever emotions flowed beneath his calm exterior. Grey raised his sleeve to his face as if wiping sweat from his lip, using the motion to hide a bottle of ril from which he drew a tiny puff of aerostatic gas. He used the extra ril to strengthen his twist.

After agreeing to join Westing's rebellion, the unpredictable man jailed Grey under the condition that he learn the basics of twisting, a technique wielded by ril users to disguise their identities. The shieldhand Callan taught Grey to twist over four weeks, helping him reshape the muscles beneath his face to develop an alternate appearance. Experienced twisters reshaped their entire bodies into many forms, but after a month, Grey was not so skilled.

"At least no one will want to look at you with that face," Kip had said when she'd witnessed Grey's efforts two weeks ago.

"You look inbred," Dilan had commented, giggling. Grey rushed to a mirror and choked. His nose had sunk into his face so that his droopy cheeks protruded farther than his nostrils. The entire left side of his face sagged towards his neck as if he'd suffered a stroke. Ugly was too gentle a description of his reflection.

"Good," Callan said now, referring to Grey's strengthened facial twist. He led Grey through the dense throngs of wandering Pillar soldiers, miles and miles from the gondola connecting the two mountains. The crowd parted ahead, keeping a respectable distance and allowing Grey and Callan's white robes to billow in the evening breeze.

When they'd walked far enough so that the bulk of the western mountain hid the eastern mountain, Callan turned towards a cliff, leading Grey into a dark cave. Darkness surrounded them, so Callan grabbed a torch from its place on a nearby hook. A fire blazed with the help of a flint box, illuminating a stairwell cut into the mountain.

The stairs were just wide enough for the two to walk side-by-side, and as they began their descent, Grey asked, "Can I resume my normal appearance?"

"No. As Westing said, the First Servant must not discover you survived." Grey tried to frown, but his mouth was so twisted that he drooled a bit. His face hurt like a foot cramp, making it hard to focus on anything but his knotted muscles.

"Why do the soldiers treat us with such respect?" he asked, trying to distract himself from the discomfort.

"Respect? What makes you assume they respect us?"

"They weren't even polite enough to step aside when Emerson led me to the First Servant's palace."

"While I suppose you might view their fear as respect, it's born of terror—not appreciation."

"I don't understand why they would be afraid. There's about a thousand of them to one of us."

"The Pillar fears the Array's power."

"Their soldiers use aerostacy, too."

"Only as novices. The Array's techniques are unknown to the Pillar, so our powers appear mystical. I imagine the First Servant perceives our true capabilities, but even our elders don't learn the full range of our ingenious methods. After all, intermingling powers is pointless."

"Why? If one Pillar fighter became a Blaster and a Flyer, they'd be far more formidable."

"Yes, someone like that would hold great power—but unless you're the First Servant or a maramor, it's an impossible combination. It takes thousands of hours to master just one ability, even an ability associated with the same aerostatic gas. Strengthening your body with dak, for example, is an almost completely different skill than using dak to speed your body. As a result, you won't find a shieldhand who is a swordhand, or vice versa, even though they both use dak."

"Then combine the learning process."

"And double the dak intake? No. If I'd trained to become a swordhand on top of my shieldhand training, I wouldn't live to be twenty-five. Add another gas, like vum, and I'd die before I hit puberty. Only Marble Zealots consume multiple gases out of a misplaced worship for maramors. None live past their teens."

"I knew the aerostatic gases are poisonous, but I never realized just how deadly they are," Grey said, trying to decide if he'd choose aerostacy. Westing claimed Grey was immune to the ill effects, but he offered no proof. "How does the gas kill you?"

"You'd have to ask Dilan for an explanation, but from my understanding, the human body falters. After a time, the mind stops functioning. The heart no longer pumps blood, the electricity in the brain ceases, and all other organs stop. I'm told it's quite sudden and painless."

"Most soldiers would pick a longer life over aerostacy."

"We have our reasons for choosing this fate. Many believe in the First Servant's Circle, the realm where you go after you die. Others, like Kip, Dilan, and Bow, are driven by horrors from their pasts. Then there are the Fizzers, who escape reality by abusing ahl to their deaths. We're on our way to meet one right now."

"And this Fizzer, he lives deep in the mountain?" They descended for thirty minutes, and the end was nowhere in sight.

"Yes, in the slum." Callan stopped and turned to Grey. "When we arrive, don't speak to anyone, even if someone asks you a direct question—and stay at my side. We'll remove our white cloaks here, for the Fizzers do not respect the First Servant's authority. A member of the Array would draw violent attention."

"But these people are right under the First Servant's nose," Grey said as he pulled the cloak over his head and handed it to Callan, who stored it in a brown sack he wore across his shoulder. "I'd think the First Servant's rule would be undisputed this close to his palace."

"Everyone has a theory explaining why the First Servant allows the slums to persist."

"Do you believe any of them?"

"Perhaps one: the First Servant is afraid to enter this chamber because he lost his liver within Harkk's mountain. The loss gave him the will to imprison the gods who had enslaved humanity for many generations." Grey raised an eyebrow. A single mural depicted the First Servant's lover, and Grey considered Callan too level-headed to trust an outrageous story.

"Now is not the time for further discussion," Callan said. "Remember not to speak to anyone and to stay close to me. Understand?"

"I understand."

"Good. Then let's keep walking. It's not much farther." Callan and Grey's opinions on distance differed, for they didn't emerge into the cavern for another fifteen minutes.

The chamber dwarfed the First Servant's palace, but where

the palace was crafted with meticulous care, this space appeared raw and untouched. Jagged rocks lined with hundreds of thousands of stalactites curved up to meet overhead. Black sludge dripped from the stalactites like oil, splattering the ground every few seconds with a resounding thwack and dripping into a vast crevasse at the center.

A covered walkway began near the stairs, with just a few wooden struts holding a tin roof over wide oak planks. It led into the most confusing set of structures Grey had ever seen, perched near the edge of the bottomless pit. Buildings—if you could call them that—were cobbled together from various scavenged materials. A single wall might contain slabs of blue stone, red brick, and gnarled wood cemented together. Grey estimated around five hundred such structures, each connected by the same kinds of walkways upon which he and Callan now strode.

"An earthquake would send this entire town into that pit," Grey said. "Why don't they build it closer to the chamber walls?"

"I don't know. These people aren't sensible, and I'm not convinced anyone planned this settlement."

The blackish fluid slid below the planks, fuming into a dark haze. Grey had thought his facial twist made breathing difficult, but he realized the fumes made the air heavy. He had to force air into his lungs, and then, instead of releasing his breath, he had to push the air back out.

"Several men are spying on us from behind slatted windows," Grey said, eying huts with suspicion.

"Yes, but don't speak to them or anyone else."

Despite his words, Callan's shoulders tensed, and his pace quickened. He stooped to enter a dark space, and Grey followed, finding the interior spacious.

The room held four rows of carts, each displaying a wide variety of fleshy objects Grey didn't recognize. The things writhed on the carts as though alive. Bondmen, Grey realized. They were organic structures created by the Array for specific tasks. One reddish bondman looked much like the massive heart in Faycliff that had pumped water from the aqueduct before the maramors had arrived in their shifter disguises.

Callan approached a merchant, a round man with voluminous jowls and tiny black eyes. He wore the ragged ruins of a suit much like the one Emerson sported, and Grey didn't doubt it was the man's only outfit.

"Ahhhhhhhhhhh," the man sighed, exhaling with a puff of smoke. "Callan, my old friend, I was wondering when you'd come crawling back. What is it this time? A bit of Fizz to take the edge off, maybe? Or perhaps there's something more… human I can offer you?"

"Gerd, I have little time to haggle with you over your unsellable merchandise. I only ever come for one thing."

"Unfortunately, I can't oblige." Gerd looked uncomfortable, backing away from Callan, who wore his sternest face.

"You can't, or you won't?" Callan could appear downright hostile if desired, and the muscle bulging beneath his cloak didn't hurt.

"Can't, can't, my friend," Gerd said, holding up his hands and backing away another step. "I'm not withholding. I have no dak."

"Then direct me to another merchant who does, and I'll deal with him. I'll compensate you for the information."

"No one has any dak to sell."

"No one? Are you certain?"

"I'm certain I'd hear if someone did. The dak supply dried up a month after the final shipment into Harkk. Our many friends in the dak trade have been transporting empty tanks from Arndak into Harkk for at least a month. Possibly longer."

While Callan spoke, Grey found a support beam to rest against, taking pressure off his injured rib.

"You're an ugly one," said an oily man who sidled next to Grey. "I don't recognize you, and I see everyone. You must've just arrived." Still, Grey held his tongue. "Ran away from your parents," the man muttered. When Grey continued to stare, the man spoke to himself under his breath.

"And an idiot, to boot. Yes, yes, you're ugly as they come, but your body is strong, firm, and so young. Yes, young and unspoiled, no doubt. Well, we can't be picky, can we? No, no, no."

He extended his bony hand to caress Grey's twisted face, but the man's filthy fingernails never found their target. Grey caught the man's wrist, twisting it hard so that his brittle forearm was near the breaking point. He held him there, pinned and unable to move.

"Kill this disgusting fool," the Gentleman snarled, stepping into the room. A stab of pain shot through Grey's temple, and a violent urge raced through his thoughts more strongly than any time he could recall since he'd killed Isa by poisoning her stew. "Slash his neck with these scraps of metal."

Grey only fought the Gentleman's will for the barest moment before giving in to the rage that filled his chest like liquid metal. Using his toe, he flipped the nearest scrap of metal into his hand, jamming the sharp end into the filthy man's neck. The jagged edge didn't enter smoothly; it ripped through flesh, shredding anything it encountered. The man opened his mouth to scream, but the shout caught in his throat as Grey twisted the metal shard. Knowledge of his approaching death widened his eyes as Grey joined the Gentleman in gleeful laughter.

A man to Callan's left shouted, and Grey threw the bloodied shard into his open mouth, severing his throat.

Two other merchants grabbed Grey's arms, pinning them

behind his back. But the thrill of battle fueled his body, filling him so that no other emotion had room to enter his mind.

Grey stamped down hard on one man's foot, feeling bones crunch. The man's grip loosened, and Grey jumped up, planting his feet on the merchant's chest. The second man still held Grey's arm, so he used the first merchant's weight to topple the second by pushing off hard with his legs. Stunned, they fell. Grey rolled away as his eyes searched for another target.

But the other merchants fled, leaving only Callan and the Gentleman. Grey charged Callan, too far gone to recognize the large man as his ally. The Gentleman filled his mind, churning his thoughts into a mixture of rage and joy so potent it overwhelmed all rationality.

Grey skidded across the room, aiming a well-placed kick at Callan's knee, but Callan moved with unexpected speed. One large hand shot out and wrapped itself around Grey's neck. The other hand snaked around his body, pulling Grey against his broad chest so he couldn't move. With the blood cut off from his brain, Grey soon lost consciousness.

Chapter 7

Grey tried to sit up, but leather restraints bound his arms, neck, torso, and head to a sturdy metal chair. Westing stood with his back turned, gripping a slender blade. He ran his fingers across the edge, stroking the sword as if petting a cat.

So I'm back within the Array's eastern mountain. Grey's head ached as he struggled to remember how he got there. He grasped at fragments of jumbled memories like leaves in an autumn breeze, with each leaf a snippet of hidden time. The crunch of a bone. Blood pouring from a severed artery. He could only hold onto one thought, each memory already forgotten by the time another floated by.

"How did I get here?" he asked. He tried to swallow to work up moisture in his dry throat, but it seemed his body had none left.

At Grey's voice, Westing spun around and approached with the light gait of a seasoned swordhand. His handsome face held no expression, and he stared into Grey's eyes for an uncomfortable stretch of thirty seconds. "Your soul is a burning flame driven by an eternity of fuel… yet your body has not yet seen sixteen winters."

"I don't know what you mean."

"There is a rage in you," Westing continued, now in a whisper. "I wish I had beheld you as Callan did…" Westing paused, then raised his voice as if addressing Grey for the first time. "Why did you kill those Fizzers?"

"I killed someone?" Grey asked. The Gentleman leaned against the weapon racks as a knowing smile creased his pale cheeks. Grey's dull headache became a searing pain.

"You killed two and injured one more before Callan stopped you." It wasn't an accusation, nor was there any anger in Westing's voice. He stated facts, observing Grey's reaction. There was none.

"I was with Callan. I remember that much. We were descending into Harkk's western mountain. Then I woke up here, tied to this chair."

"Bow, get over here," Westing said. The door opened, and both Callan and Bow entered. Bow wore a simple white gown, beaming when he spotted Grey. Grey's headache lessened somewhat at the sight of Bow—though he didn't comprehend why.

"Get him to remember," Westing ordered, handing Bow a bottle of compressed ahl. Bow accepted it, taking a deep breath from the nozzle.

"You'll have to open your mind up to me, Grey. I can't probe the thoughts of those who resist, at least not without causing damage."

"You're going to read my mind?" Grey asked, more curious than afraid.

"New memories are easiest to read, but it's difficult to parse another's thoughts as they form. Their chaos prevents true mind reading by any but the Array's most experienced Seers. Older memories are just as hard to read as new thoughts."

"Okay, that's fine. How do I open my mind?"

"You said you worked with a medic named Arlo during the shifter War?" Grey nodded as much as his restraints would allow. "Try to recall a particular surgery you performed. Walk through the procedure in your mind as if you were performing it now. Visualize the surgery to prevent your mind from rejecting my intrusion."

"Alright," Grey said, closing his eyes. A grisly day of the shifter War sprung to mind. Nestled within a forest, their medical camp came under attack by a group of twelve shifters who'd sneaked across the Defiant Empire's border. The dozen shifters were as green as the foliage overhead, and they swung from tree branches using long arms and strong fingers. Five Pillar guards fell before the shifters worked their way through the rows of wounded soldiers, killing as they went.

From the medical tent, Grey grasped Agony's Joy, ready to join in the fight. But Arlo had stopped him.

"Stay here," he'd told Grey. "It'll be a long night, and I'll need your full strength."

The Pillar fighting squad dispatched the shifters within minutes, but not before the enemy had wiped out a quarter of the camp. Grey and Arlo spent the next fifteen hours performing surgeries, amputating limbs, and sewing shut abdomens.

Grey blinked a few times when Bow said to Westing, "He didn't kill those Fizzers." Grey had to focus hard to pull himself into the present.

"What do you mean? Of course, he did it," Westing said, looking at Callan for support.

"I saw him kill those men myself," Callan agreed. "He appeared out of control. He didn't even recognize me."

"According to his memories, none of that happened. Grey's telling the truth when he says he can't recall any of that. From his perspective, one moment, he was watching Callan transact with a Fizzer merchant, and the next, he was right here in this room. It's as if the hours in between never existed."

"Amnesia?" Westing asked.

"No. Even patients with amnesia store memories, though they cannot access them. This is different. It is as though Grey did not exist for five hours."

"What does he mean?" Grey asked, looking past Westing at the Gentleman. But the Gentleman just snorted.

"I'm not sure," Bow replied. "It's troubling, but it leads me to believe I should train Grey as a Seer above all else. Perhaps he can unlock these memories where I have failed." And maybe I'll be able to block out the Gentleman without resorting to napthal, Grey added silently.

"No," Westing said. "If the dak supply is exhausted, we must uncover the First Servant's nefarious purpose."

"You'd like me to visit Arndak," Callan guessed.

"It makes sense. You're a dak user, and you're best placed to teach Grey proper self-defense."

"You want to train him, even after what happened today?"

"Especially after what happened today. You've seen how powerful he can become, given the proper teachers." Callan frowned, so Westing continued, "But you're right that he's a danger to himself and others. If today's incident had happened anywhere else in Harkk, the First Servant would no doubt have learned of it, and we would have lost Grey. He can't live in Harkk."

"Let's enroll him in a Pillar training camp or even in one of our guilds," Bow said.

"No," Callan said. "Westing's right. If Grey tackled more than a single aerostatic gas, he'd draw unwanted attention from the First Servant. That's why Westing is suggesting I take Grey with me to Arndak."

"Yes, exactly. If you journey on foot, you'll have a month to train him before you reach Arndak."

"Then let me go along," Bow said. "I can train him with ahl while Callan instructs him in dak."

"I'd like that," Grey said, unsure if he wanted to gain Bow's skills, or whether he desired Bow's company. It was a puzzling thought.

"Absolutely not. I need you here, especially when we're worried the council might catch wind of our activities. You can see trouble coming."

"But it'd speed up Grey's progress," Bow said. "Gaining control over his mind will help him master the other gases."

"It doesn't matter. I need you here. Now go back to your studies before you're missed." Grey noticed Westing's jawline tense at Bow's protest. That man is dangerous, Grey knew.

"Alright," Bow said. He winked at Grey and then left.

"Callan, prepare for the journey at once. I'll explain your absence to the council members. How soon can you be ready to leave?"

"Give me a day, and I'll have everything we need." Callan followed Bow from the room, leaving Grey alone with Westing. After the door closed, Westing loosened Grey's restraints. He stood up to rub feeling back into his limbs while Westing walked to the weapons rack and picked up the sword he'd been holding earlier.

"Agony's Joy," Grey whispered, seeing the blade up close. "I thought I'd lost it at Faycliff when the shifters—I mean, when the maramors attacked."

"Bow retrieved it and brought it to me. Tell me, where did you find it?"

"I awoke on the outskirts of a battle, gripping the hilt in my hands."

"You've had other missing memories?"

"Yes," Grey said. He opted not to mention he'd forgotten almost two years of the shifter War.

"Callan will keep a close eye on you until we figure out what triggers these episodes. I have to believe it's tied to your unusual ability to absorb any of the aerostatic gases without ill effect."

"Yes, I wonder what triggers these killing sprees," the Gentleman said, holding Grey's gaze. Grey frowned, but the Gentleman had tortured him enough for the day. The immaculately dressed man walked straight through the nearest wall.

"What can you tell me about Agony's Joy?" Grey asked, eager to learn about the mysterious sword.

"Nothing about this specific weapon, but I recognize its style from the golden age of the swordhand. The Pillar trains dak users to speed their movements, but the modern swordhand's fighting style amounts to little more than swinging a sharp stick. Whoever is faster wins the fight. Aerostacy has given us so much, but it's also eroded many great arts from ages past."

Westing stepped up to a padded steel practice dummy and swung the blade in a wide arc, blunt side first, into the dummy's arm. The dummy tilted, but Westing's arm didn't move.

"The tempered metal reduced vibration so that even the most powerful swing doesn't translate into the swordhand's arm. Its leading edge slices through solid marble and never needs sharpening, and none may shatter it—other than a smith with the skill to forge its equal."

"The hilt is broken," Grey said.

"Broken? No, this hollow end is intact. With a cable, skilled swordhands once propelled the blade at incredible speed, then recalled the sword to their hand. A trained swordhand could defeat a modern Pillar squad without breaking a sweat."

"How do you know all of this?"

"The First Servant taught me, and I have good reason to trust his words. Accompany me tonight, and I will tell you more before you leave with Callan."

"I'd like to see Bow first," Grey said, thinking only of Bow's offer to train him to use ahl like napthal to keep the Gentleman at bay.

"That is not possible. I asked Bow to attend to another matter. You may learn to use ahl after you master dak, as dak is the most useful gas in combat. If you can't protect yourself, there's little point in familiarizing yourself with another aerostatic gas."

"Still..."

"How about this? Come with me tonight, and I'll give you your first lesson in ahl. Then leave with Callan to Arndak, learn what you can, and return here afterwards. Bow will teach you. Now, we have a long night ahead."

Chapter 8

"We will accomplish much tonight," Westing whispered to Grey. The two of them perched in inky darkness below Keep Devum, near the spot Grey had left Emerson a month earlier. The Keep, an impressive metal tower with few windows, loomed above, while a hundred feet away, two men guarded the narrow entryway.

"What are we doing here?" Grey asked. "I thought you wanted to keep me away from the First Servant."

"Focus on your facial twist. It would help if you had a dose of reality, a look into the despicable filth boiling beneath Harkk's grand surface. You must understand why I fight, why I want you to help me overthrow the First Servant and save the world."

"Alright," Grey said, careful to keep his tone even. His sense of Westing's instability grew sharper the more time he spent around the man. Westing was dangerous.

"All my plans demand careful preparation. I will deal a blow to Ventrahl's outpost so large that each of the four cities will know just how vulnerable they truly are—even below their vaunted ruler's heavenly arches!"

Whatever, Grey thought. I just hope the napthal I took earlier lasts through the night. He didn't much care for Westing's cause, but the Gentleman's appearance would help no one.

Together, Westing and Grey crept towards the Keep. Drainage channels, which funneled rainwater into cisterns within the mountain, acted as camouflage until they crouched beside the Keep's western wall.

"Here, take this." Westing peeled back his coat and pulled something from a belt at his waist, offering Grey a blue metallic cylinder no larger than his index finger.

"A dak canister," Grey guessed from the color, which matched the blue marble used to store dak in Shallow Canyon.

"Yes. Of the four gases, dak has the widest range of applications," Westing said. "It allows humans to perform miraculous feats of agility, strength, and speed. shieldhands strengthen their bodies with dak, and swordhands enhance their speed. Metal holds aerostatic gas for up to twelve hours before corroding the bottle."

"You should carry a marble canister instead. Those are impervious to the gas."

"A single marble canister might not slow you during combat. But I'm carrying twelve canisters of aerostatic gas right now, and they weigh less than one marble canister of similar capacity. Perfect for combat missions. Now, press the one I gave you to your mouth, extend your lips around the end, and press the inner ring with your teeth."

Grey complied, and the dak blasted into his throat. He scrunched up, trying not to cough in case the guards might hear.

"You'll get used to the injectors," Westing said as Grey writhed on the ground. The burning in his lungs subsided, but his limbs ached, complaining at the forceful injection of dak now streaming through his extremities. Then the familiar surge of dak-strength asserted itself, like the energy gained from eating after several missed meals. Weakness gave way to boundless strength, and his body itched to move, to test itself by sprinting across the dark mountainside.

"The effect from the aerostatic gases lasts a set amount of time, based upon concentration. Gasses are diluted, centered, or pure. The centered dak you just inhaled will offer you twenty-three minutes of increased strength and speed. Diluted dak lasts twenty-three hours, while pure dak lasts only two point three minutes."

"What's the limit?" Grey asked. "How strong can I become?"

"Strong enough.

"Pure dak would give you enough strength to lift a boulder or sprint from Harkk to Arndak in a few hours—though the quantity of dak for such a feat would prove fatal. Pure samples kill unless the user has built up a tolerance over many years. The Pillar regulates concentration, and even black market gases fall within one of the three levels of aerostatic potency."

"Why not mix other concentrations? Maybe one more powerful than centered, but not as deadly as pure."

"Why is there gravity? Why do we need to drink water to live? The aerostatic gases follow a set of rules, as do all natural powers."

"I guess that's a good thing," Grey mused. "Without consistency, people would die even younger from concentrated samples."

"Most who practice aerostacy die plenty young. But now it's time we focused on more immediate concerns. Do you see that ledge overhead?" Westing pointed to a two-foot gap perhaps fifteen feet above Grey's head. "We're going to pull ourselves into Keep Devum through that window."

Grey had once leaped onto a shifter's back in Shallow Canyon, but instinct drove him on that fateful day. Westing's jump demanded absolute precision.

"I don't think I can do it."

"Not without years of dak training, I agree. But unlike anyone aside from the First Servant and his maramors, ahl will lend you an advantage."

Westing handed Grey a second canister, this one painted white like the marble from ahl tanks, which he put to his lips and inhaled. The ahl didn't burn like the dak, but it produced a wave of overwhelming nausea, along with a sharp headache like the Gentleman's migraines. Then, his mind cleared.

When he looked up towards the window, which he'd estimated to be about fifteen feet above, he knew with certainty that it sat thirteen feet from the ground. He also judged the exact amount of force required to propel his mass up to the window. A general clarity settled over his senses, and he smiled, bending his knees.

The dak gifted Grey's muscles with inhuman force, but he sailed past the window. All confidence drained as he fell, landing painfully on his side.

Westing smirked. "Understanding differs from performing. Unless..." Westing handed Grey a third canister, yellow like ril marble, which Grey inhaled. His heart stopped, and he could no longer draw breath. Had Westing been wrong about me? Grey wondered. Maybe I'm not immune to the aerostatic gases after all. Grey's eyes went wide, but Westing regarded him cooly.

"Tell your heart to beat and your lungs to inhale, like you might signal your arm to scratch an itch," Westing said. Grey did, and his heart started beating. Then his lungs inflated and deflated. He took a giant, gasping breath. "That ril. It gives you control over your own body and external flesh under specific conditions. It is also the Array's primary tool for crafting bondmen. Ril brings your body's automated functions under the control of the conscious parts of your brain."

Grey nodded his understanding, though he split his focus on keeping his heart pumping and his lungs inflating. He noticed his stomach had stopped digesting the food he'd eaten earlier, but his digestive processes could wait. Maintaining his facial twist on top of all this required intense concentration.

Westing jumped, sailed up to the window, and pulled himself in with one smooth motion. A few seconds later, his wiry arm reached out, motioning to Grey. This time, Grey commanded his muscles to supply the proper force, and he lurched once more into the air. He reached his arm towards the window, but it was no use; he'd jumped too low. Westing grabbed Grey's hand and hauled him the rest of the way in, where he fell onto the frozen metal ground.

"I don't understand what went wrong this time," Grey said. He looked around, noticing with alarm a guard slumped across his desk, blood pooling around his bashed-in head and dripping onto the floor. Westing must have smashed the butt of Agony's Joy against the man's skull as soon as he'd entered the room.

"Aerostacy is a tool," Westing said, ignoring the dead man. "The sooner you realize this, the better. If I hand you Agony's Joy, will you defeat a trained swordhand?" Westing paused, awaiting a response.

"No, of course not."

"Then why would aerostacy replace the value offered by diligent training? Each gas offers one of two powers, and you may apply each power in many ways. Most who practice aerostacy learn one gas, and within that gas, one power, and within that power, one specialty. I use dak to augment my speed, and I use that speed to wield a sword. Thus I am a swordhand. It has taken me a lifetime of training to develop this ability."

"I get it. I need to train to expect optimal results. That's why I agreed to help you so that Bow could teach me ahl. But you've kept the two of us separated for a month, and I've learned nothing."

"Then learn something new. Come, follow me, and be as silent as possible."

Westing swung the door open and crept through the halls, holding Agony's Joy. Most of Keep Devum's population was asleep, so they didn't encounter another guard until they arrived at a circular chamber. These four soldiers wore thick, flowing cloaks draped nearly to the ground and carried no weapons besides metallic gloves that Grey thought might be useful in a fistfight.

"Royal Blasters," Westing said, stepping into the hall. The guards turned to face him, momentary surprise on their faces replaced with grim determination when they spotted his sword. Three of them fanned out, while the fourth ran to the room's other entrance opposite where Grey and Westing stood to raise the alarm. He never made it, for in a blur of motion, Westing flung Agony's Joy into the man's back, which pierced his armor like no other blade could. He fell with a thud.

"Come kill me if you can," Westing taunted the three remaining guards.

To their credit, they didn't glance at their fallen comrade, instead punching the air in front of them, which sent glimmering balls flying from their metal gloves. Grey dove behind the doorframe while Westing whipped two daggers from his cloak and, with one swing, batted the projectiles to the side. A ball exploded into a storm of metal shards, which flew too slowly to catch Westing.

Faster than Grey would have believed possible, Westing skidded across the floor on his knees as the other two projectiles exploded behind him. He jumped, planting his feet against the far wall and pushing off towards the nearest Blaster, daggers in hand. He swept his arms in a wide arc, but the guards backed away, flinging more explosive metal spheres at Westing.

Westing kept close to the guards, his attacks swift and precise. Then one of Westing's blades caught in the nearest guard's thick cloak, and the large man twisted away, ripping the weapon from Westing's hand. Another guard grabbed the other dagger's blade with his metallic glove, and the sword shattered in a billow of black smoke. With the hilt still smoldering in Westing's hand, the furthest guard tossed another metal ball into the air. When it neared the ceiling, it changed direction with a loud pop, whistling towards Westing. Westing cartwheeled back, grabbed Agony's Joy from the dead guard, and spun into a low crouch. For a moment, all was still. Then Westing jumped.

The nearest guard had no chance to defend himself before Agony ripped through his throat to the left of his spine. With the back of the blade pressed against the falling man's vertebrae, Westing used the dying man's weight to redirect his own momentum, swinging into the next guard.

Westing turned, dislodged the blade, and twisted around to allow his blade arm to come down into the next guard's shoulder. A typical blade would have lodged itself into the guard's armor, but Agony's Joy was no standard sword. It cut through the shocked man, sliding into his heart.

The last guard backed away towards the middle of the chamber, keeping the cylinder at the center of the room between himself and Westing. Westing smirked at Grey, who stood in the doorway as if to say: See how easily I kill!

The guard pulled a rod from his cloak, brandishing it at Westing. A boom rattled the small chamber, and the guard launched himself ten feet in the air towards Westing, trailing smoke from his boots. He brought down the stick, and more bangs ensued as three small projectiles exited the rod. Westing sidestepped the attack, slicing through the guard's weapon even as he fell and allowing the man's momentum to bring him into contact with Agony's sharp end. With a final twist of his hand, the last guard fell from Agony, dead.

Before the dead guard hit the ground, Westing lifted two marble canisters from the room's central column. He tossed these to Grey. Red marble, he noted. They were used for vum storage.

"Come, it's time to go," Westing said. One flick of the wrist left Agony's blade as clean as the day Grey had first seen it. Nothing could lay claim to its gleaming surface, especially not blood.

"Won't someone sound the alarm?" Grey asked as he walked with Westing back to the window through which they'd entered.

"And admit that a single swordhand broke in and relieved them of one of their vum caches? I think not. Showing weakness only invites further trouble, so they pretend nothing happened."

"Then why bother at all? Surely you can get vum in the Array."

"Because they'll know it happened, and that's my goal. Plus, the First Servant's guard can't trace this vum back to the Array."

Grey followed Westing back to the window, but just as he was about to climb outside, a man appeared in the hall. Emerson, the nobleman who'd met Grey the day he'd arrived in Harkk, opened his mouth.

Grey slipped from the window before Emerson could speak and scampered across the ground after Westing, who ran around the mountain towards the House of Ahl. I don't think I'll mention that to Westing, Grey decided as his dak-enhanced muscles supplied an overabundance of force for an all-out sprint across the mountainside. A few strides later, though, he began tripping over his feet, so he slowed to an easy jog.

When he arrived at the House of Ahl, Westing was busy splashing a sticky substance containing chunks of dark stone onto the side of the building. Keep Devum was a fortress, while the House of Ahl looked much more like an actual house—the largest manor house Grey had ever seen. Five floors piled on top of one another against the mountain, with sloping roofs and grand, multi-paned windows. A weather bondman sat atop the tallest point as a statement of wealth; the residents wouldn't need to leave their home to know if a storm was coming, for the bondman sensed temperatures and barometric pressure, announcing the information each day with its primitive vocal cords. Grey thought they'd do better with a guard bondman, but Ventrahl wasn't a warlike city.

"Let's put that vum to good use," Westing said, handing Grey a canister he'd taken from Keep Devum. Grey inhaled it without hesitation, and his skin tingled as it had when Westing had first forced him to inhale vum. This time, he focused on the strange sensation, like electricity bouncing around inside his body, trying to leap from his fingers. The electricity buzzed behind his eyes, and the wall in front of him lit up a web of white sparkles, like the sun reflecting off a field of broken glass.

"I didn't just steal vum to piss off Keep Devum," Westing said. "Our true goal lies ahead, below the House of Ahl. So blow us an entrance."

"I don't know how."

"You did it before when you set off one of Jeanne's weapons at the Array. Let the electricity leave your body. Ask it to detonate one of those shining lights you see in front of you."

"What are they, the lights?"

"Vum highlights any substance with which it may interact. The brighter the object, the more strongly you can affect it. Those lights you see now hint at a rare marble that interacts with vum."

Grey nodded, focusing on a single point of light near the edge of the wall. He envisioned it exploding, and a jolt of energy flashed down his arm, forming a blinding, jagged line that connected with the wall. Instead of exploding, the piece of marble shot off towards him with a soft pop, and Westing had to step in and deflect it with Agony's Joy.

"No, not like that," Westing said. "Try again."

"How? I pictured it blowing up, and I felt electricity jump from my fingers… but the stone just popped off the wall instead."

"Picture the light as fuel. By igniting only one side, you created a rocket, like a firework. To produce an explosion, ignite the entire sphere at once. Try commanding it to move in every direction so it won't have any choice but to explode."

Grey focused on another chunk of the lit-up marble, imagining it flying in many directions. The ensuing explosion lifted both Grey and Westing off their feet.

"Now that was a proper vum blast. Follow me!"

The single explosion had ignited many other bits of marble stuck to the wall, blowing open a gaping hole as wide and tall as a normal-sized house. The edges of the shattered wood planks crackled with orange flames, and inside hung an abundance of white smoke. As Grey entered, someone nearby screamed, and a chorus of voices yelled in response.

"We must be quick," Westing said, pulling his collar up to cover his mouth and nose. "Such an explosion will draw Pillar guards and may even attract a maramor."

Grey hurried after Westing, who jogged with confidence through the suffocating smoke. They brushed past residents hurrying towards the source of the commotion, but the frightened noblemen paid Westing and Grey no attention as they darted down a spiral staircase.

"What now?" Grey asked, panting, after they stopped at a vault.

In answer, Westing wedged two hunks of marble, each about the size of his fist, against the door's hinges. "Time to make another boom," Westing said, handing Grey another canister of vum. As he lifted it to his lips, Grey noticed the bright red nozzle and hesitated.

"That's pure vum," said Westing in answer to Grey's unasked question. "You won't be able to detonate so much marble with a centered or diluted sample."

Grey inhaled the gas in one violent breath. Where the centered vum had sent electricity running through his body, pure vum permeated his whole being, vibrating his guts and turning his skin numb. The skin and muscles along his forearms felt as though they might pop from his skeleton, flaying him like a fish, but when he looked down, his arms appeared unchanged. Westing's dark marble grew too bright to look at, so Grey had to command the stone to ignite through squinted eyes.

Electricity tore from his body, smashing into the marble and unleashing its hellfire. Westing yanked Grey behind a nearby wall as flames from the ensuing explosion rushed up the spiral staircase from which they'd descended. A sharp pain stabbed against the inside of Grey's chest, thumping a few more times until it faded.

"That hurt," Grey said, surprised. He rubbed at the lingering pain.

"Yeah, larger explosions hurt the vum user. You'll have to ask Jeanne about it sometime. Here, help me with this door." The explosion had torn the door's hinges off, but the slab of metal still rested within its frame, untouched by the force of the blast.

"You can pull the door from its hinges," Westing said, handing Grey a blue aerostatic canister with a red nozzle. Though the pure vum had already left Grey's body, he remained woozy from the experience. With shaking hands, he accepted the dak canister and inhaled. Spasms ripped through his body, and his limbs convulsed.

"This is killing me!" Grey cried, falling to one knee.

"I assure you it's not. Tear the door free. You have less than two minutes until the pure dak is exhausted."

Grey stumbled forward to grasp the edge of the heavy door opposite the busted hinges and pulled. The vault door shifted in its frame. Planting one leg against the wall, he heaved forward with all his strength, using his leg to gain leverage. To his surprise, the door flew from its hinges, and Grey spun aside to avoid getting crushed. It hit the far wall, then fell to the ground with a thud.

"That must have weighed a ton," Grey said, impressed at the strength pure dak had allowed him to apply.

"About twenty tons."

Curious, Grey stepped into the vault. He'd been expecting a treasure hoard, perhaps filled with canisters of ahl, but instead found a vast, carpeted space holding rows of unadorned beds. On each bed lay an individual. Identical twins, he thought. But that wasn't quite right. While all hundred or so men and women had golden-blond hair, generous lips, and lithe bodies, there were slight differences in height and facial structure.

Many of the individuals sat up at Grey's appearance, then stood when Westing brushed Grey aside, his sword held high. Westing stopped before the nearest man and extended Agony's Joy towards his throat. Rather than turn in fear, he stood his ground as a woman walked forward to the blade, allowing its blunt edge to touch the nape of her neck. A sensual smile bent the corners of her mouth while her white, flowing garment slipped from a shoulder, revealing her breasts.

"How may I serve you?" she asked, her voice low and melodic.

"You and your brothers and sisters are to follow me right now."

"Our masters do not let us leave these chambers," the woman said, taking a step closer to Westing. The sword ran along her shoulder, pushing the remaining strap from her garment, which fell around her ankles.

"I'm giving you permission," Westing told the nude woman.

"We can't leave, but you may stay with us if you'd like. Pleasure beyond your imagination awaits you right here, in our chamber." She reached out to caress Westing's gaunt cheek.

"Do you know what death is?" Westing asked, slapping the woman's hand.

"We know death, yes."

"Good. Then you'll understand my meaning when I tell you I will kill you all, one by one, until those alive come with me. So either you come with me right now, or you die."

"You shouldn't kill them," Grey said from his spot at the door. It's wrong to kill, he thought. But I've killed many times, and I've felt no remorse. Still…

"And how else would you have me convince them to come with us?" Westing asked, craning his neck without moving his sword arm. "They are not rational creatures, these bondmen."

"They're human, not bondmen."

"Oh?" Westing asked before returning his attention to the woman. "This is your final warning."

"We're not allowed to leave. I'm sorry," she said. Westing rotated his wrist, flipping the blade so the leading edge faced her long neck, and applied gentle pressure. Agony's Joy sliced through her neck, and her head dropped to the ground, followed by her body. Grey expected screams from the others, but none came. They all shifted from foot to foot, eyes widened to hundreds of white circles glowing in the dim room.

Westing stepped towards the nearby man, raising Agony's Joy to strike again, but the man shouted, "Stop! We are not supposed to die." He looked around at his brothers and sisters, and they nodded to him. "We will go with you."

"Works for me," Westing said. "Come quickly. Grey, you follow."

All hundred of them filed up the spiral staircase, Westing at the front and Grey trailing behind.

When Grey stepped outside after the last of them filed through the door, he raised his arms against a hail of pebbles kicked up by strong winds. Lightning flashed against the black horizon, followed by the low rumble of distant thunder.

The men and women were all crouched low against the wind, but Grey spotted Kip standing at the edge of Harkk's cliff atop a pile of dead Ventrahl guards. She looked feral, her face raised to the stormy sky with her white hands grasping the ropes of three floating bondmen. These flyer bondmen were grotesque, like gargantuan pigs floating on their backs, stomachs inflated to the size of houses. Fleshy ropes held metal passenger carriages like those from Harkk's trams, which swung below the bondmen. Nearby, Jeanne bent over the dead guards, collecting her weapons from their bodies.

"You know where to take them?" Westing asked Kip, having to shout over the roar of the wind.

Kip sneered.

"Get in," Westing commanded the men and women, and they followed his instructions, filing into the passenger areas hanging below two of the bondmen's backs. "Jeanne, you go with Kip as well. These bondmen must reach their destination."

She nodded, entering the nearest cabin, while Kip launched herself into the air, letting go of the bondmen's tethers. As she floated off with two of the flying bondmen, she turned in the air, screaming, "maramor at Keep Devum!" The gale tore away her words, along with the bondmen.

"Shit," Westing said amidst a blast of thunder. The storm approached Harkk, racing across the barren land with nothing to slow its path. "Time for us to leave."

Westing and Grey hopped into the third bondman's carriage, and Westing urged the creature upwards while Grey gripped the edge of his seat, peering down at the shrinking House of Ahl. He looked towards Keep Devum as lightning flashed again, and he thought he saw a figure plunge from the roof. But the bondman had entered the clouds, and he saw nothing more.

For a minute, the carriage shook, then grew still when they breached the low clouds. Grey allowed himself a sigh of relief.

"So what now?"

"Now we wait a few hours for storm and maramor to pass," Westing answered, standing straight with his back to Grey. The chill, wet air sent shivers down Grey's spine, and he huddled within his thin clothing.

"Here," Westing said, turning to toss Grey a canister of ril. "This diluted ril should let you warm yourself somewhat. You can increase blood flow to your extremities, at least."

"Thanks. So who were those people we rescued? Or kidnapped…"

"They're not people. They may look human, but they're bondmen, created by Estril and programmed by Ventrahl to extract information from across the Empire. Ventrahl calls them dolls, and they are—or were—the core of Ventrahl's power."

"How do they get information?"

"Let's say that men and women speak to these beautiful dolls if they want to continue using their services. When the dolls return to Ventrahl, their masters read their minds. Ventrahl wields this knowledge like a currency matching or exceeding the value of any aerostatic gas."

"And what do you want with them?"

"A doll shortage will cripple Ventrahl's spy operation for a generation, making the great cities far more insular than they've been. Misinformation breeds distrust, and distrust leads to fighting. Since we've just stolen three-quarters of the dolls Ventrahl owns, it will take at least thirty years to replenish their ranks."

"Owns?"

"Yes. These are not people, Grey. Estril grows them in vats and programs their behaviors. I hope that a skilled Seer can reprogram the dolls for our own purposes, since operating our own spy network will come in handy."

"So you didn't want to free them. You only want to use them, like Ventrahl uses them."

"None of us are free while the First Servant lives. You'll come to understand that someday."

Chapter 9

The sun beat down upon the deserted plain, scalding Grey's shoulders, but he didn't dare move. He'd learned over the past week never to take his eyes off Callan, who stood ten feet away, arms hanging at his sides.

They each remained still for twenty minutes before Callan launched himself at Grey, who dove to the side. Callan landed on his feet where Grey had been standing and swung his foot low across the ground. Before Grey regained his balance, Callan had already swept Grey's legs from under him. Rock came up hard behind Grey's back as he flopped backward.

"You got me again," he said, looking up at Callan's massive form. At least Callan's bulk lent him temporary shade.

"Do you always tell your enemy when he has beaten you?" Callan asked.

"I suppose you'd like me to continue fighting to my death."

"I wouldn't call whatever you did 'fighting.' You cannot allow yourself the luxury of relying upon your instincts anymore. If your opponent outthinks you, he'll have you dead within five strikes. Instead of dodging like a fool, why not attack? If you must dodge, you should already have your next move mapped out in your mind."

"Give me dak to even the playing field. You're far stronger than I am. If the past week has taught me anything, it's that I'm unable to defeat you without using aerostacy."

"No," Callan said, shaking his head. "If you use dak, you must assume your opponent is also using dak. Even if ahl quickens the pace of your thoughts, you cannot be sure that your opponent does not have a similar advantage. You must first learn how to control your body and keep focus throughout a fight. After that, we'll discuss augmenting your strength and speed."

"I can't defeat you," Grey said.

"I saw you lose control within Harkk's western mountain. You were in an angered rage, yes, but at least you showed passion. You've shown no emotion since we left Harkk."

"Because I don't experience emotions. Not usually. I've explained this three times."

"You're never going to learn unless you want to learn. You'll never win a battle unless you want to win."

"I wanted to learn how to use ahl." Grey sipped a drop of napthal to ward off the Gentleman, but mastering ahl would prove more effective. Even the smallest dose of napthal slowed Grey's reaction time, making it even more challenging to defeat Callan in their skirmishes.

"Come, we'll reach the river's edge by nightfall." Callan dropped the irritating conversation, but experience taught Grey he'd try again before they rested.

"I don't see any river."

"It's over the horizon."

"Of course."

Their traveling bondman, a lumbering beast with six legs and a wide head, munched away at a nearby patch of grass. Neither the beast nor Callan seemed ever to tire, but Grey's legs were like weights hanging from his sore hips. Callan scooped up the bondman's rope and led it north, followed by a sighing Grey.

"What are bondmen, anyway?" Grey asked. Callan would hold his silence for hours unless spoken to, but he also seemed more than willing to answer any question Grey asked.

"They are creatures shaped by aerostacy for use by humans."

"But how are they created? What drives their minds? Are they conscious?"

"The Array creates them, and if by conscious you mean self-aware, no, they are not."

"So people at the Array build them?"

"Yes, though the process is complex. Only the eldest in the Array have the skill and training to shape new bondmen."

"Dilan used ril to heal me, though. That also seems complex, and he's only a little kid."

"When Dilan healed you back at the Array, he used ril and an aerostatic art known as Knitting to reshape the inside of your body into what it once was. He's a gifted Knitter, and he may even create a replica of an existing bondman, but he's incapable of creating a new design."

"How can we prove the bondmen aren't conscious?" Grey asked, returning to his earlier question. When he looked at the bondman that carried their supplies, its wide eyes stared back at him. It scanned the landscape for obstacles, maintaining a perfect pace to keep within twenty feet of Callan at all times.

"Because the Knitters who create the bondmen must program the creatures' minds to perform specific tasks. They do not understand the world as we do. This bondman has wonderful balance and stamina, and it can keep distance from a person. It's not capable of anything beyond this, and it can't learn new patterns or behaviors."

"Can the Knitters create conscious bondmen, though?"

Callan lurched to a halt and said, "Many thousands of years ago, ambitious aersotacy Knitters attempted this deed. The First Servant forbids the Array from making another attempt."

"Why?"

"Perhaps the First Servant may hold the answer." Callan resumed his pace, and the bondman demurely followed.

"And what about you? How did you join the Array?"

"I'm not a full member of the Array, as I wasn't born in Harkk. I only arrived in Harkk twenty years ago."

"Around the start of the shifter War," Grey said.

"Yes. My skills with dak were strong enough to allow me entrance to the Array, and I continued my education in the capital of the Defiant Empire rather than die in a shifter battle."

"I don't blame you. The war was not pleasant."

"You have a way of understating everything, Grey." Callan smirked, but Grey shrugged, for he preferred not to dwell on the notion that his perception of the world was dull.

A dark line grew against the horizon, distinguishing itself as trees lining a river. The river drew closer as the sun set and Echore rose. For around ten minutes, Echore reflected the sun's light from its mirrored surface, drowning the air with a crisscross of golden rays.

This isn't so bad, Grey thought, letting his hand run over the reassuring presence of the bottle of napthal tucked away in his pocket. And I am curious to see Arndak.

***

Three weeks later, by the time they'd reached the forest separating Harkk's territory from Arndak's lands, Callan's grueling pace and regular training sessions stamped out all of

Grey's curiosity.

"I'd hoped to have made more progress with your training before we reached Arndak, but slowing our pace further is unwise," Callan said. They'd entered the forest earlier that day, and Callan sat against the trunk of a magnificent tree that rose straight towards Echore, which hung almost directly overhead. Echore's silvery surface sparkled between the still leaves. Only the bondman's occasional shuffling disturbed the peace as it munched away at the forest's plentiful foliage.

Grey wished to learn at Callan's speed, but he wasn't capable of mastering any of Callan's techniques. His body was as dull as his mind, his connection to his limbs just as hard to access as his emotions. He sensed Callan's frustration but kept his silence.

"We're three days from Arndak. Everyone there works, so we'll find you a temporary job while I track down the dak shipments in the mines."

"Don't worry. I'll keep out of your way."

Grey had only ever fought against real danger when a single mistake separated victory from death. Fighting Callan was different because he knew the man wouldn't kill him. Hurt him, maybe. But kill him? No. The excitement he experienced while fighting did not exist during Callan's training.

He'd tried to explain this to Callan, of course, but Callan had only replied: "You must use your emotions as motivation, but they cannot drive your decision-making during battle. Your brain is your most valuable weapon, and leaving it on the sidelines during a fight makes you no more capable than two beetles fighting over a pile of dung."

As he often did whenever he pondered his absent emotions, Grey recalled the day his father died. He pushed, trying to force sadness to spill tears from his eyes, but he wound up frustrated. Emotions flowed through other people without having to conjure them. Even Isa's murder didn't summon remorse.

A loud snap interrupted his thoughts. Callan chose their campsite for its location amidst the underbrush, which would make it difficult for predators to approach without warning. His decision paid off because Callan had ample seconds to straighten his clothing before three men stepped from the darkness and into the light of their campfire.

"Why aren't you traveling on the main road?" asked the man in the center. He wore a short sword on his left hip and a hunting bow over his shoulder.

"I'm showing my son the countryside," Callan said. "He's going to enroll in the Array training program soon in Harkk, and I wanted to take him on a trip before his lessons begin."

"You're not headed to Arndak?"

"We are."

"Ah, then we have an issue. Avoiding the main road may make it appear that you are attempting to avoid the governor's toll."

"Toll? Entry to Arndak is free, just like all other cities in the Defiant Empire."

"Dak production isn't what it used to be," the soldier said. "Arndak's citizens must find other ways to survive."

"Are you certain you're collecting this toll for your governor?"

"I don't like your tone." The soldier frowned, and Grey noticed his hand now rested on the hilt of his sword.

"I suggest nothing," Callan said, raising his hands to show he wasn't preparing to fight. "Very well. What payment do you require?"

"That depends upon what you have. We'll search your bondman and take what we need. Boy, go fetch it," he ordered Grey.

Grey walked to their tied bondman, unhooked the

creature, and led it back to the clearing. The soldiers wasted no time rummaging through their many packs while Callan watched. The soldiers removed three bags of cured meats, their currency, and several spare outfits. When they reached the sack containing the aerostatic gas canisters, Callan spoke.

"I'm afraid we'll need those for our travels, gentlemen. Help yourselves to anything else, but please leave the marble."

"There's an awful lot of gas here," the soldier said.

"I belong to the Array in Harkk. Most of us do not leave the mountain without an adequate supply."

"The Array, eh? We don't get your kind much around here, save for your outpost in the city. But those hermits have lived here most of their lives with us, after all." The soldiers continued to unload the aerostatic canisters, despite Callan's request. They loaded them into their crate, which one soldier had carried over to the bondman.

"I cannot allow you to take those," Callan said, stepping forward. Two soldiers drew their swords, and five more militiamen stepped into the clearing behind Grey.

"Wait!" the soldier shouted at his men, then turned to Callan and said, "Look, you seem reasonable, so I'll be honest with you. We are members of Arndak's militia, like I said, but we are not collecting a toll on behalf of the governor, as you suspected. With the reduction in dak supply, we must find new ways to feed our families. Your aerostatic canisters will support us for a year, so we'll take those and leave your other possessions."

"And if I resist?"

"We'll kill you and your son and take them, anyway."

Callan sighed. "Very well then." He jumped at the soldier, who stood over ten feet away. Mid-jump, Callan produced a canister of dak from his sleeve, inhaled its contents, and tossed it to the side. He landed on the soldier's chest, crushing his ribcage. The soldiers to either side of Callan swung their swords, but Callan's hands shot out to grab their necks.

"Drop your weapons," he ordered. The soldiers didn't listen. Grey could hear their vertebrae crack under the force of Callan's grip. They dropped to the ground, dead.

The remaining five soldiers stepped forwards, their steady sword arms a testament to their training. Something landed near Grey's feet, and he and Callan dove to the ground before the object exploded. Two more balls fell from the tree, exploding in mid-air and raining down shards of glass around them. A tiny chip penetrated the back of Grey's thigh, and he pulled it out.

A swordhand leaped at Grey while the rest circled Callan. Grey had nothing with which to block the soldier's attacks, so he crouched and dodged to avoid the man's wild swings. The blade nicked Grey's arm and then his back in quick succession as he twisted away. Then a metal bar landed behind Grey's foot, and he tripped, falling onto his side. The soldier stabbed forward with his sword, but it dropped from his hand mid-thrust. Grey wasted no time grabbing it and plunging it deep into the man's abdomen. It went in roughly, unlike the Agony's clean incisions.

The man fell to his knees to reveal a boy standing behind him, his flushed face displaying a wide grin.

"Bow?" Grey asked, pulling the sword from the dying man and shaking it clean.

"That's three times now I've saved your life," Bow said.

"But… how did you get here? We're weeks away from Harkk."

"Never mind that now. Save Callan."

"What? Oh, yeah."

The four men surrounding Callan edged towards him, wary of his powerful, long arms. Callan, knowing he'd have no chance where he stood, jumped high over the swordhands. One man slashed a deep cut into his calf as he soared overhead, and when Callan landed, he collapsed onto one knee. He took another puff of dak, using the added strength to stand. The four men advanced, followed by the blaster who'd been lobbing the exploding missiles.

Grey dashed into the fray, a familiar well of emotion splashing through his nervous system now that he'd sweat out much of the napthal. Sword in hand, he dove headfirst into the nearest man's back. The sword penetrated his ribcage, where it stuck. Not bothering to remove it, Grey used it to swing himself around and kick another soldier in the side. Both men toppled.

The final two swordhands tipped their heads to see the action, and Callan took advantage of their momentary distraction. He punched one in the sternum, cracking the man's chest. The final swordhand dropped his weapon, yelling, "I surrender!"

Callan shook his head, grasping the man's skull in his massive hand and squeezing hard. Grey laughed, turning to face the Blaster. One, two, then three projectiles flew from the man's fingertips, propelled by tiny explosions. Grey ducked and dashed forward. Before the Blaster could pull another weapon from his cloak, Grey jumped on him. Though the man weighed much more than Grey, he couldn't balance on the uneven ground, and he fell with Grey's hands around his neck.

The man tried to pry Grey's hands free, but he slapped the Blaster's hands away and pinned them with his knees to choke the life from his neck. Callan watched, ready to help, but Grey didn't need any. The man died with Grey's hands around his neck. Grey waited for his pulse to slow and then stop, yet he remained hunched over the man, his shoulders trembling. Bow walked over and placed his hand on Grey's head.

The bloodlust drained from him, and he unclenched his hands.

"You fought well," Callan said. "You were almost a different person."

"My life was in danger. Like I said, it helps."

"Perhaps, perhaps. We'll discuss that later, after we bury these bodies and travel far from here. We had to kill them to protect our mission, but we also cannot have their deaths traced to us, for it will ruin our anonymity. Bow, keep an eye out for more soldiers while we dig."

Callan handed Grey a canister of dak and a shovel, then wrapped a bandage around his bleeding calf. Grey tended to his superficial wounds before digging. Even with his increased strength, the digging went slowly, and Echore had set by the time they'd dug a hole deep enough to bury the men. After they'd packed down the dirt to Callan's satisfaction, he led them into the forest.

When they cleared the tree line, Callan turned to Bow and asked, "Why are you here?"

"I've been following you this entire way," Bow said.

"Did Westing send you?"

"No. I came to train Grey in ahl, of course. Isn't that what you wanted, Grey?"

"Yes, but Westing asked you to stay in Harkk."

"He'll be furious, sure, but what's he going to do? Follow me here?"

"I wouldn't be surprised if he did," Callan said. "Come, let's try to enter Arndak as anonymous travelers, not wanted criminals."

An hour later, Bow said, "Grey, I noticed something while you were fighting." He and Grey had trailed far behind Callan, unable to match the man's speed.

"Yeah?"

"When most people fight, a burst of adrenaline gives their bodies an extra edge, but with you, something different happened. A massive well of feelings, primarily joy, rushed through you. The emotions weren't elevated versions of their normal selves. It was like you were a different person."

"You could sense all of that?"

"Yes, if I'm using pure ahl… which I had to do to force the soldier to drop his weapon."

"I think you're right," Grey said. "My emotions only arise while I'm fighting."

"When you killed those two men, your emotions shone."

"Yes… it was joy. I can't explain why. Thinking about it now brings me no joy, though. Or any other feeling."

"Let me try something. I still have enough ahl in my system to pull it off."

Bow squinted, and Grey experienced the strangest sensation. The world around him brightened, the barest glow from the rising sun pulsating with a vibrant warmth across distant mountains. Sounds grew so much that he could hear his heart beating in his chest. He smiled at Bow as an unfamiliar emotion fought to make itself heard. Then it all slammed shut. The curtains closed, and Grey let out a hiss of air between his teeth. Losing the sensation was akin to losing a limb or his eyesight. His mind ached to recapture what he'd just experienced.

"All out of ahl," Bow said.

"That was…" Grey trailed off. Now that the sensation had disappeared, capturing the experience in words became impossible. His longing to reclaim the excitement faded into a dull ache and swirled into nothingness. "I felt very different from what I am used to feeling," he said.

"Different how? Sleepy? Drowsy?"

"No, quite the opposite. I don't think I've ever been more awake."

"Wow! That's amazing. I expected that, but I'm still surprised. You know those Fizzers you visited with Callan? Well, they huff a processed form of ahl that banishes the topmost layer of consciousness. It puts them in a stupor, allowing them to drift off into a world of imagination fueled by the deeper reaches of their minds. I used ahl a moment ago to repress this layer of your consciousness, just like Fizz —albeit with far greater nuance."

"And it didn't put me to sleep."

"My instructors taught me that Fizz wasn't a narcotic; it was a therapeutic drug for those who'd undergone great trauma and had developed harmful coping mechanisms to deal with their mental instabilities. In these patients, the ahl erases the coping mechanism."

"You're suggesting trauma stole my emotions, but I've felt nothing for as long as I remember."

"Whatever the cause, the result is that you have a well-developed filter that makes it difficult for your emotions to surface. What tipped me off was your fight. When instincts control your actions during a battle, you lower that 'emotion barrier' to ensure survival."

"I understand. Can I duplicate the effect by inhaling Fizz?"

"Oh no. You don't want to remove this layer of your consciousness like I did a minute ago. You'll want to use ahl to strengthen what's underneath using 'Attention.'"

"What about replicating the effects of napthal?"

"Napthal is an anesthetic. I think our best bet is to strengthen your Attention."

"I find napthal necessary to focus," Grey said truthfully.

"Hm, we'll have to look into that further. It makes no sense, but your mind is unique. I figured you were special from the moment I spotted you."

Bow's comment confused Grey, so he held his tongue until Callan had stopped near another line of trees.

"We're going to camp in here for today. We could use the rest."

The sun was pushing its way above the horizon, but Grey thought it didn't look as beautiful as it had a few minutes ago, when Bow had been allowing his feelings to surge.

Chapter 10

A narrow canyon, a hundred feet wide and five miles long, pierced the metal-blue rock that Grey, Callan, and Bow had been scrambling over for the past day. Flat sheets of smooth stone jutted out at peculiar angles for miles, with no discernible pattern to their layout. Travel became a laborious exercise in repetitive ascents and descents, and Grey's knees and arms bore dozens of scrapes and bruises. Only their bondman, whose feet gripped the slick surface, was unfazed.

"How do we get across?" Grey asked.

"We don't," Callan said. "We're standing above Arndak. Come."

Callan led Grey and Bow over one last rock, where another bondman waited. They stepped onto its broad back, and it climbed into the canyon, looping its claw-like feet through hooks drilled into smooth rock. Far, far below, a fiery orange splashed up the dark canyon walls, and sweat formed on Grey's brow, dripping into his eyes. Steam swirled in wispy tufts, growing thicker the further they descended.

"We're here," Callan said, just as the bondman jolted to a halt at a metal platform bolted to the sheer cliff face. Rusty metal struts held together hundreds of similar platforms, forming a structure like a web spun by a drunken spider. Narrow entrances, mere cracks in the rock, led towards the interior of the cliff. "We're in Arndak's upper reaches, where the trade workers live. It gets somewhat nicer a few hundred feet down and then much, much worse when you reach the mines."

"I've read about this," Bow said. "But seeing it makes me wonder how anyone can live here."

"The miners suffer the most, scraping away at unstable rock to find pockets of trapped dak." Callan led them into the nearest crack in the cliff. "These sections are older and more stable."

"I suppose," Bow muttered, not convinced.

Despite Bow's doubt, Grey had to agree with Callan. The deeper they delved into the cliff, the more the tunnels resembled the Array's comfortable labyrinth. One cramped tunnel drilled into a mountain was just like the next.

Callan led them to an open space with distant walls and a raised ceiling. Merchant booths lined the hall, with colorful blankets holding a dizzying array of merchandise. Grubby, unwashed vendors peddled their wares to the crowd, and Grey thought it felt a bit too much like the cavern of Fizzers deep within Harkk's mountain.

The stench of too many bodies in a confined washed into Grey's nostrils, and he choked. Callan noticed and handed both Bow and Grey sets of nose plugs.

"I don't believe it would be wise for us to contact members of the Array," Callan said. "We've no way of guessing how they'd react to our investigation, and Westing believes Arndak's Array is disloyal to Harkk. So we'd better go to the source."

"The dak mines," Bow guessed.

"Yes, exactly. Aside from a small town called Shallow Canyon, dak only rises through this deep channel in the earth. We'll be able to track where the gas goes if we apply to work in the mines."

"Do new miners seek work?" Bow asked, sniffing at the muggy air through his nose plugs.

"Indeed. The lure of striking a dak deposit presents potent motivation. However, most miners descend from ancestors who worked in the mines for hundreds of years. Sometimes thousands. Only the death of a childless miner warrants the issuance of new permits."

"Then how will we gain entry?"

"Bribes. You and Grey will need to stay above while I try to trace the dak's path and discover where it's going."

"I grew up in Shallow Canyon," Grey said. "Could that help?"

Callan raised his eyebrows. "You know, that might work. Come, we'll talk to my contact."

Callan led them to one merchant, in particular, a thick man like all the others. Dirt was smeared up the man's arms in messy streaks, though his patchwork clothing was unsoiled. He didn't smell awful either, for which Grey was thankful.

"Ivar," Callan said, extending his muscled arm to the seated merchant.

"My friend Callan," Ivan answered, allowing himself to be pulled to his feet by Callan's iron grip. "It's been years… many, many years!"

"Too long," Callan agreed.

"You've been busy mastering that infamous Harkk magic? Running the place yet, eh?"

"Aerostacy, not magic, my old friend. And while I've learned a great deal, I'm not running the place."

"You'll have to tell me about it over dinner. Come!" Ivar rolled up his blanket, but Callan stopped him.

"Another night, I promise. Business first."

"Business, I see. Very well, but you'll be having a meal with me tomorrow, even if I have to tie you down and feed you myself."

"Okay, okay. I accept."

Ivar huffed gas, and the sounds of the crowded market faded to a distant whisper.

"We can talk now," Ivar said.

"That was not necessary," Callan said, frowning.

"What did he do?" Grey asked.

"It's Ivar showing off."

"Nonsense. It's the one aerostatic trick I have. Picked it up from another trader ages ago, and it ensures no one will overhear us."

"Unless someone else is using ahl as well and is more skilled."

"More skilled, you say? I'm offended."

"Bow, will you boost his blur, please?" Then he explained, "It's one of ahl's more interesting uses. When focused on an individual, ahl's effects can be deep and exact — as you've experienced during Bow's manipulations of your mind. You can also focus ahl's effects on a crowd and manipulate large groups of people with general instructions. Bow and Ivar are projecting a false image to our surroundings to prevent eavesdropping."

"The biggest drawback is that another ahl user of enough skill can penetrate such a deception," Bow added.

"Yes, yes, and it uses up this very pricey ahl," Ivar said. "So, let's get to the point, shall we?"

"Very well. I need a mining permit," Callan said.

"I can get you a position on one of the collection barges…"

"As I suspected. How much will it cost?"

"Five hundred Harkk coins to the station master, another three hundred to the barge captain, and a couple thousand to the scribes in the Array's record-keeping office. And that's on top of a hefty supply of gas."

"The Array scribes are so easily bribed?" Callan asked.

"They're just the librarian equivalent of mercenaries. Not

full-fledged members of the Array. The real magicians keep themselves squirreled away in their cave, down below the mines."

"The Array has always valued its privacy. At least we saved our gas from the bandits."

"Ah yes, Arndak's militia, I imagine. They've been getting quite aggressive. Anyway, those coins and aerostatic bribes should cover your permit. But you already know how to bribe your way into secret places. What is it you really want?"

"This boy, Grey, is the son of a dak miner in Shallow Canyon. I want you to help secure a work permit for him here in Arndak. It would help my mission."

"Now, that is a tricky request."

"Can it be done?"

"That depends on the name of your father, Grey."

"Gunnar Madsen," Grey answered. He died during a sudden dak-quake."

"Madsen, let me think… yes, there is a Madsen family here in Arndak. You'll hardly believe this, but all three of the Madsen sons died in a dak blowout, much like the boy's father."

"You don't say," Callan said.

"Grey may be allowed to work in the mines, though the authorities will assign him to an outermost region that's all but exhausted."

"How do we proceed?"

"We go to the Array."

"Not an option."

"Ha, you enjoy making life difficult for me. Let's see, let's see. The station master may well have an ahl clerk who can help, if you're lucky."

"I knew you'd come through," Callan said, giving the short man a tight hug. "Grey, we'll leave at once — no point in wasting time. And Ivar… I'll see you for dinner, my old friend."

Chapter 11

Grey entered the abandoned tunnels of the upper dak mines and became quite lost. Each tunnel forked into at least three offshoots, and each node continued to branch into smaller passageways. Long ago, miners had smashed their way through the rock in a desperate search for then-plentiful dak, creating a gargantuan maze of tangled, unstable pathways into the cliff. Now the entire area stood abandoned as the miners descended to more promising grounds.

Three sealant disks hung from Grey's back, and he carried a standard pickaxe, which the obese station master had handed him without instruction. In fact, the only words he'd spoken to Grey were, "Levels one through five are fine, but don't descend past level five."

After describing his father, it had been easy to get a temporary mining permit, pending further investigation into Grey's past. Arndak respected the Madsen line, at least well enough to grant Grey access to the mines. The absence left by the death of the three Madsen sons and Callan's substantial bribe summoned a permit from the station master's drawer with magical speed.

"Keep your eyes and ears open," Callan had said after leaving the station. "I'll see if I can learn anything in the dak supply chain, and we'll rendezvous tonight at headquarters."

Headquarters was Ivar's spare room, a hastily cleaned supply closet. Why Callan decided they should all stay there was beyond Grey, but Ivar seemed thrilled by the company. Bow didn't protest, but he looked displeased. After all, he would be spending most of his time with Ivar.

"It's the cost of your ill-advised trip," Callan had said when Bow protested.

Grey decided that he'd much rather receive an ahl lesson from Bow than wander this dried-up section of the dak mine. Maybe he'd sneak back early to begin his training.

He hefted the pickaxe, a lightweight metal rod with a curved blade at the end. The edge twinkled in the dim light cast by the pockets of glowing bondmen dangling every few feet throughout the tunnel. When he tapped the end of the blade against an expanse of rock, the impact sent shockwaves up through his arm. The lightness of the tool made it feel fragile, as if it might shatter or snap if he swung it any harder. Nevertheless, he raised it over his shoulder and brought it down against the rock.

Instead of a massive clang, the blade sunk into the rock like a sharp knife stabbed into a thick pat of butter. Puzzled, Grey tried to pry the axe free. It was stuck. No matter how hard he pulled, the blade would not budge.

"What in Echore is going on?" he asked himself, stepping back to examine the tool. The shaft of the pickaxe was a straight, cylindrical expanse of dull metal, save for a thin line one inch from the end. Grey pushed and twisted it to no effect. Then he pulled, and the inner shaft slid from the wall. Thinking he'd broken the fragile axe, he pressed it back together. A loud hiss emanated from the buried end of the axe, followed by a tremendous heat. The rock boiled away around the pickaxe, turning molten-red before sloshing to the ground.

Grey jumped back just as the molten rock landed near his

feet. The axe dropped to the side, next to the cooling rock. After the sizzling from the rock died down, a new hum began in the walls, and a swift rush of wind swept past Grey. Then all fell silent.

The handle holds compressed vum to melt the rock, Grey realized. Releasing the aerostatic gas into the cliff produced a heat intense enough to melt stone. That also explains the heat down in the mines.

After picking up the axe, Grey walked further into the mine, his annoyance replaced with mild curiosity. Perhaps he could learn something after all.

The deeper he walked, the more collapsed tunnels he encountered, and whenever he paused, the silence bore down around him. A chill ran up his right arm, causing the fine hairs to stand up all along his skin. He rubbed at his arm, but the goosebumps only grew more pronounced. His skin, or something just below the surface of his skin, was being pulled in a specific direction.

Now more than curious, Grey walked towards the building sensation, following the tingling pull through a series of twists and turns. The force only grew stronger as he proceeded until his skeleton vibrated, urging his muscles to propel his body. It was a pleasant feeling.

All enjoyment vanished when he rounded a corner to see the Gentleman leaning against the tunnel wall. The old man's clean, long jacket draped across his razor-thin shoulders while a smile threatened the corners of his dark lips.

"You've arrived," said the Gentleman, stepping forward. Grey reached for the napthal in the pouch at his waist, only to remember that he'd left the bottle at Ivar's home with Bow. So Grey swung the pickaxe at the Gentleman, but it sailed through his ghostly frame, embedding itself in the wall. The section of rock behind the Gentleman melted, and an explosion blew Grey back a dozen feet.

Dak hissed out through the small opening he'd created, filling the tunnel with toxic smog. Grey reached for a disk on his back, and, using every available surface of his body, he pressed the disk against the breach. The rubber-like material melted against the rock, forming an airtight seal to keep the potent dak locked in its undiscovered chamber.

Grey had already ingested a fair amount of dak, and the familiar inhuman strength pulsed through his limbs. His weariness vanished, along with any sign of the Gentleman. Eager to return to his napthal before the Gentleman reappeared, Grey used his newfound strength to sprint from the mine. He ran in the general direction of the exit until he emerged into the hot Arndak canyon.

The strange bondman Grey had ridden into the mine struggled against its tether. Its upper body, a bulging sack of floating helium, could lift five large men from the deepest levels of the mine to the upper reaches of Arndak and beyond. Thick, wet ropes hung from its inflated body, ending in balls of clotted flesh, each meant to carry a single person. Grey swallowed his distaste and sat on the ball, poking at a knob of hardened flesh.

With the tether released, the bondman rose, picking up speed as it traveled. Grey gripped the sticky rope so hard his fists turned white until an attendant at the upper station hooked the creature into a docking berth.

Grey jumped off onto one of Arndak's many metal platforms. With his memory of the Gentleman's unexpected appearance fresh in his mind, he hurried into the dak station, a large, windowless building built into the sheer cliff. A spiked metal net prevented unauthorized access from above, so miners could only enter through a guarded hallway hewn into solid rock.

Because the morning shift had begun two hours ago, the narrow passage held only three guardsmen and their inspection equipment. Bondmen, designed to detect hidden dak on any miner who might try to sneak a bottle to sell on the black market, protruded from the walls every few feet. Their wet snouts twitched, eager to spy out trace elements of dak.

Grey flinched as he passed them, but they made no further movement, so he kept walking. It wasn't until he'd reached the end of the hall that a guard called, "Stop! You're missing one of your dak seals."

"Yes, I uh..." Grey trailed off. After his brush with the Gentleman and with dak still flowing through his veins, he wanted to return to his napthal. His mind was cloudy, his thoughts slow. So he blurted the truth. "I used it to seal in a dak deposit."

"If that's true, why didn't you notify the station master?" the guard asked, eying Grey.

"It's my first day in the mines."

"Son, you're telling me you just happened upon a deposit on your first day? What level? One hundred twenty-six? I hear there have been discoveries down there."

"Level two, near the back of the southwest quadrant. Look, if you want to claim it for yourself, be my guest. I'll tell you where—"

"What are you implying?" the guard asked, standing up straighter. "That I would claim another man's dak haul as my own?"

"No, I just—"

"I think you'd better wait here while I contact the station master. Gerald, take Henry and check for the deposit this boy claims he's found. Don't forget to bring your pressure gauge and sounder!"

For a long half-hour, Grey stood in the guardroom, clenching and unclenching his fists. He considered knocking out the single guard and leaving, but that'd almost certainly hinder Callan's mission. Eventually, the two other guards reappeared, followed by the same station master who'd issued Grey's permit earlier that day.

The master had appeared large behind his desk, but it wasn't until he stood in front of Grey that Grey appreciated the size of the man. Fat rolled over his expansive waist, drooping past his knees, while each thigh was several times the size of Grey's torso. His neck lived far below the ring of skin that hung from his sizable jowl. Blond hair formed a tight circle at the apex of his globular head, like a cap.

"The guard tells me you've discovered dak," the station master said, using his thick wrist to wipe sweat from his broad, greasy brow.

"Yes, I did."

"What's your name, boy?"

"Grey."

"Do you realize the penalty for lying about discovering dak, Grey?"

"No."

"Well, there is none." The station master guffawed. "But I'll take it upon myself to revoke the permit I issued this morning if you brought me here for nothing."

"I—"

"Sir," said a returning guard. He'd run back from the mines and leaned against the door for support, his legs threatening to cave out from under him with the occasional wobble.

"Out with it!" cried the station master.

"A deposit… of dak… the largest in years. As much as six months' supply… right in level two. The boy… wasn't lying." The guard collapsed, and the station master's eyes widened within their caves.

"Fetch the governor! We thought we would not meet Harkk's quota, but this might turn the month!"

"That won't be necessary," said a pleasant voice. Grey turned to spot a girl, perhaps thirteen years old, standing over the tired guard. The guard sprang to his feet despite his exhaustion.

"Miss Winfer," the guard said, standing at attention. Even the station master straightened.

"May I present the governor's daughter, miss Leigh Winfer," the station master said.

"How do you do…?"

"My name is Grey."

"How do you do, Grey?"

"I'm fine." Grey examined the girl, noting her calloused hands and worker's pants unbecoming of a young woman, let alone a child of royalty. Her pinched nose and wide ears gave her an elf-like appearance, at once childlike and filled with wisdom. She smiled at Grey, but he returned the stare without emotion.

"Miss Winfer, fetch your father at once," the station master urged. "I have a matter of importance to discuss with him."

"My father is away," Leigh said in a calm, clear voice that portrayed an authority beyond her years. "I'm capable of handling this, Trystan."

"Of course, my lady." The obese station master backed away, planting himself on a nearby bench, which complained under his weight.

"Now then," Leigh said, turning to Grey. "How did you come upon this dak deposit when it has gone undiscovered for hundreds of years?"

"It was luck. I wandered the mines for a couple of hours, and I heard a hiss. A tiny amount of dak was escaping through the wall. I used my pickaxe to widen the hole, and then I sealed the opening before returning."

"How much is it?"

"We haven't had time to assess the size of the cavern," the

guardsman said. "But our guage indicates immense pressure, and our mobile-sounding bondman didn't reach the chamber's far side. I'm comfortable estimating more than a month's supply is beyond Grey's seal."

"Very well," Leigh said. "Trystan, process the dak and send word to the First Servant at once via Flyer. Don't send a bondman."

"Yes, ma'am. And please tell your father that the men would much enjoy a visit from him upon his return."

"I'll pass along your message."

"We would appreciate it," Trystan said, implying that he'd rather deal with Leigh's father than the proud young woman standing before him. If his attitude bothered Leigh, she kept it well hidden.

"Leave now, Trystan, and begin your work. Take your guards with you." Trystan backed out, his vast body grazing the edges of the doorframe. The three guards followed, leaving Grey alone with Leigh. She turned towards him and pierced him with her round, dark eyes.

"Such a monumental discovery demands an equal reward, don't you think?"

"I..." Grey debated refusing, but he figured odd behavior might set off more alarm bells than he'd already triggered with his discovery. Besides, he wasn't due back at Ivar's home for many hours. "I will accept whatever award you offer, my lady."

"My name is Leigh, so use that when addressing me. Come, we'll walk."

"Yes, Leigh."

As they delved into Arndak, she asked, "How did you gain entry to our mines?"

"I am a Madsen."

"Ah, I see. I remember the Madsens, though I don't recall your father."

"He left Arndak before you were born." They rounded a corner, entering a wide passageway through which many people wandered.

"Your hair's the wrong color for a Madsen, and you're too slender. And, to put it bluntly, you're far more attractive. The Madsens are a rather plain folk."

"Maybe I resemble my mother," Grey said.

"Who is she?"

"I don't remember her, and my father never spoke of her." Leigh strode into one of the adjoining tunnels, and Grey followed.

"I don't recall my mother either," Leigh said. "Though my father often spoke of her. She was from Estril, which many consider Arndak's opposite. Estril floats atop a placid sea, while Arndak is hard. All sharp edges, dirt, and blistering heat. I've never visited Estril. Have you?"

"No." Grey thought his answer truthful, though two years of missing memories suggested otherwise.

"Sometimes, I imagine Estril houses a thousand girls who look like me," Leigh said. Grey decided to smile, so he forced his lips up at the ends. He was never much good at smiling, and his awkward response ended the conversation for the rest of their walk.

Leigh and Grey emerged from the path into a far larger space than any Grey had seen in Arndak, with smooth ceilings a hundred feet above and four rows of round columns spaced from one end of the hall to the other. The deafening roar of thousands of shouted conversations echoed in Grey's ears.

The hall had seen better days. Grime clung to every surface in layers so thick that Grey doubted whether the most potent bleach could remove it. The columns were chipped and scarred a dozen feet up, and several had wide cracks running up their lengths. At the end of the hall, a single metal plate stretched across an opening. Rivets, each the size of Grey's head, dotted its circumference.

A single door punctured the metal wall, which Leigh approached. A guardsman pulled open the door, using his foot to brace himself against the doorframe to allow Leigh and Grey to slip through into a meadow of the greenest grass he had ever seen.

"Welcome home," Leigh said, gesturing towards a house several hundred feet away.

"This is very... unexpected," Grey said, and Leigh laughed.

"That's the most understated reaction I've ever seen. Whenever I've brought anyone here, they gasp and fall to their knees in shock."

"I'm not an emotional person," Grey said. "I could pretend to be more excited."

"No, no. I rather enjoy your honest reaction. Are you hungry, Grey? I'm famished. Come inside, and I'll prepare sandwiches."

As they approached the house, Grey appreciated its age. Distortions warped its glass windows, thicker on the bottom than the top, and the wood panels cracked against the underlying beams.

"Come in," Leigh said, holding open the ancient oak door for Grey. She led him to the kitchen, which contained only primitive cooking equipment and had no bondmen.

"My father told me that our ancient ancestors built this chamber during the First Servant's war with the gods, who are now locked forever in Echore. They believed they'd be able to survive down here should the First Servant not prevail in his battle with the gods. They'd intended to build an entire village, but they only wound up building this lonely house. Our line has lived here, even as the Arndak mines grew and aerostacy became the Defiant Empire's dominant currency."

"Why not build more homes?"

"Because industrializing this chamber would ruin its beauty. Do you want these pastures to resemble the rest of Arndak? No, we should keep this space to remember a time when humans lived in harmony with the land, when we had reason to be happy."

Leigh lit a fire in the wood stove and pulled out a loaf of bread, along with an assortment of vegetables.

"I'm a vegetarian," she explained. "Myself and a few trusted employees tend the fields."

"The Array's bondmen can do twice the labor in half the time."

"I do not allow bondmen in this chamber."

"What about your father? Does he allow them?"

"He doesn't have an opinion." Leigh chopped the vegetables, tossing them into a heated pan atop the stove. Sizzling tones filled Grey's ears, and his nose detected an unfamiliar yet pleasing aroma. "Slice that bread for me?"

Grey picked up a knife and cut four slices from the loaf. Leigh loaded them with vegetables, spooned sauce on top from a nearby cupboard, and took a giant bite.

"You should try it," she said through the food in her mouth. She'd eaten almost half the sandwich in one bite. Grey ate his sandwich, gazing out the window at the field.

"Now then," Leigh said, wiping her mouth with the back of her wrist. "The reward. You might live as a Harkk nobleman with the money from such a discovery."

"I don't need money."

"No? What, then? Name it, and I'll grant your reward."

Without realizing it, Grey was about to risk Westing's entire mission with his request. He meant to seek answers to Callan's questions, but he didn't anticipate the terrible power that lay at this young woman's fingertips—for if he had known, he would never have spoken his following sentence.

"I'll take payment as an answer to this question: where does the First Servant send your dak supply, if not to Harkk?"

Leigh froze, gripping the countertop to prevent herself from strangling Grey. Her eyes played across him, searching for a sign. Her face relaxed, and she released her grip. Like Grey, she'd decided to take a risk.

"We're channeling the dak to a site on the outskirts of the Defiant Empire, just past the old battle lines from the shifter War, though I'm not privy to its precise location. The First Servant claims to undertake a project vital to his Empire's very survival, so he's commanded all aerostatic gases be directed to this mysterious site. maramors oversee each of the supply routes."

Grey paused, searching for a reply. "I see."

"Now let me ask you something, Grey. How did you discover the dak? One truth deserves another."

"I share a deep connection with the aerostatic gases, particularly dak. It alerted me to its presence."

"I'm relieved you said that. Very relieved."

"Why?"

"Because I'm sworn to report spies who ask about the dak supply chain. If you hadn't been special, I would have called Arndak's maramor to kill you."

"Special?"

"If I didn't think you could help me, I'd have had to kill you."

"Don't let her threaten you," the Gentleman said, emerging from a dark corner of the room. "You should cut her unworthy throat or remove her arms and legs but let her live. Yes, that might be worse for her."

Grey's temples burned as the familiar headache took hold. The longer he stayed, the worse it would become until he gave in and followed the Gentleman's instructions. And then the pleasure would come. After he killed Leigh, he'd feel the most powerful surge of bliss, a feeling unlike any other he'd experienced. He had to leave before the Gentleman broke his will.

Nothing is more important than having Bow teach me how to use ahl to replicate the effects of napthal, Grey thought.

"Why do you need my help?" Grey asked, struggling to excuse himself.

"My father is dead, Grey. He died three years ago in a mining accident. There were seven witnesses, and the maramor killed all three. The Array replaced him with a bondman who shares his appearance but not his mind."

"You want to leave?" Grey asked.

"The only place she'll be going is to her fields, where her blood and meat will fertilize the next season's crops," the Gentleman said.

"If I don't leave, the maramors will force me into servitude as a breeding wife. The First Servant will choose a man to impregnate me; then a maramor will murder him. A Knitter will feed me ril to speed the pregnancy, and I will continue having children until I produce a male heir to rule Arndak in the First Servant's name."

"Only a man can rule?" Grey asked, puzzled. The headache was pounding now.

"Our people see little value in women. The boy I birth would not take over as ruler until he turns twenty-three, which means I will be at least in my mid-thirties when I'm freed, at the end of my lifespan given the aerostatic gases I'll have inhaled."

"I can help you leave, but I need to go see my friend first. He is from the Array, though he isn't with them."

"I've decided to trust you this far. I see no harm in allowing this. But return within the day, or I'm afraid it will be too late."

"Thank you, Leigh. It was nice to meet you, and I'll see you again soon."

"Don't leave," the Gentleman said. "Kill her. Kill her now!"

Grey turned, though his limbs shook with each step.

Chapter 12

Grey rushed through Arndak's twisted corridors towards Ivar's home, not noticing when he bumped into a woman carrying a bundle of textiles or toppled a merchant's display. The distinction between the Gentleman's intention and his own desires blurred to nonexistence. Every ounce of Grey's willpower kept him moving instead of turning back to murder Leigh in the horrific fashion laid out by the Gentleman. His headache had transformed into a constant stream of agony, as if a dull blade scraped the inside of his skull.

The last hundred feet were the hardest, and three times he turned back towards Leigh's home. No, he told himself. Keep going. Find napthal.

"You won't make it," the Gentleman said, his stick-thin form barring Grey's way.

I will, Grey thought as he ducked under the Gentleman's outstretched arms.

Grey reached Ivar's quarters, shouldering his way through the door before collapsing onto the ground. Bow jumped to his feet, alarmed.

"Bow," Grey cried. "Help me!"

He saw Bow reach for a flask at his side. Then he lost consciousness. His dreams were bloody. With a gleeful howl, he charged into a shifter horde, blobs of flesh that writhed across the landscape like amoebas. He held Agony's Joy aloft like the deadliest arrowhead ever created and slashed shifter flesh. Blood filled craters on the battlefield, turning the soil into an unsettling deep red and drenching Grey's ragged clothing. Only Agony's Joy remained untouched in a world turned red.

Grey woke with his head cradled in Bow's lap, his cool hand cupping Grey's face. A calming energy flowed through his mind. All thoughts of violence vanished, and the Gentleman's pain had subsided.

"What happened?" Grey asked.

"Your thoughts were disappearing, sinking to an area of your mind I couldn't follow as something else slid into their place. I used ahl to strengthen your sense of self." Grey sat up, wiping sweat from his brow.

"I need you to teach me how to do that myself. Please."

"That's one reason I came with you, to teach you how to use ahl like you asked."

"And the other reasons?"

"After you surface your emotions, you'll figure out my other reasons yourself."

Grey watched Bow clean the compact room, noting the precision with which his hands lifted and maneuvered items. His thin neck curved into his blond hair, and Grey caught the outline of his narrow shoulders through his worn shirt. Grey's breaths deepened while he watched Bow work, relaxing him as the sweat dried in a stale sheet covering his exhausted body.

Knowing the napthal lay within reach brought significant comfort. The Gentleman had nearly won this time, and Grey vowed with new determination to place his ahl training above all other priorities.

"Callan," Grey said as soon as the large man lumbered into

the room. "I have something to tell—"

He never finished the sentence because Westing stepped through the door behind Callan. His bald head gleamed in the sharp light of Ivar's unshielded glow worms. Dark eyes glittered beneath furrowed brows, and his wiry form appeared ready for immediate action. His hand tensed by the sword Grey had been dreaming of minutes before, Agony's Joy, which swung at his hip. Bow sprang to his feet while Grey remained seated.

"You were saying, Grey?" Westing asked. His expression didn't match the light tone of his voice.

"I, uh…"

"Please, don't let my presence distract you from what you were going to tell our mutual friend Callan." Grey looked to Callan for instruction, but he kept his expression neutral.

"Right. Well, I discovered where the dak is being shipped. Not the exact location yet, but I know how we might trace it." Grey recounted his day, from his discovery of the dak to his conversation with Leigh.

"So Leigh's father is dead," Westing said.

"Yes," Callan said, sensing Westing's thoughts. "But we should focus on tracing the dak, a task for which we need Leigh's help."

"I disagree," Westing replied. "Let's consider our situation. The bondman the Array crafted to replace Leigh's father won't hold up under scrutiny, so the First Servant ordered an heir from Leigh. Of the four cities, Arndak is by far the most patriarchal, relying on a single male bloodline to maintain authority since the city's founding ten thousand years ago. The Empire is betting that Leigh can rule with the bondman supplementing her authority until a proper ruler reaches adulthood. If Leigh dies, the city will erupt into chaos. The dak supply will cease. Stockpiles will dry in a matter of months—sooner if the First Servant needs it in such quantities for his secret project."

"If you kill Leigh, you won't be able to locate the missing dak."

"Dak is a valuable commodity, and eliminating its production is of higher strategic value than finding the First Servant's stockpile. Grey's discovery presents a golden opportunity for us to cripple the Pillar for years to come."

"You'd be murdering an innocent young woman," Callan said.

"Innocent? Leigh presides over a forced labor system that kills thousands of miners annually."

"But a maramor enforces her servitude," Bow said. "You're blaming Leigh for the First Servant's actions."

"Do not yet speak," Westing said. "I will deal with your disobedience later, after we develop our plan." Bow opened his mouth but shut it when Westing's hand tightened around Agony's hilt. "This isn't up for debate. Our goal is to topple the Defiant Empire by deposing the First Servant, so our next move is clear. Grey and Bow will stay with Ivar while I assassinate Leigh and her false father. Callan, you will gather dak, then lead Grey and Bow to the Lonely Tree southwest of Arndak."

"You're going to kill her now?" Grey asked. After winning his battle of wills against the Gentleman, he didn't want the unstable swordhand to kill the girl he'd just saved.

"If that's alright with you," Westing said.

"I'd prefer that she stay alive," Grey said, missing Westing's sarcasm.

"Then I'll apologize in advance for my actions and thank you for your service. Did Leigh tell you how she calls the maramor?"

"No, she just said she could call it and have it kill me. Nothing about how."

"Very well. I'll join you at the Lonely Tree in four hours."

Westing slipped from the room. The door shut, and both Bow and Grey sat in stunned silence.

"We shouldn't allow Westing to kill Leigh," Bow said. "The decision is rash. We haven't even attempted to unravel the potential outcomes an action like this could cause."

"Westing's actions are not your burden," Callan said. Then he, too, exited, leaving Grey alone with Bow.

"Why do you follow Westing?" Grey asked. "He might be insane."

"And yet his goal, to topple the Defiant Empire, is worth pursuing. Do you imagine a sane man would undermine the First Servant? Westing may be unhinged, but he's the most skilled swordhand the Empire has seen for a thousand years."

"He would kill you if he expected it would help him," Grey said with certainty.

"Then it's a relief that I'm the only Seer he trusts."

"Still…"

"Yes, I understand. Perhaps more completely than you do, Grey. Westing's past losses drive him to bold action. Revenge is a powerful motivator, perhaps powerful enough to lead him to success against the First Servant."

"Did the First Servant murder his wife? His children? What makes him so obsessed with the First Servant?"

"Something like that, yes. He may tell you one day."

"Very well." Grey accepted Westing's need for privacy.

"Still, I don't expect Leigh's assassination will stop the flow of dak. Her death may even prompt the First Servant to assume direct control over Arndak."

"That's forbidden. The First Servant guarantees the four cities a certain level of autonomy."

"Guaranteed by tradition, not law."

"Ah, you're saying Leigh's murder will only strengthen the First Servant's hold of the dak supply."

"It is a distinct possibility."

"Then we should stop Westing," Grey said.

"Stop him? How?"

"By warning Leigh. If we reach her before Westing, we can leave with her, locate the dak supply chain, and uncover the First Servant's plans. If she flees Arndak, it'd have the same effect as killing her in destabilizing their society. Simple as that."

Bow laughed. "Grey, you have a funny perspective."

"I'm serious. Let's go now, before it's too late."

Bow examined him. "You are serious, aren't you?"

"Absolutely." Though Grey wanted to save Leigh, his primary motivation was separating Bow from Westing so Bow could teach him how to wield ahl.

"Alright, let's do it. I've already disobeyed Westing once. What's another time?"

"We'd better get moving," Grey said, and Bow helped him to his feet. Grey swayed for a moment, still off-balance from his episode with the Gentleman, but his strength returned once they walked towards Leigh's home.

Arndak stood abandoned at two in the morning. During the deepest depths of the night, stories suggested that the gods could reach down and pluck unsuspecting humans up into the sky and torture them within Echore's impervious mirrored surface for the rest of eternity. Most preferred not to stray within Echore's grasp. The stories ensured children didn't run off at night, but the fear lasted into adulthood.

"Westing got here first," Bow said, pointing to the open door at the end of the great hall.

"Come on." Grey broke into a run, reaching the door within a minute and slipping through. Westing had slit the guard's throat and propped him against the interior wall where his blood stained the grass red.

"Bow, stay here. I'll go find Leigh and bring her back."

"I've saved your life three times. Don't tell me I can't come."

"This is different. Westing won't hesitate to kill you if you intervene."

"Fine..."

"Good, see you soon," Grey said before Bow changed his mind.

"At least take this canister of dak," Bow said, tossing Grey a slim marble cylinder. Grey pocketed it and took off across the grass, stepping gingerly so he didn't make a sound. As he neared the house, he slowed, coming to a halt outside a side window. He peeked his head over the sill, but the interior was dark.

He crept around the house, looking through each window for movement until he caught Westing's thin form edging against a corridor towards Leigh, who had her back to him.

Grey inhaled the dak and threw himself forward to crash through the window, flying towards Westing with incredible speed. Westing moved faster, side-stepping Grey's blurred form with an agile pivot on his left foot. He used Grey's weight against him, swinging his elbow into Grey's back to send him flying into a wooden column instead of Westing's body. Grey's shoulder hit with a crunch, his collarbone bending from the force of the collision.

Still, Westing's movement had given Leigh the extra second she needed to dart from the room. Westing dashed after her, with Grey right behind him.

Westing skidded around the corner, ducking under two knives Leigh had thrown. Grey pressed himself against the doorframe as the knives thudded into the wall next to him. He threw himself at Westing's legs, but Westing's foot shot out to send Grey skidding across the floor, this time with two bruised ribs. Agony's Joy shimmered as it flashed towards Leigh.

Leigh raised a heavy pot to block the swing, but the blade cut through it like butter, slicing off two fingers from her right hand. She fell back against the cool stovetop, pinned with nowhere to go as Westing thrust the sword towards her heart.

Westing's blade never found its mark because, at that moment, the ceiling exploded downwards. Beams splintered, plaster shattered into thousands of chips, and metal pipes burst as a heavy object fell onto the spot where Westing had been standing. Sensing the intrusion, Westing tossed Agony's Joy into the air, backflipped out of harm's way, and dislodged the sword where it had stuck in an intact part of the damaged ceiling.

For a moment, all was still. Then the fallen object moved. Speckled-blue shoulders, like the polished tops of a marble dak canister, rose from amidst the debris. The blue marble melded with the creature's metallic neck, which held an enormous head and a smooth, dark face with two black eyes. The creature's torso was bare, an armored mass of marble plates that grated against one another. As the beast straightened, its trunk-like legs came into view, two massive pillars that looked like stone but bent and flexed like flesh.

Grey recognized the maramors as pale and motionless statues looking down from atop tall buildings, but this maramor was different. It was alive and deadly. As soon as it landed, the maramor lunged after Westing, who had just drawn a deep breath of processed dak he kept in a metal canister at his waist.

"Let's do this," Westing said, leaping into the creature's icy embrace.

The maramor swung its arm, but Westing moved faster, ducking beneath and allowing Agony's Joy to scrape along the creature's thick leg. To Grey's surprise, even the blade's leading edge made no mark, and he saw that the maramor's sluggish attack had been a ruse.

It brought its considerable bulk down on Westing as he slid past. Westing avoided being crushed by using the maramor's bulk as leverage to push himself clear. But he wasn't clear for long. The maramor twisted with astonishing speed and agility, given its size, somersaulting off of its hands with a spinning kick aimed at the sword. Agony's Joy flew from Westing's hand and landed by Leigh.

Grey scurried across the ground on his hands and feet, grabbing with one hand Agony's Joy and the other Leigh's arm. He tugged her out of the kitchen as Westing and the maramor fought. She came to her senses, running with Grey as blood streamed down her arm from her missing fingers.

They exited the house through the front door, with Leigh running just as hard as Grey to escape the mayhem behind them. Bow was sprinting across the grass towards the house, but Grey stopped him.

"maramor," Grey explained breathlessly. "We have to go."

"But Westing—"

"Nothing we can do. I fought these things at Faycliff. They're too fast, far too strong. Westing's gone, and so are we if we stay."

"Grey's right," Leigh said, tearing off a strip from her shirt and wrapping it around her hand with a grimace. "I can't call off the maramor. Our only choice is to leave. Now!"

Bow nodded, though he didn't look happy. Grey, on the other hand, celebrated in silent victory. If they escaped Arndak alive, he'd have accomplished his goal more effectively than he could have imagined. The insane Westing would be dead, and Bow could teach him to use ahl against the Gentleman. But they'd have to meet Callan first. He guessed Bow wouldn't abandon him, and he worried how Callan might to react once he'd learned of the night's events.

Aside from the night-shift miners deep below, most of

Arndak hadn't yet awoken, so Leigh, Bow, and Grey had no problem reaching the elevator bondman at Arndak's uppermost level. A single guard dozed by the bondman, but he was startled awake when they arrived.

"Take us to the surface," Leigh commanded. Grey noticed blood penetrating her makeshift bandage, and he tapped her on the wrist. She shoved her hand deep into her pocket. The guard didn't notice, blinking twice as if trying to convince himself that the governor's daughter was just a part of the dream he'd been having. "Never mind," Leigh said. "I'll go myself."

She stepped onto the bondman's back, and Grey followed. The guard, still stunned, faded from view as the bondman ascended to the surface. Though the Lonely Tree sat only a mile southwest of Arndak, each step over the undulating ground brought pain to Grey's ribs and shoulder. As he walked, though, the pain faded. I must not have broken any bones, he thought. If he had, the pain wouldn't lessen as he moved.

The Lonely Tree, a bent and gnarled husk of ancient bark that stuck up from the dry ground, appeared when they crested a hill. Grey wondered how such a large tree flourished, when no other trees grew for miles. Its towering trunk was a sad reminder of ages past, before the land devolved into a barren husk. Maybe another result of the First Servant's battle with the gods, Grey thought as he spotted a single figure below the tree's wide trunk.

Bow rushed to Callan and said, "Westing is dead. A maramor killed him."

"I see," Callan said after a moment's pause, no emotion coloring his voice. His face, too, remained tight and inscrutable.

"Didn't you hear?" Bow asked. "What are we going to do now that Westing's gone?"

"You're going to come with me," Callan said.
"Where?" Grey asked.
"To visit the shifters."

Chapter 13

"Should we turn back?" Bow asked in a whisper. Callan marched a hundred feet ahead, leading Grey, Bow, and Leigh north from Arndak. His broad form was familiar, but something else about him had changed upon their departure from the Lonely Tree. His posture straightened so much that Grey imagined an invisible rod tied his back to the ground, and his torso looked as though it floated across the rough terrain as his legs kept his upper body stable.

"Let's see where we're going," Grey said, accepting that Callan could force his obedience, even if he tried to escape.

Leigh shared none of Bow and Grey's uneasiness. After years in the sweltering stagnancy of Arndak's air, the cool breeze brought welcome goosebumps to her flesh, which she rubbed with sweaty palms. A wide smile brightened her plain features as she enjoyed a freedom she'd never known. Such was her joy that she even ignored her wound, which, though the flow of blood had slowed, still dripped onto the ground as they walked.

After five hours of steady hiking, Echore sank below the horizon while the sun warmed the chill air. Leigh's mood brightened further. Without the looming threat of Echore hanging overhead, she stared in wonder at the orange sky, a sight she'd not seen for many years. And still they walked, following a silent Callan into the forest northeast of Arndak.

As soon as they reached the first trees, Grey sensed they'd entered shifter territory. He tried to recall if he'd been here during his years of missing memories, but all he mustered was a general feeling of unease. As the day dragged on, Grey's agitation grew, and Callan still marched onwards through twisted trees and thick underbrush.

"We're here," Callan said at midday. He stopped in a clearing, at the center of which lay a circular rock that protruded from the cracked dirt. The sun reached its zenith, so the trees provided little shade as it beat down on Grey's head.

Ten monkey-like shifters swung into the clearing, appearing without warning to surround the four travelers. Although Grey tensed, Callan held up his hand in reassurance. He sat cross-legged near the center of the flat rock and invited the three of them to join him. Leigh did, sitting near Callan to rest her legs, weary from the long hike. Grey and Bow stood in front of the shifters, who peered inwards with black, beady eyes.

"I brought you here to converse without fear of being overheard by anyone from the Defiant Empire," Callan said.

"You speak as if you are not part of the Defiant Empire," Bow said.

"Observant, as always. The Defiant Empire would not accept my kind in their midst, for I am a shifter."

"You can't be!" Bow retreated, bumped into a shifter, and tripped over its hairy legs. The shifter's arms shot out, and Grey jumped—but the creature caught Bow, helping him to his feet. Flustered, Bow said, "I'd have sensed the difference if you were one of them. Their thoughts are unlike those of any human."

Grey studied Callan and wondered what prompted the man to expose himself. Was it Westing's death?

"Camouflaging my thoughts was a challenge I had to overcome before traveling to Harkk. Years of experimentation presented a solution that has allowed me to travel undetected, even under a Seer's examination. Your shifter War presented a perfect opportunity to study humans, after all."

"The shifters are monsters. Inhuman creatures with only death and destruction in their minds."

"Mind," Callan corrected. "Singular mind. The shifters, as you call them, have but one mind."

"What about these other creatures?" Leigh asked. "Are they bondmen? Pets?" She'd recovered more quickly from shock than Bow, and her eyes shone with curiosity. After living under a maramor's thumb, she feared little else.

"They are also me. I am them. We are a single organism. While I can form new shapes as needed—creatures, as you call them—I cannot create any separate life forms."

"This is all very interesting," Grey said. All he cared about was forging ahead to a point where Bow could teach him to use ahl, but Callan had thrown a wrench into his plan. "Why tell us this now? Why announce your identity?"

"Because I have what I need."

"What's that?" Bow asked.

"Me," Grey guessed.

"Yes, you. Westing's death is unfortunate, but I will succeed where he failed in turning you into a weapon aimed at the First Servant. It was I who first alerted Westing to your existence, and I will finish Westing's mission my way."

"I'm confused," Bow said, sitting down and pressing his fingers into his temples. "How did you discover Grey?"

"Grey introduced himself during the shifter War." Callan shot Grey a withering look, and all the monkey-shifters also faced him, piercing him with an accusatory glare. "You killed thousands of my forms on the battlefield. You were as unstoppable as the First Servant himself, a force of nature that appeared during major battles to swing the tide toward the Defiant Empire. And then you disappeared after Arlo found you. I won many battles, but the War had diminished my consciousness. Each time a body dies, it takes a part of my consciousness, of my soul, if you will. I can't create new life; only the First Servant can do that. Or perhaps the old gods, if they aren't fictitious. So I began to die. I won battles, but I would have lost the War."

"But then the War ended," Leigh said. "We appeased the shifters... I mean, we appeased you... by agreeing to limit our population, so we would not impede upon shifter lands."

"The Treaty of Limited Population is a lie. The First Servant claimed I demanded the Empire limit its population growth, but he chose to end the War. He stopped fighting—lucky for me, as I would not have survived much longer."

"If we were winning, he should have continued and destroyed you as a threat forever," Bow said.

"I'm no threat to you, Bow. The First Servant started the War, and I sought only to survive. Westing was correct in surmising that the First Servant is killing citizens of the Defiant Empire. The treaty is a cover to explain why the population stagnates as he kills his citizens en masse. When I lost my ability to continue killing his citizens, he ended the fighting."

"What are you, though?" Leigh asked. "Are you an alien? A bondman experiment gone awry?"

"I guess you could say that I am like a bondman. And perhaps the First Servant is my creator or even my father. My thoughts don't outlive my physical bodies, so I lose memories over time. I guess that after the First Servant's alleged heroics, after he claims to have locked the old gods within Echore ten thousand years ago, he created me. Or perhaps the old gods created me before then."

"How?"

"The answer to your question may well save my life. If the First Servant renews his campaign against me, I will die."

"Okay, then why did the First Servant create you? It is said he does nothing without purpose."

"Would you like me to guess?"

"No," Grey said, growing impatient. "What do you want from me?"

"I want what Westing wanted from you: to enlist your help in destroying the First Servant. At the rate Westing calculated, the First Servant will kill everyone within five years. That's fifty million people. Ten million each year."

"And because I can use the aerostatic gasses without harm, you expect I will defeat the First Servant?"

"Precisely. You will become the First Servant's equal, Grey."

"I can't even defeat you, let alone a maramor or the First Servant."

"Because you are not whole. Our fights highlighted that a piece of your mind is missing, the same piece that drove you to murder so many of my kind during the Shifter War."

"I remember nothing from those years, and I won't become your mindless weapon."

"Who said anything about mindless? Grey, let me help you control your power, so you may choose how to direct it."

"Wait," Bow said. "You haven't explained why you'd like to defeat the First Servant. Why do you care if he kills everyone from the Defiant Empire? You killed my—I mean, you killed so many people, hundreds of thousands, during the shifter War."

"Survival. If the First Servant destroys me before I figure out how to reproduce, I'll be the first and last of my kind. I am useful to him now as a looming threat, a reason to limit the Defiant Empire's population, but when there's no population left to limit, I am certain he'll end me."

"Westing didn't learn why the First Servant is killing his people, but perhaps you know?"

"No," Callan said with finality. "His actions appear as inexplicable to me as they must to you."

"This is a lot to process," Bow said. He removed his hands from his forehead and closed his eyes.

"I understand."

"Why should I help you?" Grey asked, curious.

"Consider what I can offer. Westing regarded himself as unique in his machinations against the First Servant, but I created dozens of resistance cells across the Defiant Empire. My plans stretch back hundreds of years. Even now, my consciousness extends across a web of connections that will blossom into the Empire's downfall."

"Ten thousand years have passed without a successful rebellion," Leigh said. "The Pillar will crush your allies, and if they fail, the maramors will finish the job."

"Ah, but I am not planning a rebellion. You're right. What would be the point? The First Servant has the power to defeat any existing force of arms, so only Grey might rival his unmatched strength. My task focuses on dismantling the aerostatic economy, the fabric from which the First Servant wove your society."

"You're as insane as Westing," Grey whispered.

"Insanity offers a clarity of vision that others cannot grasp."

"Or a chemical imbalance in the brain," Bow said.

"I am not mentally ill, not by any existing definition. My conclusions are sound; if we sabotage the mining of all four aerostatic gases, the Pillar will collapse, leaving the First Servant vulnerable to Grey's attack."

"Grey needs time to consider your plan," Bow said.

"Yeah, I do." Despite all the new information, Grey's

priority remained learning how to use ahl to block the Gentleman. His napthal supply would run dry in a matter of days, and he needed an alternate coping mechanism.

"Of course. You may have as much time as you'd like, for I will not pressure you with any tactic beyond words. Just remember that the First Servant tried to assassinate you once in Harkk. If he rediscovers you, he will try again. My considerable resources are at your disposal."

"I'd like to speak with Bow first. Alone."

"Very well. I will depart until you signal for my help." Callan paused, then said. "When you have finished speaking, I can help heal your wound, Leigh." Grey looked at her hand, which had turned an unhealthy shade of purple from the tourniquet. She'd need treatment soon, or she'd likely lose the whole hand. Callan turned and disappeared amidst the trees with his monkey-like shifter companions.

"Do you, uh, want me to leave, too?" Leigh asked.

"No, it's fine. You can stay. Bow, my priority is still to learn how to use ahl to replicate the effects of napthal."

"I can start your training tomorrow after we've rested."

"Perfect. It's safest for now to stay with Callan. With Westing dead, I'm worried about what Kip, Dilan, and Jeanne might do."

"Who?" Leigh asked.

"Our co-conspirators back at the Array," Bow explained. "Kip worships Westing, so his death will not sit well with her. Jeanne will continue carrying out Westing's plans, and Dilan will follow her lead. But I wouldn't worry about them. It's that maramor from Arndak we need to worry about the most."

"Yeah," Leigh said. "My father told me a story about a maramor who spent fifty years tracking its prey. Those beasts are relentless."

"So that's why you should be worried, Grey. Westing

won't resist its interrogation, so it might already be on our trail."

"Great." Grey could worry about the maramor after he finished using Bow for his experience with ahl. He didn't intend to stick around afterward, so perhaps the maramor would lose interest after he dissociated from Callan's rebellion.

"I figured out how we can track the dak to its source," Leigh said.

"How?"

"I'll speak with Callan and then share the plan if he's able to help."

"Alright," Bow said. "I'm exhausted. Let's tell Callan what we've decided. Tomorrow, I can teach you a thing or two about ahl."

Chapter 14

"It's nice to talk to you alone," Bow said. He sat opposite Grey in a secluded grove on the outskirts of the shifter forest amidst a sea of tall, yellow bamboo. They'd left Leigh and Callan behind at camp to find a secluded spot for ahl training.

"What do you mean?" Grey asked.

Bow laughed. "I mean, I enjoy talking to you, so I'm happy."

Grey regarded Bow, confused. "We're here for a lesson, not idle chat."

"Sure," Bow said, smiling. "You're impatient, but can you bear with me a little while longer if I promise what I'm explaining will help you use ahl?"

"Yes."

"Great! My Seer training began when my nanny fed me each of the four aerostatic gases as a toddler. I tolerated ahl with few ill effects, so the nanny assigned a Seer to manage my lessons. Eight years of daily practice, from the ages of six to fourteen, transformed me into a competent Seer."

"I don't have eight years to spare."

"My goal is to speed up your training by incorporating vast quantities of ahl, skipping rest days, and cutting out the Array's propaganda. Most crucial is practice. You'll need to train your subconscious to respond to ahl because your conscious mind will forget between sessions."

"That's confusing. Are you suggesting I won't remember from one practice to the next?"

"Yes and no. Imagine a third eye grows into your head. It sends confusing signals to your brain, which you untangle to see a black hair on your scalp. Then the eye vanishes, and when it reappears, you've already forgotten how to use it—even though you remember the black hair. Each time the eye reappears, you must learn anew to interpret its signals."

"Then what's the point of practice if I must constantly re-learn?"

"Because by the thousandth time your third eye appears, it takes only seconds to learn how to use it, not days or weeks. Your ability to withstand pure, unfiltered ahl might speed this education process, turning years into months or weeks."

"You've considered how to teach me," Grey said, examining Bow with mild interest. The boy was flushed, and he smiled again.

"Yes, I figured out how to teach you months ago!" Bow's excitement didn't dim in the face of Grey's indifference. "It's quite a thrilling prospect, seeing what someone without normal aerostatic limits can do. Let's begin by discussing why ahl is the strangest of the four gases."

"They're all odd. No one has ever discovered their origins."

"True enough. The gases seep up from the ground in specific locations, and the Array is quite familiar with their effects. Dak is of the body. It enhances your muscles, skin, and bones, strengthening them and allowing physical feats that should be impossible. Ril is of creation, allowing control over external organic matter. Vum is of destruction. Ahl is of thought."

"Westing told me that ahl enhances my brain."

"He practiced reductive logic. Ahl doesn't physically alter your brain; instead, it affects the invisible substance that separates humans from bondmen."

"You mean consciousness."

"Consciousness, a soul, or whatever gifts us with self-awareness. Ahl is most potent when used to affect one's perception of reality. At a most basic level, it makes you smarter. At its most advanced level, it can allow you to see the future, or at least the probable future."

"Like fortune telling?"

"Not at all. It's more like an intelligent prediction. For example, a Pillar regiment may hire an expert Seer from the Array to help in an upcoming battle. The Seer uses pure ahl to watch a fight and predict the opponent's next move, projecting the likely direction of attack into a Pillar warrior so that the Pillar can react before the enemy has even started moving. It's seldom used since an ahl aerostician can only inhale pure ahl five or six times before it kills them. Plus, the Seer can only work with a Pillar fighter with whom he has a strong emotional connection."

"I get it. Callan taught me to study his tensing muscles and predict his movements. But ahl also lets you control your own thoughts?" Grey asked, trying to lead the conversation in a helpful direction.

"Oh, yes. You can strengthen and weaken different parts of your mind with the proper training and practice."

"I'd like to learn how to change my emotions, like you did to bring me from my stupor."

"No," Bow said.

"Why not?"

"Because you have to explain why you're so determined to learn. I believe in Westing's cause to defeat the Defiant Empire or at least overthrow the First Servant. Now that Westing's dead, I intend to help Callan if what he told us proves true. If I'm going to teach you, I must trust your motivation aligns with mine."

"I..." Grey couldn't tell Bow about the Gentleman. Seeing the Gentleman meant he was crazy, and he didn't want Bow to pity him. Also, the Gentleman was personal, a terrible part of Grey's personality that only he accessed. But I can be honest without telling the whole truth, Grey decided. "I'd like to suppress a terrible part of my personality," Grey said finally.

"The part that arose during your periods of amnesia?"

"I assume so, yes. When I was twelve, I fled Shallow Canyon after a shifter attack. The next two years were a blur until I awoke with a medic named Arlo leaning over me at the edge of a battlefield." Grey spoke without emotion of his experience while Bow listened in silence. "Now that I'm fifteen, my goal is to prevent another extended period of loss."

"It doesn't frighten you?"

"No. My teacher Arlo was afraid many times during the shifter War. He would tremble with a bottle of napthal in his hands as he lived battles through his attempts to heal the wounds of dying soldiers. That fear is foreign to me, as is happiness, sadness, and all other emotions. My motivation revolves around controlling my body, so I don't unintentionally kill again."

"And that's the only reason?" Bow asked.

I want the Gentleman gone, Grey thought. That's it. Or was it? When Bow had neutralized the Gentleman, he remembered a sensation that was now impossible to imagine or describe.

"The world became brighter when you altered my mind," Grey said. "I want to experience that again."

Bow nodded. "This is the perfect place to begin since you're asking me to teach you the first skill all ahl users must learn. In the Array, Attention provides the foundation for every ahl discipline."

"I am paying close attention already."

Bow snickered. "Not 'attention' but Attention. A strengthening of the self."

"I see."

"No, you don't, Grey. But you will. Building your Attention is like kindling a fire. Have you ever built a fire? Not a simple campfire, but a fire intended to forge steel?"

"Not steel, but Arlo and I built many fires to craft medicines for injured Pillar troops in the shifter War."

"Perfect. Then you know that placing even one log can direct the heat, strengthening it and focusing it where it's most needed. How do you decide where to set the wood?"

"Experience, I guess. You understand fire and how heat flows through a furnace. Then you look at the fire and decide how to fuel it."

"Like I said earlier, you must strive for an instinctual understanding of how to use ahl to stoke your fire. The fire is your consciousness. Strengthening your consciousness increases your Attention, allowing you to learn the many skills that ahl can offer."

"Consciousness doesn't exist," the Gentleman said, stepping into the clearing. His crisp suit stood out against the bright yellow bamboo. "Kill this pitiful child and end the Array filth he's spewing."

Grey's arm twitched towards Agony's Joy, which lay at his side. Bow noticed the movement, but he said nothing. "Do it," the Gentleman urged. "Spill his intestines into the soil. The worms will make better use of his body than he."

"What's wrong, Grey?" Bow asked. Grey shoved his hand into his pocket to grab the bottle of napthal.

"You left it back at camp," the Gentleman said as Grey grasped at empty air. "Now, why would you forget your medicine? Deep down, you want to kill this boy. Take your sword." An itch spread across Grey's palm, and he yearned to reach for Agony's hilt.

"Do you have ahl with you right now?" Grey asked Bow through gritted teeth. His chest vibrated, and his hands shook as if freezing cold.

"I do, but—"

"I'm going to kill you if you don't give me the ahl!" Grey screamed. Bow regarded him. Grey's eyes bulged, and saliva dripped from the corners of his mouth, but Bow's smooth forehead remained uncreased, his eyes unafraid. Bow reached into his pocket and produced a slim marble canister. Grey swiped it from Bow's hand and inhaled the potent gas. "Now tell me what to do."

"Close your eyes," Bow said.

"Keep them open," the Gentleman ordered. Grey shut them with great difficulty, squeezing his entire face to keep them closed. Thoughts of Bow's dismembered corpse flashed across the back of his eyelids, and the sight pleased Grey.

"Do you sense your body?" Bow asked. "Your arms, your chest, your head. Can you feel them?"

"Yes," Grey said, forcing the grisly images away.

"Good. What else do you sense?"

"Nothing." But Grey noticed a faint glow even as he spoke. "There is something like a tiny flame."

"Make it brighter."

"How?"

"How do you tell your arm to move? Command it. Give it fuel. Tell it to grow."

"Kill him," the Gentleman said, and Grey fell over, pounding his fists into his temples. The pain became unbearable.

"You can do this." Bow placed his dry, cool hand on Grey's forehead. I must do this, Grey thought. So Grey commanded the flame to grow, brightening it ever so slightly.

"Kill!" the Gentleman screamed, but his voice came from a distance.

"Brighter!" Grey yelled aloud. The silent flame expanded, pushing the Gentleman from his mind.

Grey's eyes popped open to see Bow above him, his hand still on Grey's brow. Grey wondered if Bow knew how close he'd come to death. Bamboo cast shadows across Bow's tense shoulder, confusing Grey because it had only been midday when they'd entered the bamboo forest.

"How long have I been laying here?" Grey asked.

"Almost five hours," Bow said, standing up with effort.

"I would have guessed a few seconds."

"Ahl affects your perception of time."

Grey noticed an incredible sight behind Bow. He'd seen the bamboo's color earlier, but now, when he looked at it, he became lost in wonder. Green hues faded to a golden yellow, made warm by the evening light.

"It's so beautiful," Grey said. His face was wet, and he raised his hand to his cheek, surprised to find tears. Had he ever cried? Not even when he'd seen his father's corpse in the Shallow Canyon dak field. His father…

The simple man had cared for Grey. And he'd died. Grey pictured the sight of his father's lifeless body half-buried in the sand as he'd visualized so many times. But now, the image conjured a tightness in Grey's chest, followed by a lump in his throat. He sobbed once, then again and again as tears streamed down his cheeks. What is wrong with me?

Isa raised him after that. She didn't have to, but she did. And how did Grey repay her? By murdering her. He'd poisoned her stew at the Gentleman's urging for no logical reason. He'd killed Isa in cold blood. This, too, he'd relived many times since it happened, always with a sense of cool detachment.

Grey's tears changed to heaving as his stomach turned, and he vomited. How many people had he killed? Five that he remembered? And how many during the two years he'd lost his memory? Five hundred? Five thousand? Grey threw up all the food in his stomach, but still, he continued to heave as great sobs wracked the length of his body.

Bow came over and placed his hand on Grey's back.

"Don't touch me," Grey said, slapping Bow's hand away. He didn't deserve the care Bow showed him. He didn't deserve life after his terrible deeds.

Grey stood, stumbled a few steps, and then fell to the ground, all energy drained from his body. Still, he cried. Bow walked over to him again, putting his hand on Grey, who lacked the power to move.

They remained in that position for an hour, with Bow stroking Grey's back and Grey sobbing into the dirt. The sobs grew less frequent, only rising once a minute, until they subsided, and Grey's body was still. He struggled to sit.

"What happened?" Grey asked, his voice shaky.

"I'm uncertain," Bow said. "By definition, empowering your Attention means you've become more yourself than ever. My best guess is that your consciousness has been so weak that your brain's ability to process emotions has withered. Long-suppressed emotions are surging to the surface."

"I don't know what this is."

"Describe it to me."

"A weight pushes me to the ground, consuming my body, chest, throat, and head. It's heavy, hopeless."

"That's sadness."

"I also want to punch the ground and tear apart those beautiful bamboo shoots while punishing myself for the terrible violence I've committed."

"That's anger. And guilt."

"But your presence lightens my shoulders. You rescued me three times, and now you've also helped me in another way. I understand what you said earlier, that it was nice to have time to talk to me alone." Grey paused, then whispered, "I share that feeling."

"That's happiness."

"I never realized what it means to experience emotions," Grey said.

"No one can process so many powerful emotions at once. The ahl I gave you while you were unconscious will wear off soon, and you'll lose these feelings once more."

"Maybe that's for the best." Grey didn't want to understand his guilt and sadness about the people he'd killed.

The bamboo rustled, and Callan stepped from the forest.

"It's time to leave," he said. "Leigh and I have discovered a risky method of tracking the missing dak."

Chapter 15

"This is your plan?" Bow asked incredulously. He knelt behind a rock alongside Grey, Leigh, and Callan, overlooking the western reaches of Arndak canyon, where the sheer rock walls came together at a point. Complex machinery smothered the rock with gears and pistons, ending with spikes like claws reaching towards heaven.

"Leigh insisted it will lead us to the dak, and I don't have a better idea," Callan said.

"If it was Leigh's idea, why isn't she coming?"

"Callan asked me how to trace the dak, not to join you on this suicide mission," Leigh said.

"What is the plan?" Grey asked.

"The maramor transports dak," Callan said. "So we will follow it to its destination. Simple."

"Impossible," Bow snapped. "Those creatures can sense if they're being followed."

"Ah, but that is why Leigh's devious suggestion is brilliant."

"Right," Leigh said. "Remember, Grey, when I told you I had an alternate plan to escape Arndak?"

"Yeah."

"Well, a few weeks ago, when my maramor captor left on one of its weekly dak deliveries, I set about flushing the sewage bondmen. The maramor was unable to find me upon its return…"

"I don't like where this story is leading," Grey said.

"Yes, well, you can imagine my surprise at hearing the maramor's call. That close, the beast should have been able to sense my presence. But it didn't. Something about the bondman's flesh hid me from its senses."

"Who would have tested hiding inside a bondman to evade a maramor?" Callan asked. "Brilliant."

"I waited inside the bondman for over an hour, then returned home. The maramor found me there at once."

"I'm claustrophobic," Grey said. "There's no way I can ride inside a bondman."

"Especially not a sewage bondman," Bow agreed.

"Seeing as this may be our only opportunity to follow a maramor to trace the dak, you must go… unless you no longer accept Westing's cause?"

Bow frowned. "Why don't you go by yourself?"

"I intend to ride in another bondman, in case its hide doesn't also shield shifters. Should the maramor sense me, you must continue following it."

"Fine," Bow said with an exasperated sigh.

"Do you have a supply of ahl?" Grey asked Bow.

"Of course. Seers always carry ahl."

"Then I'll go as well."

"The ahl is the only reason you're coming?" Bow asked, sounding a bit annoyed.

"Unless you'll lend me a supply," Grey responded, thinking, Why else would I do something so dangerous, unless to avoid falling under the Gentleman's control? Napthal was rare enough that he'd be unlikely to stumble upon more before he exhausted his meager supply, so he needed ahl to strengthen his Attention in an emergency. And yet, there was another reason he wanted to go with Bow, something he couldn't quite grasp, an understanding he'd achieved when he'd used ahl but now lay out of reach.

"There's Ivar with the bondman," Callan said.

Grey turned to spot Ivar atop a nearby hill, leading an enormous bondman by a rope. The creature lumbered along on six legs, its round belly scraping the ground as it moved. Its neckless head bulged from a vast, smooth body so that its mouth and eyes stretched across the width of its torso. Its gaping maw was over three feet in diameter.

"Hello there." Ivar clasped Callan's arm. The sewage bondman towered over Grey, at least twelve feet tall and stinking of rot. "I cleaned it, but I'm afraid it has crud still gumming up the works."

"The maramor will smell this monstrosity," Bow said.

"So? These sewage bondmen trample all over the Empire, dumping waste. They're one of the Array's most reproduced specimens. The maramor can smell one wherever it goes."

"Get down," Callan said. A maramor appeared in the distance, climbing from the canyon towards the mechanical claw. Grey squinted, peering between blades of grass and attempting to pierce the haze radiating from the hot ground. The creature jumped atop the claw in a single leap, at least thirty feet straight into the air, and lay down against its metal fingers. The claw tightened, and the maramor's body ballooned within its metallic grasp, stretching to four times its typical size. A piercing hiss echoed across the barren landscape as the maramor fell from the claw and marched north.

Callan stood back up and said, "We must leave before we lose the maramor's track. Bow and Grey, you two will ride in this bondman."

"What just happened?" Grey asked.

"The bondman absorbed dak into its body for transport. It will release it via a similar mechanism at its destination. Ivar, did you leave the other creature where I requested?"

"Of course," Ivar answered, helping Bow climb into the bondman's gaping mouth.

"That's my cue to leave," Leigh said, reaching out to shake Grey's hand. "Perhaps I'll be able to repay you someday… or perhaps we will never meet again. Good luck."

"Thank you," Grey said, returning her handshake before following Bow, whose feet had just disappeared into the bondman.

"We'll reconvene at our destination," Callan said. "Meet me at Arndak's Lonely Tree if I don't arrive and take these dak canisters." Grey nodded, accepting two marble cylinders before diving headfirst into the bondman's mouth. Its short throat swallowed him, and he slithered into the creature's massive stomach, an ovular space covered in a thin slime with thousands of digestive flaps lining every fleshy surface.

"This is disgusting," Bow said. Enough light penetrated the creature's flesh to illuminate the grotesque details of their surroundings.

"Yes," Grey agreed. "And it smells."

"Best we go." Bow inhaled a breath of ahl, then touched the creature's flesh with his bare hand, and the beast moved. At the first lurch, claustrophobia slammed in around Grey. He tried to take a deep breath, but his body only allowed him sharp gasps. Stars spun across his vision, which narrowed until he looked at Bow through a tunnel.

"What's wrong?" Bow asked.

"Claustrophobia," Grey said between quick breaths.

"You can't be claustrophobic if you're asleep."

"I can't possibly sleep. If I had napthal, then maybe…"

"You don't need napthal. I can help you. Just close your eyes."

"Fine." Grey shut his eyes. It didn't ease his claustrophobia, but it didn't make it worse, either.

"Good. Now tell me something about yourself."

"Why?"

"Trust me. Tell me the first personal detail that pops into your head."

"I wouldn't know what to say."

"Let's start somewhere simple. Tell me about your mother."

"I don't remember my mother, only my father and Shallow Canyon."

"Were you born there?"

"I don't remember anywhere else."

"And then what? Why did you leave?"

"The Pillar recruited me to battle the shifters. Two years passed, the two years I cannot remember, and I woke up on a battlefield gripping Agony's Joy with a man named Arlo standing over me. I spent the rest of the shifter War with him, helping heal wounded soldiers. He's the one who introduced me to napthal, the only protection I have against…"

"Against what?" Bow asked. Grey almost told him of the Gentleman, but he held his tongue.

"Against losing control of myself. The last time I lost control, two years passed. I knew I couldn't let it happen again. By the time the War ended two years later, I'd become so dependent upon napthal that I realized I'd have to find a steady supply. So I left Arlo and headed to Faycliff, the perfect location."

"Faycliff was little more than a cobbled-together shantytown. Why'd you want to live there?"

"It's far from Harkk, yet it had enough materials to brew more napthal. Plus, if I lost control, I wouldn't kill too many people. Each day, I worked in a tavern to distract myself from misery."

"What did you do at night?"

"I used napthal to sleep, though sleep was never restful

because of the nightmares, bloody dreams I don't want to recall. I think they might be memories."

"That sounds awful," Bow said. Grey had never shared these dreams, but telling Bow was a relief. The very act of sharing, of speaking his thoughts out loud, created a bit of distance between himself and the memories, and during their conversation, Grey's breathing had slowed. To his surprise, his claustrophobia eased.

"I can't imagine suffering alone for so many years," Bow said. He rested his hand on Grey's forearm, and Grey suppressed his instinct to recoil. Bow's touch was comfortable, a small realization that made Grey quite uncomfortable.

"I'm hoping your lessons in ahl will allow me to avoid using napthal," Grey said, changing the subject. Bow removed his hand.

"I hope so, too, but your first try was upsetting."

"Guilt," Grey said. "I can't summon the sensation, but I remember disliking it.

"You've never had to process your emotions. I'm not even sure you can access them without using ahl to strengthen your Attention. I'll try to teach you how to understand your emotions."

"Thanks, I'd like that."

Bow spoke no more, and a wave of exhaustion washed over Grey. The next thing he knew, Bow was poking him and saying, "Hey, wake up."

"Huh?" Grey sat up, struggling to place himself in his surroundings. "Was I sleeping?"

"For ten hours. Echore rose over two hours ago."

"Where's Callan?"

"I'm not sure, but I watched the maramor enter a cave. After it leaves, we'll explore."

Grey rubbed his eyes. Ten hours, he thought. I haven't

slept so long without napthal in years.

"How can you see the maramor?"

"By tapping into the bondman's senses."

Grey sat back and waited. Though they'd stopped moving, the bondman's heart beat through its stomach walls, a pleasant sensation if only the rest of their surroundings weren't so disgusting. An hour passed in silence before Bow spoke again. "The maramor emerged from the crack in the rock a few minutes ago. Let's move."

Bow commanded the bondman's mouth to open, and they crawled from its orifice, slithering onto a grassy patch. Grey took a deep breath of fresh air to discover the bondman's foul odor lingered. He stood, shivering in the brisk wind blowing from the north.

"A storm is coming," Bow said, studying the clear night sky.

"How can you tell?"

"Moisture saturates the air, driven by the northern mountains that often send storms rushing towards the south. Now let's hurry and get changed. We can't sneak around covered in this slime, smelling as we do."

Bow pulled a bag from the bondman and handed Grey a towel and a change of clothing. Grey placed Agony's Joy on the ground, then stripped down and used Bow's towel to scrub as much of the bondman's fluids from his body as possible.

As he pulled on a fresh pair of trousers, he noticed how Bow's pale skin glowed in Echore's reflected light. Grey stood still, struggling to understand his reaction to Bow, but the strange emotion lay too deep to grasp, like the distant flapping of a fish trapped under thick winter ice. Grey jerked his head away in embarrassment when Bow caught him staring.

He turned towards the cave and jogged to the entrance

while Bow pulled on fresh clothes and followed. The narrow arch opened into a white hall, where Bow tackled Grey to the floor. Two maramors stood on either side of a metal door, their powerful, gaunt forms black against the white walls.

"Those must be statues," Grey whispered. "They'd have already seen us if they were real maramors, and we'd be dead." Still, the marble statues were indistinguishable from the actual monsters, with sinewy muscles tensed as if they might spring from their perches.

"Only one way to find out." Bow stood and walked towards the demons.

"Perhaps we should wait for Callan," Grey suggested.

"I didn't spot him outside, nor do I trust that shifter creature. I'd rather explore before the living maramor returns."

Bow walked to the metal door, pushed it open, and waved. Beyond the door lay an immense cavern, sprawled out below the platform on which Grey and Bow now stood. Walls divided the arena into roofless rooms with tens of thousands of people.

"What… is this place?" Bow asked.

"It looks like a nursery." Grey pointed to an area holding hundreds of babies, each laying in cribs encased by transparent bubbles connected to tanks of dak and ril.

"And a school," Bow said, noting a section divided into classrooms. Children sat in rows behind their adult teachers, all sipping on aerostatic gas. "Those teachers are members of the First Servant's Circle. See the bracers?" Tall bands of metal with inward-facing spikes choked their owners' necks. All members of the First Servant's Circle wore them as signs of complete devotion to their ruler. "I've seen cribs like these in the Array, though we use them to grow bondmen. Ril accelerates their growth, but I'm unsure what purpose the dak serves."

"We should go," Grey said. "The First Servant has brought all his resources to bear on this project, which means we're dead if anyone catches us."

"There's lots of adults here as well," Bow said, ignoring Grey's concerns. Thousands of men and women queued in a snaking line that ended at a gated arch.

"Excuse me, sirs," said a man who had crept onto the platform. Bow spun around to face the newcomer, who wore a curious expression. Grey reached for Agony's Joy, then hesitated, for the young man was unarmed.

"We'd like a full report," Bow said, approaching the man with false confidence. "The First Servant's description was one thing, but seeing such an astounding accomplishment in person is another matter." Bow's voice changed, adopting the drawl of a nobleman. He sounds like Emerson, Grey realized.

"You're from the First Servant's Circle?" the young man asked. He shifted on his feet, and Grey tried to spot any hidden weapon beneath his baggy clothes.

"We're too young for that," Bow said, chuckling. "Leigh sent us to guard the recent dak shipment."

"If your help resulted in a successful delivery, I am grateful."

"The maturation tanks are operating well?" Bow asked, eager to gather more information. The man nodded. "Perfect. But why are those men and women standing in line?"

"They're waiting to die, of course."

"Die?"

"Yes, right on schedule," the man said.

"How old are they?"

"Four."

"Four? How old are you?"

"I'll soon be three."

"Three what?" Bow asked. Grey grew uncomfortable with

the questions. Each second increased the chances the man would realize they were intruders, so he gripped Agony's Joy tighter.

"Years, of course—three-quarters of my way to my ascension."

The boy looks eighteen at least, Grey thought, three years older than himself. He was tall, wore a man's beard, and appeared quite muscular beneath his clothing. Bow must have been thinking the same because he asked, "You've seen only three winters?"

"You're referring to the seasons. We don't have them in here. But yes, three winters have passed."

"Excellent," Bow said, realizing the danger in his line of questioning. "What's your name? I'll report your fine service to the First Servant."

"4,591,371." That is an unusual name, Grey thought.

"Thank you, 4,591,371, for the brief tour. Now we must be on our way."

"You're welcome. But you're not going anywhere." 4,591,371 glanced up, and Grey followed his gaze to a maramor perched on a beam near the cavernous roof. That creature wasn't there before, Grey thought, the pit of his stomach flipping. The maramor dropped like a stone from the beam, its knees barely flexing from the impact.

"You called the maramor," Bow said.

"Of course, as soon as I spotted the two of you. Our protocol for intruders is quite clear. May your souls offer the First Servant with the strength he needs." Then 4,591,371 retreated from the platform, leaving them alone with the maramor, who approached Bow.

Grey stepped in front of Bow, drawing Agony's Joy from its sheath. The blade flashed as he held it aloft, pointed at the maramor. "Bow, I can't kill this thing, but we might escape if we're fast enough."

"Here, take this," Bow said, tossing Grey a canister of ahl. He inhaled Callan's dak and Bow's ahl in quick succession, shivering as the aerostatic gases enhanced his body and mind. Clarity descended, relegating the world to points of data. The maramor stood twenty-five feet away. Bow lay seven feet behind Grey. The tip of Agony's Joy hovered five feet above the ground. Grey waited for emotions to overwhelm him, as they had the last time he'd ingested ahl, but adrenaline suppressed his feelings.

As the maramor advanced, Grey examined its unusual body. He'd encountered the maramor that had attacked Westing, of course, but that one hadn't stood still. This creature moved in a tall crouch, its head at least as high as the tallest man Grey had ever seen, and its powerful legs operated with bondman-like precision. Its body was as wide as two men, a thick trunk of interweaving marble plates leading up to its ghoulish head. Eyes, more like black voids from which no light could escape, stared ahead, while its hinged lower jaw protruded beyond its sharp upper teeth with two fangs. The surface of its skin was as blue as the marble that held dak, though the maramor's skin wasn't smooth like a dak canister. Segments of stone, like armor plates, shifted in complex, overlapping patterns as it walked.

Grey tried to edge towards the door, but the maramor swiped out with one of its sharp claws. The world slowed, and Grey watched the maramor's arm swim through the air with languid grace as he blocked its claw with Agony's Joy. The creature cocked its head and stared at Grey with its jet-black eyes.

Its jaw hinged open in a wicked smile. The maramor took another swing, which Grey dodged as easily as he'd deflected the first blow. But its attack was a ruse; as Grey twisted aside, it brought its leg up faster than Grey could see, and its knee slammed into his chest like a sledgehammer, sending him skidding across the platform. Only dak kept his aching body in one piece.

The maramor jetted across the ground with unbelievable speed and lifted Grey by his neck. It held him aloft like Grey might lift a feather, squeezing with its stone claw. This close, Grey gazed into the pits of its eyes, which held wisps of bluish gas.

Through all this, Grey had kept his grip on Agony's Joy, which he slammed into the maramor's torso. The creature only smiled at the blow, immovable and unstoppable. Just as Grey's vision closed in, a meaty arm appeared around the maramor's neck.

With a mighty roar, Callan flung the creature over his head, sending it sailing across the platform with Grey still in its grip. Callan stamped on its arm, and it released Grey. Bow ran to Grey's side, helping him towards the exit.

They looked back at Callan, who had dodged two of the maramor's blows before the maramor caught one of his arms, pinning it behind him. Callan said, "Run," and Grey stumbled through the door. The last sight he caught before Bow swung the door shut was Callan's pained expression as the maramor tore his arms from his body.

Chapter 16

Grey rode atop the lumbering bondman with Bow at his back. At any moment, he expected the steel-blue maramor to jump from the trees, ending their lives as swiftly as it had Callan's. Grey couldn't shake the image of Callan's calm face, his lips forming the word "run" while the monster plucked his limbs from his torso. He remembered the image more vividly than any other death he'd witnessed, for the diluted ahl he'd inhaled hours ago made it difficult to repress the thoughts.

But the maramor didn't appear, and the sewage bondman carried them to the south under Bow's command, towards Arndak. As they rode, cold air blew at their backs, pushed south by the approaching bad weather Bow had predicted. Soon, the wind strengthened into a mighty gale, bending tree trunks and kicking pebbles in their path.

"I can't believe we made it out of there alive," Bow shouted over the wind.

"If Callan hadn't intervened, we would not have. That maramor was unstoppable."

"I suppose we should be thankful that Callan's on our side."

"He's on his own side," Grey said with finality, and Bow spoke no more beneath the fat raindrops that splashed against the bondman. The storm gathered as they approached Arndak, drenching them in a torrential downpour. Rivers of mud flowed across parched ground, and water soaked Grey's clothes, chilling him to the bone while washing away the remnants of the bondman's digestive fluids. Visibility shrank to five feet in every direction.

Despite the rain, Bow directed the bondman towards the Lonely Tree, which appeared on its squat hill, emerging from sheets of rainwater like a boat from fog as it clung to the wet soil with old, deep roots. Grey spotted a figure its base. Another shifter?

Bow brought their bondman to a halt, and Grey jumped from the creature's back, wading through knee-deep water towards the gnarled tree. Jeanne and Kip huddled by the tree's base while a man stood above, his cloak spread to shield the two women from the downpour.

"Callan," Grey said, waving to Bow, who came to stand next to him.

"You're alive!" Bow shouted. Of course he is, Grey thought. The shifter owned many bodies resembling Callan, even if the maramor slaughtered one hours ago.

"Why wouldn't I be?" Callan asked. So Jeanne and Kip haven't learned his secret, Grey thought, deciding whether to declare Callan's true nature.

"Now that you're back, tell me what in Echore happened," Kip said. She stood and moved right up to Bow's face. "Westing insisted he'd be gone for a few nights, but when he didn't return, we set out to investigate."

"Westing's dead," Bow said, and Grey shot him a look of surprise. Bad idea, he thought, for Kip was quick to anger and unpredictable.

"Dead?" Jeanne asked. "How?" She stood, bending to prevent from being blown over by the strong wind.

"He died by doing something foolish," Grey said, annoyed

that they should speak of such things instead of seeking shelter. With ahl allowing him limited access to his emotions, he realized he didn't much care for Kip or her attitude.

"How?" Kip asked. "How did he die?"

"Let's find shelter first. We can tell you what happened later."

"Tell me now!"

"No. We need to get inside, or we'll drown."

"You killed him," Kip said, tears somehow visible against the rainwater streaming down her face. "He shouldn't have trusted you."

"What are you talking about?" Grey asked with disgust.

"I bet you lost control again, like you did in the Fizzer cave." Kip's face was inches from Grey's, and he took a step back. Kip followed, raising her hand and slapping him, her palm flat against Grey's cheek.

At that moment, something inside Grey broke, or perhaps ahl mended a broken piece of him. In either case, ahl released an unfamiliar sensation—less foreign than the Gentleman's influence but quite different from his typical stoicism. This novel emotion smashed through his mind, burned in his chest, and filled his throat with acid.

"Shut the fuck up!" Grey screamed, as shocked by his words as Kip, who stumbled backward, startled. Grey stood over her, continuing to scream, "I didn't kill Westing! A maramor murdered him, a fate we've escaped twice now. That maramor is still hunting us."

"Perhaps you didn't kill him yourself," Kip said, her anger burning hot. "But your lack of devotion to our cause led to his death. You're a murdering, disloyal little shit."

"You're right, Kip. I'm a murderer who is not interested in your cause because your cause is insane. Complete lunacy."

"Westing had a plan—"

"Oh, a plan? He had a plan, did he? The maramor might

appear from this storm and kill us any second. Do you understand what would happen to Westing's plan? It wouldn't exist, like you won't exist, if you continue trying to solve an unsolvable problem. The maramor who killed Westing will kill us all since that creature will follow us around forever." I'm furious, Grey realized with a jolt. Arlo and Bow had tried to describe the emotion to him, but he'd never understood.

"If we just—"

"I'm not finished yet," Grey said, embracing the pleasure his newfound rage brought. "If the maramor can kill us, what do you suppose the First Servant would do?"

"Westing insisted you're his equal," Jeanne said. She didn't appear to share Kip's anger, only a deep confusion.

"Are you stupid?" Grey asked. "The First Servant jumped a mile and landed on a marble slab without even flexing his knees. Not even pure dak would allow me to survive that fall. No human would. The First Servant is a law, like gravity. Would you fight gravity? Can't you see your foolishness?"

"Grey, please calm down," Bow said, holding his hands out.

"I've appreciated your help, Bow, but your fight isn't my concern. Westing sought to turn me into his weapon, and it got him killed. Callan, too, has paid the price in seeking my help. All I ask is you leave me alone, so I might return to Faycliff or any other town far from those I might kill."

"Wait," Bow said, barely audible above the rain. "I understand that you don't care about the cause. So forget about maramors, immortal dictators, and all the rest. Just consider me. We've become friends, and I need your help. Isn't that enough? For now, at least?"

Another unfamiliar emotion tempered his anger. Bow's blue eyes watched Grey from beneath his furrowed brow. They were soft with genuine concern, and Grey noticed

Bow's exhausted body vibrated with chills. Grey lifted his hand to comfort Bow, but anger slammed back into place. "It's not enough," Grey said with finality, taking immense satisfaction from turning away from these fools, these idiots who sought to topple a god.

Grey drained the centered dak Callan had given him from its canister, tossed the marble aside, and ran into the night. Bow yelled, "Find us in Estril if you change your…" But the sound ebbed as Grey bounded over land with inhuman speed. He wanted to run as far as possible, as quickly as possible. While he ran, the storm raged, releasing a month's worth of rain into the parched earth and toppling any tree too young to have formed deep roots. Each dak-powered stride sent up a mighty splash until soon, mud covered Grey's body from head to toe. He didn't care. He only wanted to keep running.

When the dak left his body, he slowed but kept moving, ignoring the stitch in his side and the chill in his bones. The downpour eased into a steady rain, then a fine mist before stopping. Clouds parted, revealing Echore's flawless surface overhead.

Reflected against Echore was a stretch of sand, punctuated on either end by short cliffs. Shallow Canyon. I was running south, Grey thought, puzzled. Somehow, he'd run northwest to his old home, to Shallow Canyon. In a daze, he wandered towards the canal, now filled with sand and mud. Wind buried the shacks, leaving a handful of spikes protruding every dozen feet. The town's abandonment proved the dak fields were exhausted.

Nothing at all remained of Isa's hut, but Grey spotted a mound in the sand where her home used to be. He kicked it with his foot, then pulled away the sand to uncover Isa's giant stew pot. She was the first person the Gentleman made me kill. But not the last. Grey touched his cheeks to find tears, and he thought his stomach would turn again if it weren't empty. He wished the ahl would leave his system. The Gentleman's will would be preferable to this emotion, but the ahl remained, forcing him to suffer beneath the total emotional weight of recent events.

A rustling caught Grey's attention, and he straightened, pulling Agony's Joy from its sheath at his back. The rustling grew louder, and a figure approached, shrouded in a dark cloak.

"Arlo…?" Grey asked, blinking in confusion. The medic's ruddy, round face smiled at him from beneath a layer of grime.

"Grey, it's so good to see you again." Arlo stepped forward to hug him, and Grey let it happen. The surreal moment stretched to several seconds before Arlo released Grey, stepping back.

"What are you doing here?" He hadn't left Arlo on the best of terms, having stolen the man's supply of napthal.

"Ah… well, that. I was, uh, well, I was looking for you."

"And you just happened to find me tonight by an insane coincidence?"

"No, no, not a coincidence at all. I had it on decent authority that you were headed in this direction."

"Oh, Echore. Don't tell me you're a shifter too. Callan, is that you?"

"No, no, no, I'm no shifter. Although… it was Callan, the shifter horde itself, who told me where you'd be this night. Surprised?"

"Perhaps I would be if I weren't so exhausted."

"You're pallid. We'd better get you food. Come, come, away we go." Grey was far too tired to argue, so he trudged behind Arlo until they reached a covered wagon hitched to two mule bondmen. "Here, change into dry clothing," Arlo said, tossing Grey another change of clothes. Grey discarded his soaked garments and pulled on a fresh pair of dry pants and a sweater.

While Grey dressed, Arlo brought him a bowl of soup, which he sipped. He followed the soup with a bowl of stew, a loaf of bread, and fish jerky. Though his hunger diminished, his exhaustion only increased. His arms shook, and tears once again threatened the corners of his eyes.

"You've subjected your body to greater stress than most ensure in a lifetime," Arlo said. "Aerostatic gases demand a heavy toll."

"If I hadn't absorbed those gases, a maramor would have slaughtered me. Or Kip would have attacked me… though I'm not sure I understand why she did that. When she hit me, I only wanted to get as far away from her as possible. As far away from everyone as possible."

"So you ran."

"Like I ran away from you."

"I didn't say that."

"You didn't have to."

Arlo didn't speak for a few seconds, but his brow creased. Finally, he said, "You're right, Grey. Your unexplained departure was disappointing."

The sadness in Arlo's tone exposed more than his words, and the ahl in Grey's system allowed him to experience the brunt of the emotional blow. Arlo was a friend who had cared for Grey during his most desperate year. He'd adopted Grey, taught him to heal wounded soldiers, and introduced him to napthal, without which Grey the Gentleman would have regained control.

"I'm dangerous, Arlo. I've killed many times that I can remember, and I fear many more times that I can't. When my presence endangered your life, I fled."

Arlo considered him with grave importance, but his perpetual smile soon returned to brighten his features. Then his eyes squinted with humor, and he laughed, a deep, rolling laugh that echoed across the empty desert.

"I'm not joking," Grey said.

"Not at all, not at all. It's just that the whole situation is quite amusing."

"I don't see how."

"Let me ask: was it luck that brought you to me and my never-ending supply of napthal? Napthal isn't a common substance, not by a long shot."

"What are you trying to say?"

"That I used napthal to snap you from your murderous trance, then continued to feed you napthal because I'd seen your monstrous side. Callan, or the shifters, deserves most of the credit. He sacrificed a legion of himself to allow me to subdue you, all because he trusted you were the best chance we had to defeat the First Servant."

"You never spoken of this."

"Callan wanted you to recall what happened in your own time," Arlo explained, shrugging. "Now, can you understand my amusement? You took off to protect me, though I'd accepted the risk… and if I had mentioned my knowledge of your past, you might never have left. Despite all the confusion, we're together again!"

Grey didn't share Arlo's amusement, which didn't stop Arlo from chuckling as he collected Grey's empty dishes and carried them back to the wagon. Grey watched while Arlo arranged branches around kindling, stoking the fire until it roared to life. The light threw uneven shadows across the remnants of Shallow Canyon's village, the only visible evidence of Grey's childhood home. Somewhere, in the exhausted dak fields, lay his father's body, long since decayed and lost to the desert sands. For a moment, Grey yearned to join him, to lie in the sand and submit to his exhaustion.

"Callan's plan with you has failed," Arlo said, drawing Grey from his trance. "It's time we tried a different approach."

Grey stared into the fire. He'd considered Arlo his friend, but now… now he was yet another manipulator, attempting to use Grey for his own purpose. Grey wanted only to rid himself of the Gentleman. He'd been willing to join Westing's rebellion, and he'd even continued to go along with Callan's plan to learn from Bow. But Arlo, too?

His anger returned, and he stood to leave—but then his anger dissipated. Ahl vanished from Grey's system as quickly as a blown-out candle, and his emotions descended once more to their place beneath conscious thoughts. He was no longer upset with Arlo, only curious. Grey realized his feelings had been clouding his judgment, for he'd missed the most obvious question.

"Who are you?" Grey asked.

"I see you've exhausted your ahl," Arlo said, grinning. He handed Grey a bottle of napthal from within his coat, which Grey accepted. "I imagine you'll need this soon, lest you lose control again."

"You're not part of the Array, the Pillar, or the shifters," Grey said, ignoring for a moment the napthal. He needed his mind to work, and the potent drug would slow his thoughts. "You aren't in league with the First Servant, so you're not one of his creations. You're not a maramor or a bondman. With your knowledge and association with Callan, it's unlikely you're acting independently. That means you're with a faction I haven't yet discovered."

"What's your hypothesis?"

"You must be part of a group working against the Defiant Empire, perhaps within Callan's rebellion. He mentioned he has many cells working across the Empire to destabilize the supply of all aerostatic gases."

"The members of his rebellion, as you call it, work with no knowledge of other cells. Should the First Servant discover one plan, this protects the rest from discovery. Callan has shared his entire plan, so I'm not part of his rebellion."

"I give up."

"Here's a hint: humans and their progeny aren't the only life on this planet."

"Right," Grey said. "bondmen and shifters share our world. I suppose there's maramors as well."

Arlo waved his hand. "There's other intelligent species."

"Where? I'd have noticed."

"Haven't you, though? You've even fought vorsters, who are more clever than any bondman."

"They're animals, a pest."

"Have you visited a vorster colony? They build complex shelters with tools and care for their children while adult males inventory all their loot. They're not humans, but they're self-aware."

"You're suggesting you're not human?"

"Exactly!"

"Your appearance suggests otherwise, Arlo."

"Nevertheless, I am no more human than the vorsters you killed near Faycliff. I grew into this shape during my time in the Defiant Empire, for the bodies of my people shift to accommodate their surroundings."

"There are others like you?"

"Grey, I accept your anger about hiding all this from you, but you must understand the risk I am taking by revealing my true nature. My people are called transeel, and they'd execute me on sight if they learned of my meddling in the First Servant's affairs."

"Why?"

"My independent life as an herbalist conflicted with the wishes of the other transeel, for they believe we are best hidden as the servants of human nobles. However, my people tolerated certain eccentricities because it was I who discovered how to speed up the biological changes that enabled our survival of the First Servant's purge of my people thousands of years ago."

"Then why risk your people by telling me?"

"Because you are new. You're something different. For ten thousand years, the world hasn't changed. My people dedicated their everlasting lives to servitude, but I am unsatisfied, just as the First Servant grew weary under the old gods' control."

"Are the First Servant's tales true?"

"The purge ended our memories of that time," Arlo said sadly. "The changes we underwent affected our minds as much as our bodies, and the First Servant destroyed all historical records. He preserved only one of my kind, a transeel named Ezra, whom we must rescue so that he may teach you how to fight. As the original swordhand, his knowledge runs deep."

"The transeel were sores on this planet's surface," the Gentleman said. Grey sipped napthal, expecting the Gentleman to disappear, but he didn't budge. Grey's eyes widened, and the pit of his stomach dropped. The Gentleman's black lips bent into a wicked smile.

"Do you have any ahl?" Grey asked Arlo.

"Maybe somewhere. Why?"

"There's no time to explain." He could feel the Gentleman taking hold of his mind. When Grey looked at Arlo, he saw only his body splayed on the ground, his flesh peeled back like a dissected pig, and his organs spread across the sand. Rather than repel Grey, the thought enticed him. He wanted to bring his vision to life. Grey opened his eyes to find his hands around Arlo's neck.

"No," he screamed, pulling himself away with a surge of

willpower. Did he still trust Arlo? I trust him more than the Gentleman, Grey decided. He gulped down the napthal until only a few sips remained. Still, the Gentleman remained. Grey downed the rest of the drink, and he fell into an unconscious stupor.

Chapter 17

Grey awoke to a forest of plants hanging from the canopy of Arlo's bouncing wagon. Blue, red, and purple roots tickled his face while jars of seeds rattled in cabinets along the walls. He tried to sit, but restraints pinned him to the wagon's bed.

Arlo popped his head through the fabric at the front of the wagon. "So you're alive!"

"Sort of," Grey said, slurring his words through the napthal that would circulate in his blood for many hours. "Can you cut me loose?"

"I don't know. Are you going to try to kill me again?"

"No."

Arlo examined Grey, then nodded. "Okay." He climbed in next to Grey and loosened his bonds. "Come, join me outside."

Grey rubbed his wrists and legs to urge the blood back into his tingling extremities before following Arlo into the hot, dry air and taking a seat on the short bench next to Arlo, who gripped the reigns. Desert stretched to the horizon in an unending sea of burning white sand. Midday sun reflected against the sand through the cloudless sky, singing Grey's pale flesh, so he leaned against the wagon where overhanging fabric cast a wedge of shade.

"We're heading west, towards Estril," Grey guessed.

"Very observant. Now drink." Arlo nodded towards a hose that ran into the wagon's canopy. Grey eyed it with suspicion, for he suspected the water must be from the same source that fed Arlo's plants. Still, water was water, so he took an experimental sip before filling his stomach and laying down the hose.

"I take it we're going to rescue the man you spoke of," Grey said.

"Ezra? Yes."

"I didn't agree to help you."

"Then leave. I'll drop you off at the nearest town so you don't die of thirst." Grey said nothing. "No? I'll take you anywhere in the Defiant Empire, then. Perhaps you'd like to return to Faycliff if they've rebuilt? Or I can leave you in Harkk, where the First Servant sent assassins after you. Might you prefer Arndak? Rumor suggests they're killing one another now that they've discovered Sir Winfer is dead and his one heir escaped."

"Just keep driving," Grey said. As if I have a choice. The amount of napthal he'd consumed last night to banish the Gentleman was startling, perhaps five times the volume he'd expected. Drinking such a large swig of napthal brought unconsciousness, which meant that another incident of the Gentleman taking control had transformed from a terrible possibility to a horrifying inevitability. If the Gentleman appeared during a fight, a drop of napthal wouldn't banish him. Ahl was the proper solution.

"You've been running for years now, Grey. It's time you stopped to focus on what's important."

There's nothing more critical than banishing the Gentleman, Grey thought, but he said, "I can't stop running because there's a maramor chasing me."

"You know that's not what I mean."

"Anyway, you don't understand why I have to run. If you

did, you wouldn't bother me about it."

"Then make me understand. Please tell me what's so frightening that you push away all those around you. What is it that drives you mad, that turned you into a deadly weapon during the shifter War and made you drug yourself to stupidity for a year in Faycliff?"

Grey shook his head, refusing to tell Arlo about the Gentleman. He wouldn't ever tell anyone. The Gentleman manifested Grey's darkest tendencies, and he decided that speaking aloud would lend the Gentleman greater power.

Arlo didn't attempt to converse until hours later, when the sun sunk low in the western sky and a thin, vertical line appeared against the horizon.

"Ezra's there," Arlo said, pointing to the line.

"What is it?"

"A guarded tower, holding a single cell at its peak. The First Servant built this prison to preserve the last living transeel—or so he believed. Any who survived his purge went into hiding, but Ezra miscalculated. He trusted the First Servant to guarantee his survival in exchange for his help training new swordhands."

"The First Servant kept his word."

"Yes, but Ezra didn't expect to live as a prisoner for ten thousand years."

"I'd bet isolation drove him to insanity thousands of years ago."

"Unlikely. transeel don't need companionship or stimulation, for we can exist within our minds. We'll soon discover if I'm correct."

"How will we break into this tower? You're not a fighter, Arlo, unless you lied about that, too."

"Oh, no, it's you who must rescue Ezra. I suggest you sneak into the tower to avoid confrontation because the First Servant assigned an entire Pillar regiment as guards." Arlo brought the wagon to a stop behind a gentle dune, and Grey slipped from his seat, stretching his stiff legs. The sun would set in another hour, followed by Echore's inevitable ascension.

"Do you have any aerostatic gas?"

"A canister of diluted dak…"

Grey frowned. "Just give it here." Arlo handed him the canister, and Grey inhaled the aerostatic gas. No surge of strength materialized as it had when he'd inhaled centered or pure dak. Instead, the diluted gas added a spring to his step and eased his lingering weariness. Better than nothing. The effect would last twenty-three hours, enough time for a Pillar squad to slaughter him.

"I also have this," Arlo said, handing him a spyglass.

Grey accepted it without a word and turned from Arlo. He broke into a slow jog towards the tower, which, for its height, was unusually thin. It stretched hundreds of feet into the open sky, a smooth, rounded cylinder the circumference of a spiral staircase. Even from a thousand feet away, Grey recognized the same material that allowed the First Servant's palace to stretch over the chasm between Harkk's two mountains.

He peered through the spyglass and scanned the prison's defenses, spotting only a single guard near the tower's base, and though he panned the scope across the landscape, he could find no other signs of life or fortifications. Puzzled, Grey made a full circle around the tower. Still no one.

Better safe than sorry, he thought, crawling across the cooling sand until he reached the rear of the tower, opposite the guard. He ran his hand across the stone—if indeed it was stone—marveling at its smoothness. Even biting sand carried by the desert's winds couldn't erode the seamless material.

Grey edged around the tower until he reached the ancient guard dressed in a shabby Pillar uniform. He leaned against the building in a worn chair beneath a ragged umbrella, which cast just enough shade to cover his bulk. Arlo's description of the tower's protections must be outdated, Grey thought.

Grey knocked the man out with a bump to the temple and hoped he didn't cause any lasting damage. Inside, a staircase wound up the tower, lit by the occasional glowing bondman wedged into narrow crevices in the curved wall. Even though the diluted dak gave Grey plenty of energy, he still paused every few seconds to listen for unexpected sounds. He heard nothing but his breath, for the howling wind didn't make its presence known through the tower wall.

The staircase ended abruptly at a room, which Grey entered. Furnished no better than a jail cell, the undecorated space contained a single bed upon which lay a man, his back turned to Grey. Thick, rusted bars planted in front of the stairs prevented Grey from proceeding further, while the single window provided the only light source.

"Hey," Grey called to the man, who didn't move. "Hey!" he shouted, grabbing the bars and rattling them in their settings. The man turned over, swinging his thin legs over the edge of the bed. Grey averted his eyes, for the man was nude.

"What do you want?" the man asked, examining Grey with mild interest. Grey returned his stare and noted his resemblance to Westing. His bald head reflected the last of the sunlight, while his gaunt cheeks and thin lips matched the dead rebel's features. Even this man's body was lean and wiry, like Westing's.

"I'm here to rescue you," Grey said, feeling foolish. From Arlo's description, Grey had imagined himself enacting a heroic rescue, infiltrating a trained Pillar squad and taking out prison guards on his way through the tower. Instead, he'd crawled across the desert like a rat, conked an elderly guard's head, and strolled up a flight of stairs.

"How'd you bypass the guards?"

"Just one guard, an old man dozing on the stoop."

"Only one!" The man laughed, his eyes narrowing in mirth. He stood up and stretched. "The First Servant's laziness never ceases to amaze."

"Are you Ezra?" Grey asked, growing more confused by the second. Surely, this strange, naked man wasn't the mighty warrior Arlo had spoken about.

"Forgive me. It's been hundreds of years since I've had to meet someone." Then, as if noticing he wasn't wearing any clothes, he draped his worn bedsheet over his shoulder, tying it around his waist like a toga. "Yes, I am Ezra, and though customs may have changed over the centuries, I'd imagine it's still polite for you to introduce yourself."

"I'm Grey. Arlo sent me to, uh, rescue you. Like I said a minute ago."

"Arlo! How is my old enemy?"

"Enemy? He asked me to fight an entire Pillar regiment on your behalf."

Ezra raised one eyebrow. "When the First Servant realized I wouldn't try to escape, he withdrew his troops. Besides, I'm sure the mighty Pillar has more important matters to contend with besides an ancient transeel, eh?" Without waiting for a response, Ezra continued, "Anyway, say hello to Arlo for me. If the First Servant dies, he's welcome to visit."

"You won't come with me?" Grey asked. He'd expected gratitude, not for Ezra to shoo him away like a pest.

"No. While the First Servant lives, I stay. He is alive, isn't he?"

"Yeah, he is."

"Then goodbye!"

Grey examined Ezra. The man stood at ease, but he carried himself like a swordhand, light on his toes and ready to move at a moment's notice. Grey contemplated taking Ezra from the prison, but that would prove pointless. Arlo needed his cooperation, not his limp body. Besides, if Ezra could fight like Arlo claimed, he'd never be able to take him. I don't have any choice, Grey decided. "Fine," he said. "I'll go."

Ezra shrugged, but as Grey turned to leave, Ezra called out, "Wait one moment!"

"Yes?" Though Westing and Ezra looked alike, Westing's smile had been a cold, unfriendly smirk. Ezra's wide grin portrayed joy, and Grey even smiled back.

"Show me the sword dangling from your back." Without hesitation, Grey swung his scabbard around and drew Agony's Joy, holding it out. He couldn't recall deciding to show the sword to Ezra, yet there it was, on display in the open, where its flawless surface picked up the last glints of daylight shining through the window.

"How surprising," Ezra said, releasing a deep chuckle that rolled from the depths of his belly. "I never expected to see my sword again, not after where I left it."

"Your sword?"

"Well, I suppose it's yours now." Ezra laughed again, walking over to the prison bars and pushing open the door, which was unlocked. "You are carrying it, after all. I forged it a long time ago, so it was once my sword."

All Grey knew about Agony's Joy was what little Westing had told him. Suddenly, Arlo's pointless quest didn't seem so irrelevant after all. If he could learn about Agony's Joy, perhaps knowledge would unlock his memories from his two years in the shifter War.

"There's someone else in the stairwell," Grey said, for he listened to footsteps echo up the tower, accompanied by the swoosh of someone's clothing brushing against the railing. He pressed his back to the wall by the stairs, readying Agony's Joy for a fight.

"Missed a guard or two in your hurry to save me, eh?" The

amusement hadn't left Ezra's voice, but Grey supposed he had no reason to worry. Only Grey's own life hung in the balance.

"Be quiet," Grey whispered, and Ezra shrugged, sitting back down on the bed. The footsteps grew louder. Grey wrung the sword's hilt with his hand, pulling his arms around for a swing.

"Don't shoot," came Arlo's familiar voice, followed by his raised hands.

Grey let out a whoosh and said, "I nearly chopped your neck off."

"But you didn't. Hey, Ezra," Arlo said, waving at his old companion or enemy.

"Still having others do your work for you, I see."

"And you're still sitting in the same spot I left you thousands of years ago."

The two transeel glared at one another for several unbearable seconds before Ezra clapped and said, "This has been a pleasant reunion. But all this socializing has exhausted me, and Grey was leaving."

"I suppose Grey didn't convince you to escape."

"Why? Because he has my old sword?"

"Because of how he might use it. Ezra, you've been wasting away for so long that you imagined I thought a sword would change your stubborn mind?"

"Then why send him? What's so special about this boy?" Clearly, the ancient transeel didn't enjoy Arlo's attitude. Grey, though, leaned forward with rapt attention.

"This 'boy' has a name, which you already know. Grey can inhale the purest aerostatic gases, all four of them, and come away unharmed. Aerostacy doesn't kill him." Arlo let his words sink in while Ezra cocked his head. Arlo nodded, which set Ezra pacing about the room. Grey edged towards the staircase, but Arlo grabbed his shoulder and motioned him still.

"Oh, Echore...." Ezra trailed off, stopping and letting a long hiss of air escape between his teeth.

"Yes," Arlo said. "Ponder the implications."

"Fine, Echore-damnit. I'm interested. Slightly interested."

"Grey, Ezra crafted weapons and trained swordhands for the First Servant after the purge, but after he'd vanquished all major threats, he no longer needed Ezra. The First Servant is immortal, a god. He offered Ezra a choice: die or live in prison. While I helped the rest of our people go into hiding, Ezra opted for imprisonment."

"Our people are in prison, whether or not they see the bars."

"Until the First Servant dies, Ezra considers his own whereabouts unimportant."

"He'll kill me if I leave, just like he'd kill you if he knew any other transeel survived the purge. And don't fool yourself — he will find out. It may not be today. It may not be a hundred years from now, but it'll happen. Remaining here is our entire species' best hope for survival."

"Come with us," Arlo said. "Grey will defeat the First Servant with the proper training. The shifter Callan tried to teach Grey, but while Callan may be excellent at combat, he's unfamiliar with the aerostatic arts. Grey needs a true instructor, a swordhand who can show him the subtle interplay between aerostacy and weaponry."

"Too risky."

"Your cowardice matches the other transeel whom you once mocked!" Grey shrunk from Arlo's passion, for the medic never raised his voice. "Our people have survived as long as you by hiding among humans as servants, so you're not suffering in noble isolation to prevent transeel extinction."

"Needn't I remind you who transformed us into these

human forms?" Ezra asked, thrusting out his pale arms in disgust.

"I acted. I helped all willing transeel survive, so we could bide our time and turn our best virtue into a weapon: patience. But the time for waiting has ended. Now is our chance to act… though our brethren disagree."

"You'll always be an outcast, Arlo, blinded by the truth that the First Servant is unkillable."

"I see what others do not. I see that our patience has delivered Grey, a young man who may defeat the First Servant — but only if we help him do so!"

A headache welled beneath Grey's scalp, and he turned to the window for fresh air while Arlo and Ezra continued their argument. The room triggered his claustrophobia, so he inhaled a deep breath of desert air.

The sun set, leaving a gentle glow on the horizon. Over the next two hours, the sand would cool as the temperature plummeted, while Echore would begin its ascent behind the tower. He took another deep breath, focusing on the open expanse below until his heart slowed and his headache faded.

Near the horizon, a line of dust trailed off towards the east, catching the fading daylight, and Grey raised Arlo's spyglass to his eye. He followed the dust to a dark speck passing across the desert towards the tower. Expanding the glass brought the figure into closer view, and Grey froze.

A maramor sped across the sand with incredible speed, and as it moved, its flat head twisted towards Grey. He dropped the spyglass, and it shattered against the stone floor.

"What is it?" Arlo asked.

"A maramor," Grey sputtered, sinking to his knees. The maramor's stare had unnerved him.

Arlo grabbed the scope from the ground and shoved it against his face, then spun to face Ezra. "Now is the time to decide," Arlo said. "You've wasted ten thousand years. Help

Grey escape this maramor and defeat the First Servant."

"I can't kill that creature," Ezra said.

"You don't have to," Arlo replied, sensing Ezra's wavering certainty. "We can continue running. Grey can kill it with your help. He'll be able to move faster than a maramor and strike with equal force. You can show him how. Make your decision now, for we can't escape across open terrain without your aid."

Ezra said nothing, but his whole body tensed. A deep shudder ran through his spine, down his body, and into his legs. Grey wondered whether he was seizing, but Arlo wasn't concerned. After a minute, Ezra stopped shaking, and he spoke with clear intent.

"We have ten minutes before the maramor reaches the tower. I can lead it off, but I need your scent, Grey. Your clothing smells putrid, so that should suffice."

"It was a hot day," Grey said.

"Good, the sweatier, the better. Take off all of your clothes, and give them to me. Then scrub yourself off as best you can."

"With what?"

"There is a hose in the corner. I have diluted aerostatic gas, a bit of dak, and ahl if you need it. Take Arlo, and I'll deal with the maramor."

Grey followed Ezra's instructions, then inhaled the twin gases, while Ezra donned Grey's filthy outfit.

"Do you want the sword?" Grey asked, reaching for the weapon on his back.

Ezra paused but shook his head. "Even that weapon won't mark a maramor's flesh, if indeed you can call it flesh." He flew down the stairs, with Grey and Arlo racing behind. At the bottom of the stairs, Ezra sprinted east, towards Arndak, and Grey marveled at the man's confidence. Now that Ezra had decided, he'd become a whirr of endless motion.

"We'd better move," Arlo said moments later.

Arlo led Grey back to his wagon, where the mule bondmen waited in their tethers. Arlo urged the creatures forward, and they soon pulled the wagon west at a good clip. Grey noticed that the evening winds covered their tracks almost as soon as they rolled past, so the maramor would have only his scent to track. Hopefully, Ezra's ruse would fool the creature.

"We should keep going to Estril," Grey said, surprising himself. Arlo raised an eyebrow, for it was the first time Grey had shown any interest in their direction.

"You insisted you didn't care about Callan's cause."

"I still don't. It's just... Estril is where Bow might be."

The napthal had worn off, and the diluted ahl he'd inhaled allowed a sliver of his emotions to surface. His memory of Bow, standing drenched in the storm by Arndak's Lonely Tree, stood out in his mind. Bow had saved his life at Faycliff, Harkk, and Arndak, while risking Westing's wrath to train him. As thanks, Grey had abandoned Bow. Guilt swelled in his chest, but another desire joined that unpleasant emotion: eagerness to reunite with his friend.

Chapter 18

"We're clear," Arlo said. Even the mule bondmen, creatures Grey had considered tireless, panted after their five-hour run through the chill night. The hardy animals now strained to pull Arlo's wagon, plodding past the sparse vegetation with their heads held low to the ground. Steam rolled from their nostrils to disperse into the dry air while their feet dragged through deep sand. Fifteen minutes later, the sand thinned and gave way to smooth rock, spotted with areas of soil holding the occasional ragged tree. Mountains sprouted from the horizon, a mighty barrier between desert and sea.

"If Ezra didn't kill the maramor, it will come after us again," Grey said.

"Ezra is a formidable warrior, but no one has ever killed a maramor. I'd imagine only their creator, the First Servant, might face those monsters and live. Our best hope is that Ezra misled that monster before he returns to meet us in Estril."

"Great..." The ahl Grey inhaled earlier would soon wear off, and he dreaded facing the Gentleman. "I need more ahl."

"I have a bit of diluted ahl, enough for one more dose."

"Will they have more in Estril?"

"I haven't been there since the last time I visited Ezra's prison, and you saw how outdated my knowledge was."

"In other words, you have no idea."

"Nope," Arlo said, nudging Grey with his elbow. "Come, Grey, smile a bit. Few have escaped a maramor's grasp once, let alone three times. The sun will rise, and a glorious day awaits."

Grey said nothing, only leaned back and closed his eyes. With the ahl enhancing his Attention, sleep wouldn't come no matter how much he willed it, so he instead ran through his options.

Bow, and by extension, the Array, were his best chance of securing a reliable stash of ahl. But Bow intended to follow through with Westing's plan and topple the First Servant, an immortal, all-powerful god. That meant danger, incredible danger.

When Grey opened his eyes, the mountains no longer loomed in the distance. Dark rock jutted five miles into the cloudless sky, becoming a series of snow-covered slabs halfway up. The slabs shone so brightly that Grey had to shield his eyes.

"There's pure ice up there," Arlo said, letting slack into the bondmen's harnesses. They slowed, sinking to their knees and laying to rest.

"I guessed snow."

"One of the world's mysteries, eh? An undiscovered geological force melts the snow before freezing it into solid ice. It's quite beautiful but dangerous when it falls from the mountain." Of all the world's mysteries, inexplicable ice didn't catch Grey's imagination.

"The Array knows how to craft strong bondmen," Grey commented, eying the beasts. Powerful muscles, larger than any naturally born animal, quivered from exertion. "I didn't know they ever ran out of energy."

"Bondmen tire as we do," Arlo said, unhitching two feed bags hanging from the sides of the wagon. He placed the bags in front of the bondmen, and they munched. "The difference is that the Array programs them without emotions or pain, so even when they tire, they will continue moving until dead or ordered to stop."

"So we wait for them to recover?"

Arlo pulled two packs from the wagon and tossed one to Grey. "No, we continue on foot."

"Don't tell me we need to hike over those mountains."

"No one takes the mountain pass, at least not since the last time I checked," Arlo said, shouldering his pack. "No need to worry. We'll take Estril Tunnel." Grey raised an eyebrow, so Arlo continued, "I keep forgetting how little you know of the world. Estril Tunnel is one of the First Servant's great works, a true engineering marvel. We'll have to leave the bondmen and my wagon here."

"What will happen to these bondmen?" Grey asked, pulling on his pack. The compact satchel weighed a surprising amount, so he had to lean forwards to prevent from toppling backward. "Echore, what's in this bag?"

"Metal," Arlo answered. Before Grey pressed him, he continued, "To answer your other question, the bondmen will rest and pull the wagon to a safe location before awaiting my return. A bandit may grab them while they're in transit, but I'll chance it. Otherwise, we'd have to wait several days for them to recover."

"Fine. Let's get moving."

"Right, off we go!" Arlo moved with surprising speed for someone so round, a fact that had always perplexed Grey. Perhaps the transeel's organs worked under different principles than the human body.

An hour later, the tunnel entrance appeared as they crested one last hill, which sloped towards a wide bay filled with murky water. The tunnel was as wide as the First Servant's palace atop Harkk's western mountain, a gaping archway hewn into the heart of the mountain range. Mosaics, like those inside the First Servant's palace, lined the rim of the arch, reaching perhaps one hundred feet from the tunnel against the mountainside. Grey wondered at the expense. Marble stored the aerostatic gases, but the First Servant possessed it in such quantities that he used it in his art.

The southernmost part of the mosaic began with the First Servant's imprisonment of the gods, followed by a familiar sequence of his alleged heroics to establish the Defiant Empire. The gods, as usual, resembled balls of amorphous light trapped within Echore. One scene, however, stood out.

"I've never seen that image before," Grey said, pointing to a mural section near the northernmost region of the tunnel entrance. The mosaic depicted Echore hanging above the First Servant's palace in Harkk, between the eastern and western mountains. A light shone down, hitting the palace's great overhanging half-arch before lighting up the palace like a star.

"It depicts the day the First Servant summoned Echore into existence from his throne atop the mountain." Arlo led Grey toward the shore, where a lengthy boardwalk stretched towards the tunnel entrance across the lake.

"Do you believe that story?" Grey asked between breaths, for Arlo's tone suggested doubt.

"Well, if you admit that the First Servant created Echore to imprison the gods and you accept the First Servant constructed his palace atop Harkk, then I don't see how this mosaic can show Echore's creation."

"Because the gods wouldn't have allowed the First Servant to keep his palace after constructing their prison."

"Right, unless the mosaics aren't in chronological order. So many questions! What if these alleged gods never existed at all?"

"There were gods," Grey said with certainty. "If they lacked physical forms, the First Servant depicted them as light."

"Only the First Servant holds the truth. Since you asked for my opinion, I maintain that the First Servant invented the gods to control his population with fear, just as he began the shifter War to kill his citizens."

Grey pondered Arlo's notion, but he shook his head. He was confident that the gods existed. The First Servant's incredible powers were godlike, and the Defiant Empire's impressive longevity implied a solid foundation. The First Servant freed us, Grey thought, so he deserves our respect. Another side of his brain thought, Do we also deserve to die if he wills it?

Grey followed Arlo onto the boardwalk that held only a handful of fishermen who dotted its length. Placid, dark water radiated a chill fog, which, combined with his dripping sweat and the shade cast by the mountain, set off a deep shiver in his chest.

Arlo stepped towards an old man resting beside the most decrepit boat in the harbor, a chipped, wooden vessel not much larger than a canoe. The sun-hardened man nodded at Arlo, and Arlo handed him his pack.

"Give him your bag," Arlo said, and Grey dropped it into the boat. The sailor pulled out a solid bar of metal, nickel-colored and half a foot thick, which he secured with a set of cracked leather straps. Arlo sat on a bench opposite Grey as the boatman lifted his oars and paddled.

Bored, Grey leaned over to watch the occasional bit of seaweed float in the gentle current. Now that the imminent danger from the maramor had passed, Grey pondered Arlo's motivations. No matter how he framed it, the old transeel sought to use Grey's immunity to the aerostatic gases. Westing, Callan, and even Bow viewed Grey as a tool in their arsenal, and though Grey resented the others, he didn't judge Bow. Bow cares about me, he thought, wishing the boat would sail faster. The thought of Bow waiting for him in Estril made him smile, an expression his facial muscles had little experience producing.

A deep shadow descended, and the seaman pulled his oars into the boat. Arlo dipped his hand into the lake, and to Grey's surprise, the water pulled at his fingers, forming a wake beside the hull. The boat propelled itself, picking up speed until the wind rushed across Grey's exposed cheeks.

Complete darkness descended, and claustrophobia clamped around Grey's heart, stealing his breath. The deep black smothered him like it had in the coffin at Harkk. He pictured the weight of the mountain above, miles of rock pressing down against the tunnel's support beams. What if an earthquake struck, shattering the tunnel and bringing down unspeakable tons of stone? No one would ever discover their crushed bodies.

I need a distraction, Grey thought. During his ride inside the sewage bondman, Bow had asked him about his life. That distraction had worked, but since shouting his life story over the roaring wind would be foolish, he instead yelled to Arlo, "How are we moving so fast?"

"A bondman, perhaps the world's largest, lives beneath this river. It's like a serpent, swimming forever in a loop beneath the water and pulling along any metallic objects with magnets attached to its torso."

"Ah, that's why we brought metal."

"Yes! We'll soon emerge into Estril Sea, ending a journey that would take days of rowing to complete."

A dim point of light appeared in the distance, and it brightened as they neared the tunnel's end. As they approached the opening, the sailor unstrapped the metal slabs and tossed them overboard. The boat shot from the tunnel, emerging into another bay, this one smothered in a dense layer of cool mist sliding off the mountain.

"A shame to waste good metal," Grey said.

"It's no waste. The bondman that pulled us through the tunnel either eats the metal or it eats the boat with the metal. I prefer to hand over the metal."

"The metal is its food?"

"Care to dive and see for yourself?"

Grey ignored the question, for the city of Estril emerged from the morning mists. The city was unlike any Grey had seen or predicted. He'd imagined Estril as a peaceful city, nestled by the sea, since ril was a healing gas. Instead, Estril floated upon the sea and looked more like the disorganized Fizzer camp within Harkk's western mountain, a jumble of floating barges tied together by metal ramparts and algae-covered ropes. Only the city's center appeared solid, a massive coliseum built from gleaming yellow stone.

"We'll have to board a ferry to the city."

An aquatic bondman with broad flippers propelled the ferry across the sea, and as they neared Estril, Grey noticed a figure standing on the dock. The boy was thin, leaning into the wind, with a shock of blond hair.

Chapter 19

Grey stepped onto the dock and laughed. The sound burst from his throat, and he choked. Have I ever laughed? he asked himself, but he had no time to ponder, for Bow ran down the sloping dock and flung his arms around Grey. To his great surprise, Grey squeezed Bow's shoulders before disentangling and stepping back.

"I'm so glad you're okay," Bow said, his pale cheeks flushed with excitement. "When you ran off—"

"I shouldn't have left," Grey said. "It's hard to explain, but I became so angry that I lost all sense of logic."

"You're not used to your emotions, and anger is one of the most powerful."

"Still..." Grey trailed off, realizing that Bow didn't hold a grudge. Only now, when the weight of his worry had lifted, did Grey realize how much Bow's possible reaction distracted him. "I'm so sorry. All you've done is help."

"It's okay," Bow said, beaming. "I forgive you, though there's nothing to forgive."

Grey returned Bow's smile, and they stood in awkward silence until Arlo coughed. "Who's your friend?" Bow asked.

Grateful for Arlo's interruption, Grey said, "The medic from the shifter War, the one who found me with Agony's Joy."

"Arlo, right?" Bow asked, extending his arm.

"That's me!" Arlo took his hand, and Bow shook it. "I can already see why Grey likes you so much."

Bow blushed, so Arlo said, "We'd best be moving, lest the maramor track our scent."

"You needn't worry about the maramor," Bow said.

"How's that?"

"Just follow me, and you'll soon see..." Arlo eyed Grey, who just shrugged, still too happy that Bow wasn't upset with him to focus on maramors, immortal dictators, or anything else.

Bow led them through an orderless configuration of ships, barges, and other floating platforms connected by rolling wooden walkways. The barges bobbed in the calm waves, making it difficult to walk without slipping, and Grey wondered how a storm would affect the floating city. He decided he'd rather not find out.

"We're here," Bow said, stopping at a gleaming white ship the size of a small building. Grey had to crane his neck to view the impressive pyramid of narrowing levels piled twelve stories atop the ship's wide hull, an improbable mass that looked like it shouldn't float. Two bondmen stood near a metal gangway stretching to a narrow door set into the hull twenty feet above the waterline. The bondmen's tall, flat bodies merged into a fleshy door while ten spiked arms pointed at Grey as he approached.

"This must be the Array's outpost in Estril," Arlo guessed, eying the sophisticated bondmen.

"Good thing I have my Array credentials," Bow said. The bondman extended a tendril, which touched Bow's arm before whipping back into place. It lowered its spiked arms to allow them passage.

The ship's interior matched any other vessel, with tight corridors punctuated by watertight doors. Six steep ladders brought them to the first level above the hull, where Bow led Grey and a wheezing Arlo to a room facing inward towards the heart of Estril.

Callan sat in a plush leather chair with his back to the window, legs crossed. "Good to see you, Grey," he said.

"Took you a while," Ezra said, stepping into the room. He crossed his arms across his chest, which was now covered in a plain white shirt draped over loose pants.

"You couldn't have made it here before us," Arlo said, still out of breath and leaning on his knees for support. "Not with that maramor chasing you."

"That maramor won't be troubling you for a while." Ezra smirked, enjoying Arlo's shock.

"I brought Ezra here," Callan said, and Ezra pouted, unhappy that Callan had spoiled the surprise. "He would never have been able to make it otherwise."

"Yes, I had a bit of help from the shifter. He lent me a hand, or one of his flying appendages, I should say." Ezra paused for laughter, but when none came, he plowed ahead. "No one helped me defeat the maramor, though."

"You can fly?" Bow asked Callan, ignoring Ezra's assertion.

"I can form any shape I please," Callan said, a hint of pride entering his voice. "I have an assortment of flying forms; some built for distance and others speed."

"Why not fly us everywhere, then?"

"The First Servant would not tolerate shifters fling across his lands. If he learned of my ability to challenge his Pillar's flyers, he might resume his war against me."

"Oh yeah, good point…"

"Anyway, is the maramor dead?"

"Goodness, no," Ezra said. "I don't believe anyone has ever killed one of those monsters. It's buried in Arndak's deepest mine, though, and it'll take weeks to dig itself free."

Grey shuddered, imagining himself trapped beneath all that rubble. "How did you get into the mines?" Grey asked, forcing himself to concentrate. "Security around the mines was quite strict during my short time there."

"Amazing how disorder can shatter a society's structures! Leigh's disappearance led to the discovery that her father had died, which of course sent Arndak into chaos. The Perdue mining family first attempted to grab power, but the other mining families contested their authority. In Arndak, power flows from those who control the dak mines. In desperation, the Perdue family began destroying the mines. If they couldn't control dak, then no one could."

"Men are foolish," Callan said, shaking his head.

"Completely," Ezra agreed, and Arlo, too, nodded. "The ensuing fight destroyed most of their productive mines, so I encountered little resistance. After a clever ruse involving a mule bondman dressed in Grey's filthy clothing, I used an Arndak pickaxe to collapse the cliff, trapping the maramor."

"Now that Ezra has thrilled us with his heroics, perhaps we'd better discuss our plan," Arlo said. "We've crippled dak production, so now we turn our sights to ril."

"Westing's plan was wise," Callan said. "Ril bubbles up from beneath the ocean through the king's chimney, so if we destroy the chimney from inside, Estril's ability to harvest ril will be gone."

"Oh no," Bow said. "Absolutely not. I won't let Grey do that."

"Do what?" Grey asked.

"You see that arena?" Bow pointed towards the center of Estril, where the enormous coliseum rose from the sea. "That's the top of the chimney, where the yearly ascension occurs. Royals battle in that arena to join the King's Circle, a pale imitation of the First Servant's Circle in Harkk."

"Westing had planned to fight in the tournament himself,"

Callan explained. "But he is dead, and as it's still six months away, it makes the most sense for Ezra to train Grey to compete. Grey will win, enter the Chimney, and use vum to demolish its outer wall."

"People die in that tournament."

"Knitters stand by to heal most wounds," Arlo said.

"Why don't we dive and blow up the chimney today?" Grey asked.

"Because the First Servant designed Estril's chimney to withstand the ocean's incredible currents. Exterior pressure, even from vum, won't collapse the stonework from the outside, while stealth won't get us past its guarded entrance to attack the interior. Only tournament champions may enter, so we must help you win the contest and destroy the chimney from its vulnerable belly."

"As long as Bow trains me with ahl, I'll agree to Ezra's lessons—but I don't promise to fight in the tournament."

"Of course I'll teach you," Bow said. "Still, I didn't realize you cared about defeating the First Servant."

"I don't." But this wasn't true, not anymore. Before, when he'd imagined the First Servant killing Defiant Empire citizens, he'd pictured an amorphous mass of dead bodies, a common sight in the shifter War. Now, he imagined Bow's body among them, and he cared enough to prevent Bow's death.

"Well," Ezra said, clapping his hands. "Let's get started."

"What? Now?"

"No time like the present! Bow, is there somewhere we can train?"

"Yeah, the ship has a few sizeable chambers, but I'm not convinced Grey should expose himself to scrutiny in such a public tournament. What if a soldier from Harkk recognizes him?"

"Grey will not compete unless we agree that he is

prepared," Callan assured Bow. "He has six months, during which all of us will contribute to his training, and Grey will practice his facial twist to hide his identity."

"Enough talking," Grey said. All the details of their plan would evolve over the next six months, and he was eager to stretch his legs.

Bow led them to a chamber containing a sunken pool surrounded by a wooden deck. At least three hundred feet long and half as wide, the pool's empty bottom sloped towards a covered drain near its center. Glow-worm bondmen hung overhead in fixtures that swayed with the ship's gentle rocking, casting a light as powerful as the sun.

"This is one of the ship's fisheries," Bow said. "When it's filled with saltwater, fish can live and even breed in this pool to provide the sailors with food during long voyages. They've gone unused for decades, though, since this boat became a permanent fixture in Estril."

"Hello!" Ezra shouted, and the sound echoed against the tiled walls and smooth floor. Grey hopped from the deck, landing five feet down on the pool's unforgiving surface. "Eager to begin, I see."

"Eager to finish," Grey said. Bow crouched at the pool's edge while Callan stood behind, thick arms crossed.

"Hand me your blade," Ezra said. Grey removed Agony's Joy from its sheath at his back, and Ezra hefted the sword, balancing it on his fingertip. "I forged many weapons for the First Servant, but this sword is my greatest achievement, a masterpiece beyond any weapon crafted by mortal hands. When the First Servant delivered the marble from which I carved the blade, its texture directed me towards its finished form."

"Marble?" Grey asked. "It's made from metal."

"Nope. I crafted Agony's Joy from a rare marble capable of storing each aerostatic gas. Through an aerostatic technique lost to the ages, I forged the blade, so its leading edge is sharp enough to slice through stone and never dulls. The handle dampens vibrations from any strike—but you're missing its most valuable part."

"Westing said a cable sits in the handle, allowing it to be thrown and retracted."

"Right and wrong. A bondman once lived within the sword's hilt, and its tentacle merged with the wielder's hand. The Array has not crafted such a complex creature in thousands of years."

"But you remember how to make one? How did you make the blade? Where did you hide it? I don't recall finding it…" Grey's questions rushed out in a flurry, but Ezra held his tongue.

"How about this for motivation? I'll answer one question for each blow you land during your training."

"I need to learn about Agony's Joy," Grey said, with mild anger flushing his pale cheeks.

"The sooner you fight me, the sooner I will answer your questions."

"Fine. Hand me the blade, and let's get started."

"We're not starting with this weapon," Ezra said, tossing the blade aside, so it hit the ground hilt-first and leaned against the wall. "How can you control a sword if you cannot even master your own fists?"

No sooner had he stopped speaking than did Grey swing his fist at Ezra's face. In a blur of motion, Grey found himself on his back with Ezra's foot against his chest. With an annoyed sigh, Grey jumped to his feet. He expected to see Ezra's haughty grin many times over the next several months.

"Again!" Ezra shouted.

***

* * *

"I didn't even get to ask one question," Grey said. He sat with Bow in one of hundreds of empty living quarters for a crew that had abandoned the ship years ago. Only fifty Array personnel remained, and they kept to the upper deck.

"Well, you didn't land a blow," Bow said. They sat side-by-side atop the room's bare mattress, and Grey pressed himself into the metal wall to allow heat to drain into the ship's hull.

"Ezra's too fast. He moves faster than Callan, and I never even beat him."

"I know you can do it."

"How? Ezra's as fast as a maramor."

"I watched you hold your own against a maramor in Faycliff. Something awoke inside you, like it has during many of your fights. We'll discover a way to harness your primal instinct."

Grey fell silent. Bow wanted to help, but he didn't understand the Gentleman's unrelenting pull. He didn't know that Grey's fighting prowess arose from the Gentleman's murderous words and that without the man's evil presence, he lacked notable skill. Grey might defeat a few bandits, but he would never triumph in a duel against Callan or Ezra—and certainly not against a maramor or the First Servant. Still, Bow's unwavering confidence ignited a sliver of hope.

"I'm happy you believe in me," Grey said. With ahl's help, he grasped the edges of his feelings towards Bow. I like him, Grey realized. But that wasn't it. He liked Arlo, and this emotion differed from simple friendship.

Bow lay his cool hand on Grey's bare knee, and, as usual, Grey wanted to pull away. But he didn't. Instead, he leaned against Bow, allowing their shoulders to touch and relishing in the flutter of sparks that flowed between them.

Chapter 20

"You need another lesson," Bow said. Drained to his core after another day with Ezra, Grey replied with a grunt. Each morning, Ezra dragged him to the empty pool and only allowed him to rest once Echore rose late in the evening. Grey hadn't once left the Array ship since he'd arrived, for Ezra's methods made even Callan's attempts to train Grey seem gentle. And yet, Grey admitted, he'd made no progress.

"I've had nothing but lessons for weeks," Grey said. "And with all that training, I haven't been able to hit Ezra. Not even once." Ezra's movements were so swift, his predictions of Grey's attacks so precise, that Grey doubted he'd ever be able to land a blow on the transeel. Grey even wondered if Ezra was cheating, using ahl to predict the future as Bow had described to him months ago. Ezra had promised an answer for every hit, but weeks of punishing training left Grey with the sinking notion that he'd get no answers.

"I meant a lesson in ahl, not more training," Bow said.

"Oh, right..." Grey hadn't worried about the Gentleman since they'd arrived in Estril. Saturating himself with diluted ahl produced a mild effect that held the Gentleman at bay while keeping Grey's emotions at a low and ignorable background hum. A perfect solution, as far as he was concerned. "As long as I have access to ahl, I'll be fine."

"You don't want me to teach you anymore?" Bow crossed his thin arms, blocking Grey's path as he trudged down the hall to his room.

"I suppose not. You've already taught me enough." Grey tried to pass, but Bow moved to stop him.

"Bow snorted. "You begged me to teach you, but now that you have a supply of ahl, you're no longer interested?"

"If Attention helps me control myself, then that's enough."

"Not acceptable," Bow said.

"What?"

"You heard me. I'm not taking no for an answer. In fact, we're going to take a brief trip tomorrow morning so I can continue your lessons in ahl."

"Ezra won't like that."

"Are you Ezra's pupil or his servant?" Bow spit Ezra's name from his mouth like poison gas, for he despised the ancient swordhand. Grey didn't blame him. Ezra insisted everyone recognize his talents, whether his prowess with a sword or his golden tongue. Even Arlo refused to share a room with Ezra for over ten minutes.

"Okay," Grey said. "If it's that important to you, I'll go."

"It should be important to you." Bow huffed, his face red. "Don't act like you're doing me a favor." He turned on his heel and stomped off down the hallway.

"Wait, does that mean we're going or not?" Grey asked, but Bow didn't stop or answer. "I suppose I'll find out tomorrow." Grey returned to his room and closed his eyes, but sleep didn't come. It never did, not since he started using ahl in place of napthal. A couple minutes of sleep here and there provided all the rest his ahl-fueled brain would accept. Too physically exhausted to move but too wakeful to sleep, Grey did nothing but wait all night for Echore to set, alone with his thoughts.

All his life, Grey's expectations had been clear. He'd

considered only practical matters, like how to feed and protect himself. Even the bloody dreams that began after the shifter War didn't affect his waking mind. Now, ahl introduced an unfamiliar fuzziness to his perception. Emotion colored his judgment, altering his opinions and twisting logic in unexpected directions.

When his thoughts turned to Bow, he smiled. He'd noticed that reaction more and more, but his feelings about Bow were difficult to decipher. Perhaps another try with pure ahl would help, he thought. But no, that would be too risky. The last time he'd ingested pure ahl, guilt almost drove him to insanity.

Grey must have dozed because Bow's appearance startled him awake. The pale glow against the horizon hinted at sunrise, but it'd be an hour before the sun shone above the mountains. "Let's go," Bow said.

"Did you tell Ezra we're leaving?" Grey asked, standing up and pulling on a clean shirt.

"No." Bow rushed into the corridor, forcing Grey to jog after him.

"Are you upset with me?" Grey asked after a minute of silent walking.

"Yes." Bow didn't speak another word while they disembarked. He maintained silence during their walk through Estril and ferry ride to shore.

When Grey stepped onto dry land, he almost fell on his back. A month on the sea had done something odd to his balance. The solid dirt swayed beneath his feet as if the land spun atop a swivel, and Grey stumbled ahead in uncomfortable silence as Bow hiked south along the coast.

"Where are we going?" Grey asked, but Bow didn't respond. Fine, Grey thought. After two hours, the sandy beach they'd been following turned to pebbles, rocks, and soon impassable boulders.

"We're here," Bow said, turning inland.

"Where?" A thin pine forest provided much-needed shade from the rising sun, and Grey's body temperature dropped under cover of trees.

"A fishing town, one of many that provides dehydrated fish as rations for the Pillar." Grey wondered whether Isa's stew meat had once swum in these waters.

The forest thinned, making space for stone buildings that were several stories tall and far larger than any structure in Shallow Canyon or Faycliff. Piers extended into the sea like fingers grasping an array of boats. Despite the town's size, it appeared abandoned.

"Where is everyone?" Grey followed Bow down the central avenue, a cobblestone road lined with shops. Then Grey noticed them. "Those look like blood stains," he said, pointing to a blackened patch of ground around which flies buzzed.

"Yes. They do."

"Another maramor attack?" Grey asked.

Bow nodded. "Callan says the maramors attacked in shifter guise a week ago. They slaughtered the entire town and brought the severed heads back to Harkk just like they did in Faycliff. They threw the bodies into the ocean."

"Is that why we came here?"

"We came for your next lesson. I already told you. Now take a seat." They'd arrived at a park, little more than a few benches surrounding a dry fountain. At least none of the seats were covered in human remains.

Grey sat, and Bow picked another bench. "Take this," Bow said, offering Grey a vial of centered ahl.

"I already have diluted ahl in my system."

"It's fine. The centered ahl will take effect for twenty-three minutes. Then you'll go back to experiencing the reduced effects of diluted ahl. It's not additive."

"The last time I took pure ahl…"

"Don't be afraid," Bow said, But Grey hesitated. "Are you going to inhale the gas or not?"

"Fine." Grey breathed in the gas, bracing himself for its effects to overwhelm him. Instead, Bow spoke, drawing Grey's attention away from his rising emotions.

"I've taught you how to strengthen your Attention, the basis of ahl's two gifts: shaping your thoughts and reading others' thoughts. Seers examine and manipulate others, while Thinkers look within. When you inhale ahl, or any other aerostatic gas, it becomes part of your body. A Seer pushes ahl into the minds of those around him, like sensitive tendrils that tug at others' brains."

While Bow talked, Grey noticed a halo floating above Bow's head, a ring of light that vanished as soon as he focused on its glowing presence.

"Once ahl leaves my body, where does it go?"

"To disperse in the atmosphere. Or down into the ground. Who knows? The point is, you can use it like an extra appendage. Either reach into a stranger's brain, or delve into your own, strengthening the parts you want to emphasize to reshape your perception. If you out-think Ezra, then you will beat him."

Bow's halo grew brighter, and Grey swore he spotted his reflection in its undulating display of colors. "There's something over your head," Grey said, focusing hard to bring the object into view.

"Wow, it took me years to develop my sight."

"What is it? It looks… it looks like Echore…" The halo expanded into a sphere, and it didn't glow; it only reflected the sun's light, just as Echore mirrored its surroundings.

"That, Grey, is the human soul. Or as close to it as anyone's ever been able to perceive. Master Seers alter its composition to inflict permanent changes upon their targets."

Grey's focus lapsed, and the Echore-like soul snapped out of existence, or at least visibility. In its place, dread built in the pit of his stomach.

"It's okay," Bow said, noticing Grey's distress. "You need your emotions to fight. Let them flow, and I'll help you deal with it this time."

"I can't."

"Yes, you can. Grow your inner flame. Give it strength!"

Grey boosted his Attention, and thoughts raced through his consciousness faster than he could comprehend them, jumping in and out of his perception.

"Hold a thought in place," Bow ordered. "Grab it like you might grab a fish in water. Don't let it get away."

Grey grasped at the first thought that surfaced, but it slipped from his awareness. Then he pinned a memory from the day the Gentleman first appeared.

"Vocalize your emotions."

"Terrible sadness. And regret. Also, helplessness." The Gentleman taunted him from the past, dredging up more memories of the people he'd killed. "They each had lives like Isa. I murdered them. Their deaths were as terrible as hers. They didn't deserve to be slaughtered like animals."

"Did you want to kill them?"

Grey moaned. "No."

"Then why did you kill them?"

"He made me!"

"Who made you?"

"The…" Grey forced himself to stop talking by biting his tongue. He tasted blood, but it didn't matter. He couldn't speak of the Gentleman.

"Tell me," Bow said. He squeezed Grey's wrist with one hand and raised his chin with the other, forcing Grey to stare into his blue eyes.

"The Gentleman!" Grey screamed, his vocal cords

straining. "He orders me to kill everyone I meet, no matter how old or young, because he relishes death. But he's invisible, imaginary. Only I see him, with his foul suit and white cheeks, taunting me. Pushing me. Torturing me. It never ends…"

"And so you used napthal."

"Yes."

"And ahl."

"And ahl," Grey agreed.

"But you don't want to kill anyone?"

"I'd kill the First Servant," Grey said, blood dripping from his punctured tongue. "I'd tear him apart."

"Why?"

"Because… because he would kill you, and I like you. I don't understand why or how, but I care more about you than anyone I've ever met." Saying these words aloud also marked the first time he'd allowed himself to dwell upon these uncomfortable sensations.

"You're special, Grey. And I'm not just talking about your aerostatic abilities. Your thoughts are pure. From the first time I watched you drive the vorsters from Faycliff, I liked you."

"But the Gentleman…"

"The Gentleman isn't you. I don't pretend to understand him, but I promise he's not you. Trust me. I've examined your soul, and it doesn't hold his horrible spirit, nor does it resemble the souls of real murderers… like the killer who slaughtered my entire family."

"How did they die?" Grey asked. Tears streamed down his cheeks, but he wiped them away to offer Bow his full attention. Grey had shared his most vulnerable truth, and now Bow meant to repay his trust.

"Though I was born into the Array in Harkk, my family summered in the south at a house that's been in our family for generations. When a shifter attack destroyed a nearby town, we welcomed refugees into our home, providing food and shelter to any who needed it. One refugee killed my parents and sister. He killed them because they were in a room that held the couple canisters of ahl he wanted to steal."

"That's horrible."

"I was only ten, the same age as you when the shifters attacked Shallow Canyon. Notions of revenge sent me into a rage, and I tracked my parents' killer through a torrential storm to his makeshift shelter. Then I inhaled pure ahl for the first time." Bow took a shuddering breath before continuing. "I reached into this man's soul and twisted it apart. Flashes of past murders showered my young mind with images no adult should endure, scenes of torture, dismemberment, and worse. As he screamed in an insane fit, I knew I'd sensed true, unfiltered evil. So believe me when I promise that your soul is free from the wicked rot that corrupts the hearts of many men."

"Now come, walk with me," Bow said, taking a deep breath and wiping away his tears.

Grey accepted Bow's outstretched hand and allowed himself to be led towards the water and onto a pier. The centered ahl faded, leaving Grey with only the dulled emotions allowed by the diluted ahl. From the first moment he'd experienced his feelings, he'd regarded them as a threat. But now? He wanted more.

"Isn't the sea lovely?" Bow asked, still holding Grey's hand. Though the water shimmered, Grey's eyes rested only on Bow.

Chapter 21

Grey stood ten paces from Callan, much as he had nine months ago during their spars on the way to Arndak. The Array boat rocked beneath his feet, which added to the challenge as he watched Callan's left leg tense. Was Callan finding his balance, or was he about to leap into action? Grey decided on the latter, so he'd already begun his counterstrike before Callan launched himself more than a half foot.

As Callan's right knee rose, Grey dropped low and swept his foot along the ground, knocking Callan's left leg from beneath him. Callan flopped onto his back, his right leg unable to find grip in time to brace himself.

"You're getting slower," Grey said, standing and offering his hand to Callan.

"No. You are much, much faster, even without dak." Callan allowed himself to be helped to his feet.

"He's right," Bow said from his perch along the wall. "It makes little sense, but he's right. You're moving far faster than you should be able to with no dak in your system. Are you doing anything special with the ahl?"

"Just what you taught me." At this, Bow smiled. He'd continued Grey's lessons, taking one day a week from a begrudging Ezra. "I guess Ezra must be a good combat instructor."

"He is a better teacher than I," Callan said.

"Not bad," Ezra said about Grey's performance. He dropped into their makeshift arena from his spot near Bow. "But not great, either. Your movements were lazy, and a more skilled opponent would have used your sloppiness against you."

Grey shrugged. Six months of Ezra's training hadn't altered his feelings about the ancient transeel. His unbearable ego had grown to the point that he'd driven Arlo away. The medic had mumbled something about gathering herbs a few weeks ago and hadn't yet returned. Callan either ignored or didn't mind Ezra's attitude, while Bow made his displeasure clear whenever he had the chance. Grey kept his own annoyance in check by appreciating his considerable progress and the blissful absence of the Gentleman.

"Now that you're warmed up, let's practice with Agony's Joy."

Grey lifted the blade with excitement. Swordplay had become his favorite activity each day, and his palm itched to hold the deadly weapon at all times. Grey weighed the blade in his hand, settling on a loose grip about halfway up the hilt. Closing his eyes, he pictured the blade's precise position as he swung it through the air to loosen his shoulder.

Ezra selected a thin, curved blade from the weapons rack and wasted no time approaching Grey, who knew not to trust Ezra's movements. When Ezra danced forward, then twisted so that his blade whirred towards Grey's right ear, Grey allowed his instincts to take over. Without conscious thought, Grey directed Agony's Joy into place at a slight angle, deflecting Ezra's blade.

The blade cleared his head, and Grey jabbed his elbow into Ezra's throat, which had retreated just out of reach. When Ezra's curved blade threatened Grey's midsection, he barely had time to tuck Agony against his body and brace for impact. The blade struck the blunt edge of Agony's Joy near its pommel, sending Grey skidding back along the floor. Grey hit the wall, but he remained on his feet.

"Get him!" Bow shouted, and Grey smiled. I can do this, he thought, strengthening his Attention. His thoughts sped up, and he pictured Bow in danger, threatened by a maramor. I have to use my emotions, like Bow taught me.

Ezra's astonishing speed allowed him to sprint towards Grey in a fraction of a second, but Grey was ready. He caught Ezra's wrist mid-swing, pulling Agony's Joy in a tight arc. Unbelievably, the blade drew a thin line of blood against Ezra's arm as he flipped away.

"Not bad," Ezra said, repeating his comment at Grey's earlier performance.

"Woohoo!" Bow cheered. "You got him!"

"But not good, right?" Grey asked, snorting at Ezra's false indifference.

"You have plenty of room for improvement. I feel sluggish today since I didn't sleep well last night. But I daresay: if you can draw blood from me, you're more than prepared for the tournament. All the noblemen will fall into pieces before you, severed by Agony's unmatched blade." Grey winced at Ezra's words, for the Gentleman might have spoken them. Then his mood brightened.

"Where did you hide Agony's Joy?" Grey asked.

"Huh?"

"You promised to answer one question for each blow I landed. Well, I landed a blow, so answer my question."

"Ah, your skills have developed so slowly that I forgot all about that. But very well! A promise is a promise. I took it to the endless pit beneath Harkk."

"Where the Fizzers live?"

"If you say so," Ezra said.

"Why would you hide the blade there?"

"Ah, that's another question. Are you up for another spar? Remember, one question per hit."

"No," Grey said, disgusted. "The tournament is tomorrow, so I'd better rest."

He turned to leave, but Callan said, "We should review the plan."

"I've already submitted my false name to the tournament committee. There's not a lot more I can do but fight."

"And if you win?"

"I'll enter the Chimney, throw the marble you've given me at the wall, and create a blast with pure vum. You'll be waiting for me in one of your aquatic forms outside to carry me to shore."

"There's more to it than that..."

"Don't worry. I promise I remember everything, okay?"

"Alright," Callan said, nodding. "The Defiant Empire's future sits in your hands."

"Now you're just being dramatic."

"Am I? Arndak's production hasn't resumed since we rescued Leigh. If we destroy Estril's chimney, we eliminate ril production, and the First Servant will lose access to two aerostatic gases."

"C'mon," Bow said, taking Grey's hand. "You might not sleep much anymore, but your body still needs rest."

Callan didn't stop him, so Grey left with Bow. "Are you excited?" Bow asked. "Nervous?"

"Should I be?" Despite Bow's lessons, emotions had remained fleeting. Extreme emotions, like hatred or fear, were inaccessible without centered ahl, while lesser ones, like anxiety, rose in gentle waves.

"Probably," Bow answered.

"Ezra's right, though. The aristocrats won't pose a threat."

"You shouldn't say things like that. It's bad luck."

Grey raised an eyebrow. "That's not very rational."

"Sometimes I'm not rational, especially when protecting our most important war asset." Grey snorted, for he recognized Bow's sarcasm. "Let's rest before you upset me further."

"Fine," Grey said, throwing himself onto his bed. Bow lay on another mattress he'd dragged into Grey's room a few weeks ago. They'd never discussed him moving in, but Bow had slept in Grey's room every night since.

When Bow snored, Grey turned to look at him. His light blond hair had grown long during their time aboard the Array ship, almost to his shoulders, and while he slept, it swung in front of his nose with the rhythm of his breath. This is nice, Grey thought. Too bad it can't last. Even if Grey destroyed the chimney, they'd need to move towards Ventrahl and Devum.

With those thoughts, Grey drifted into a trance, not asleep but not awake, until dawn brought Callan to his door.

"It's time to go," he said.

"Where's Ezra?" Grey asked

"Gone."

"Where'd he go?" Grey asked, annoyed. "I still have questions for him."

"What an asshole," Bow said, yawning and stretching.

"Arlo returned, though. He said he'd meet us outside the coliseum."

Grey inspected his legs as they walked. Six months of training with Ezra had made Grey strong. He'd added at least ten pounds of muscle to his thin frame, broadening his shoulders and widening his arms so they no longer hung at his sides like twigs. Still, he knew his opponents in the tournament were likely to be much larger.

A crowd surrounded the coliseum, swarming around the public entrance. Up close, Grey marveled at how much the stadium looked like a poor replica of the First Servant's palace atop Harkk. Its stonework wasn't clumsy, but it didn't shine with inhuman perfection, and the ocean's winds eroded its chipped surface.

Arlo waved and jogged over to Grey, handing him a metal canister heavier than any aerostatic container. "It's a potion I brewed," Arlo said.

"What does it do?"

"Inhale it before you blow up the Chimney. It'll coat your lungs and allow them to store more oxygen for hours. You'll cough it all out over the next week, but it'll be worth not drowning."

"Alright," Grey said, looking around before adding it to one of the empty slots in the holster strapped to his right thigh.

"It's time," Callan said. They stood before the squat entrance, and Grey turned to leave.

"Wait," Bow said. He placed his hands on Grey's shoulders, pulled him down, and gave Grey a quick peck on his cheek. "Good luck."

Chapter 22

Nineteen challengers shuffled beside Grey in a narrow hall, waiting for the tournament to begin. A dim roar filtering through stone walls hinted at the thousands of eager spectators beyond the gate, while a deep rumble shook the inside of Grey's chest and vibrated the ground beneath his feet like a gentle and unceasing quake. I bet it's from all the people headed to their seats, Grey thought.

The other fighters waited in anxious silence, and their nauseating scent of stale sweat soured Grey's stomach. He took a seat and lifted handfuls of sand to let the gritty particles slip through his fingertips. The contestants paid him no attention. These were men in their twenties, all in peak physical condition with swelling biceps and protruding chests. Grey appeared to them as a child, the spoiled offspring of one of Estril's wayward families, included in the tournament as a favor in a trade negotiation or another triviality.

The men's inattention allowed Grey to examine them. Observing a foe before battle could decide the fight, Ezra had insisted during one of their first lessons, and Grey had already noted the men's size, a sign that they'd value strength and defense over speed and aggression. Their frayed nerves suggested that none had fought in the shifter War. If they had, the prospect of this tournament wouldn't faze them, especially with a team of Knitters ready to heal almost any wound.

Grey reached to grab Agony's Joy before remembering he'd left the blade with Callan. He agreed with Ezra that the sword's ability to pierce armor would draw far too much attention, but he still yearned to grasp its hilt in his palm. Agony's replacement was a clumsy imitation of a peerless sword.

"Don't draw your weapon before the tournament begins," said a man who loomed over Grey. His massive thighs were wider than Grey's torso, and his clear, blue eyes twinkled with distant calculation.

"Huh?" Grey asked, standing.

"I haven't seen you before," the man continued, stepping forward, which forced Grey back against the wall to avoid a collision.

"So?" The other contenders shot nervous glances in their direction. Grey's intention to stay unnoticed had failed, but he returned his blade to its sheath on his back, hoping it would calm the angry man. It didn't.

"Where are you from?" the man asked.

"Arnshu," Grey said. Along with his facial twist, which widened his face, furrowed his brow, and lengthened his nose, Callan demanded he memorize an intricate backstory.

"Ah, that's far from Estril."

"An hour's run."

"Quite a boast. Only a dak prodigy could sprint fifty miles in an hour."

"It's no boast," Grey said. "Truth neither magnifies nor reduces a fact."

The man clenched his fists and asked, "What's your name?"

"Bradley," Grey lied.

"No one will remember your name after the crowds cheer 'Dale' over your corpse." Dale faced the gate, which cracked open. Grey would never understand man's need to dominate his peers, so he gave Dale's attitude no further consideration as the rising gate allowed the crowd's cheers to wash over him with such force that Grey slapped his hands over his ears.

Dale led the fighters into the arena, with Grey following last. After his eyes adjusted, his mouth dropped open in amazement. From the outside, the stadium appeared large… but not as tremendous as it did from its interior. Bleachers filled with a sea of cheering spectators curved away from the compact arena, creating an impression that a wall of human bodies might topple inwards.

Grey clamped his mouth shut, annoyed by his emotional reaction. It must be the ahl, he thought. Though the aerostatic gas allowed him to fight with passion, he continued to struggle with its emotions.

The fighters circled the edge of a gravel ring surrounding a raised platform, which sloped inwards towards a drain for blood.

As soon as the fighters stopped, a voice said, "Welcome to the nine hundredth Chimney Tournament!" Amplification bondmen boosted the announcer's voice to reach the ears of ten thousand spectators.

"For eight hundred and ninety-nine years, our regal kings have welcomed the finest warriors from the lands of Estril to this venerable contest for a chance to join the King's Ring. Forty distinguished warriors are with us today, champions of past tournaments." The crowd roared while Grey wondered why Estril's king mimicked the First Servant's circle with blatant envy.

"We celebrate the nine-hundredth year of the King's Ring with great joy, but the rules of this holy contest are unchanged. Each contestant shall fight against a competitor in a battle of skill, leaving us with ten survivors for the second round. Upon the king's entry, we shall begin!"

Grey pressed his fingers into his ears to drown out the crowd's deafening roar, but all fell silent when the king entered and took his seat halfway up the stands.

"Dale of Estril-Dafilant will be the first contestant," the announcer shouted, and Grey thought, Please pull my name next. "And his opponent will be… William of Estril-Cadent." Damn.

Dale hopped into the ring, along with William, a larger man with a much heavier step than Dale. The two stood at opposite sides of the raised platform while the crowd waited with hushed anticipation.

"Let the fight begin!"

A bell rang, and William stomped forward to swing his mace. Dale ducked, spinning across the stage with a speed that belied his size. Grey hadn't seen Dale inhale any dak, but he must have missed it. All fighters used dak to seek an advantage.

A minute into the fight, it became clear to Grey that Dale was toying with William. Dale fought with restraint, forcing his enraged opponent into a series of attacks that depleted his stamina. William didn't figure this out for another ten minutes of wild punches, but when he did, Grey noticed his shoulders droop in defeat.

Still, Dale dragged the fight on until the crowd started shouting, "End the fight! End the fight!" At their calls, William's eyes lit up with a furious rage, granting a terrible energy to his attacks. But even William's increased vigor fell short of breaking Dale's footwork, and William's anger burned out. He dropped to one knee, exhausted.

Over twenty minutes had passed since the fight began, and Dale took his time walking towards William. To Grey's surprise and the crowd's delight, William sprung up at Dale as he approached, forcing Dale to dodge to the side and end the fight sooner than he'd intended. His sword struck William in the gut, penetrating through his back. Grey heard the crunch of William's spine as he fell forward and grimaced.

Within a minute, Knitters had rushed William off the platform, the announcer had declared Dale the victor, a bondman had washed the platform of blood, and the announcer selected the next fighting pair. Dale's extended fight had made the other combatants restless, for the following six pairings passed in rapid succession, each battle lasting only minutes. Grey observed the brawlers in calm silence, noting the victors' strengths and weaknesses.

After the seventh round, the announcer called Grey's pseudonym "Bradley," along with Johansson, one of the more nimble-looking fighters. Grey climbed atop the arena platform. His shirt clung to his sweaty torso, and his mouth had become dry in the afternoon sun, which hung overhead, bathing the arena in a shadowless glow. Humidity from the sea mixed with the intense heat to create a mental sluggishness Grey recalled from his life in Faycliff. He swallowed a few times to work up saliva and hopped from foot to foot, encouraging his heart rate to rise.

Johansson, a man several inches taller than Grey's six feet, stood across the platform with a round shield and long spear. Grey would need to avoid the weapon's polished steel tip, but its wooden shaft presented a vulnerable target for his sword.

The bell rang, and Johansson charged, spear pointed at Grey's chest. Grey dove to the side to avoid the attack, rolling to his feet to prepare for another strike. He guessed the man would spin to his right, so he raised his sword in advance to block an incoming attack. Grey raised his head just in time to see Johansson's sandal slip from his sweaty foot and catch on the platform.

As Johansson tripped, he thrust his spear into the gravel, hoping to arrest his fall. But the shaft splintered, and his head smashed against the platform's edge. Grey recognizes the familiar crack of bone. Blood gushed from Johansson's head, and the stadium fell silent, waiting to see if Johansson would rise. Grey knew he wouldn't, for the blood formed an expanding pool around Johansson's prone body.

"A record!" the announcer shouted. "A victory in under five seconds… incredible!" Grey's win prompted only tepid cheers and more than a few boos, so he left the platform to sit with the other winners. Dale smiled, but Grey returned a blank stare. That was very unlucky, Grey thought. The swiftest victor would face nine opponents in the second round, which is why Dale drew out his fight for almost half an hour.

"Let the second stage commence," the announcer said after the final fight ended. "Bradley will face Harl, and the winner will continue until he falls." They're assuming I'll fall, Grey thought with a wry grin.

Grey climbed back onto the platform as a mixture of boos and jeers flooded the stadium. One man called, "You don't deserve to be here." A woman shouted, "Kill him, Harl!"

Grey ignored the crowd and drew a canister of centered ahl from his sleeve to inhale. As the gas unlocked a more intense emotional awareness, he willed an image of Bow to his mind until he could almost see Bow before him, his white-blond hair and smirk imbuing his delicate features with mischievous intelligence. I'm doing this for you, he thought. I will win so the First Servant doesn't kill you with the rest of the Defiant Empire. Grey's heart sped up as adrenaline surged through his limbs, and he opened his eyes with determination.

The crowd still booed, but the sound faded from Grey's awareness as his world narrowed to just two people: himself and his opponent. His sole task became ending each fight as quickly as possible, all nine of them, with Dale at the end.

The bell rang to mark the first round, and the man dashed forward, leaping high into the air with his sword aimed at Grey's neck. Grey threw himself down and stabbed the man's left ankle with the tip of his blade. Though the sword was no Agony's Joy, Grey had applied plenty of force to sever the man's tendon.

Grey readied himself for a second strike, but Harl had already collapsed into a sobbing pile. "Incredible!" the announcer shouted, his voice booming. "Bradley ended this round faster than his last!"

The crowd fell silent, unsure how to process the thin figure they'd taunted. Boos met the scattered cheers, but Grey didn't notice their confusion. His attention shifted to his next opponent, a towering man who lumbered onto the platform.

"I'm going to tear you apart," the man roared, and the crowd chanted his name: "Bear! Bear! Bear! Bear!"

The fight began, and Grey moved, ducking under the man's trunk-like arm and plunging his blade through his thigh. The exchange had lasted perhaps three seconds.

"He's cheating," yelled a man from the stands. A woman responded with, "How?" A chorus of confused voices rose, arguments and fevered discussions drawing their focus from the third round, which ended much the same as the earlier two. This time, the fighter's last-second block forced Grey to thrust his sword between two of the man's ribs. He punctured a lung but missed his heart so the Knitters would save him. This third victory broke through the crowd's anger and elicited gasps, followed by a cheer that built into a thunderous roar.

Grey's win in the first round had been luck—albeit lousy

luck for him—but the successive, decisive victories erased luck as a workable explanation. Perhaps this lanky boy from Estril's outer provinces wasn't the spoiled aristocrat he appeared to be. Estril's citizens wondered whether they bore witness to a spectacle without precedent in the tournament's nine-hundred-year history. Competitors trained their entire lives, yet Grey dismantled Estril's most skilled fighters within seconds.

The arena's change in mood didn't penetrate Grey's focus. Months of Ezra's training, paired with Bow's lessons, had paid off better than he could have imagined. Facing trained fighters demanded far less skill than defeating Ezra, and Grey's improvements were astonishing.

The following five fights passed as quickly as the first three, with the crowd's excitement growing each time Grey struck down an opponent within seconds of the bell's toll. The intermittent cheering became a continuous sound, filling the stadium with deafening proof of the crowd's excitement.

When the announcer called Dale's name, fewer than fifteen minutes had elapsed. Dale climbed onto the platform, and Grey noticed Dale no longer smiled.

"So, you're skilled," Dale said, angry pride hiding any evidence of fear. "We'll see how you handle a proper fight."

Grey said nothing, only pointed his bloody, chipped blade at Dale's neck as the bell rang for a nineteenth and final time. Dale inched towards Grey, and Grey let him come, lowering his sword to his side. He noted Dale's tensed calves, the tightness in his right shoulder, and, most of all, his darting eyes. Five feet away, Dale feigned right, then moved left with a powerful jolt of energy.

Sluggish, Grey thought. He blocked Dale's strike with the side of his blade, letting Dale's sword slide up to his own weapon's hilt. A sharp twist tore Dale's blade from his hands, leaving bloody strips of skin hanging from his palms. To his credit, Dale didn't flinch, pulling two daggers and flinging one at Grey, who batted it away with his sword.

Dale had used the distraction to get close, and he slashed at Grey's right side, forcing him to bend to the left. But in doing so, Dale had opened his torso, allowing Grey to elbow him in the sternum. Dale's footwork failed, and he tripped, trying to catch his breath. His stance broke for only a second or two, but it was enough for Grey, who thrust his sword into Dale's right shoulder to disable his favored arm.

Hatred seethed from Dale's eyes, and he opened his mouth, no doubt to shout an obscenity at Grey. Grey didn't give him a chance. He smashed Dale's head with the hilt of his sword, and Dale fell to the ground, senseless.

"Astonishing!" the announcer yelled yet again. "It's been 136 years since a single challenger carried the second half of the tournament. But not with such speed! This is just incredible. I am left speechless." That's untrue, Grey thought with amusement, his attention returning to his surroundings. The crowd's excited howling drowned out the rest of the announcer's words as he tried to conclude the tournament.

Now that he'd won, exhaustion spread through Grey's limbs, and his legs quaked. There's more to do today, he reminded himself as the king descended from his platform to greet the newest addition to his Ring.

The king rode a bondman, only stepping off the creature's broad back within feet of Grey. Here was a man whose life of leisure and excess added layers of bulk to his muscled frame. At around fifty, the king's formidable body hid beneath a generous, sagging layer of pale flesh. His toga exposed much of his chest and protruding stomach, though the white fabric draped to cover his legs.

"Long ago, this was the outfit of all rulers within the Defiant Empire," the king said, noting Grey's eyes wandering over his robes. "History teaches us valuable lessons, so I don this uniform to pay tribute to our glorious ancestors. Do you respect the past, Bradley?"

"My performance in your tournament speaks for itself," Grey said.

"Was it the past that taught you to become such a fearsome warrior at your young age?"

"In a sense. A master swordsman taught me to fight."

"No matter," the king said. "You'd give even a maramor a run for its money, I reckon."

"A maramor is unmatched, aside from the First Servant." Grey didn't lie. His encounters with the maramor taught him another confrontation would likely end with his own death.

"You will make a fine addition to my warriors of the Ring. maramors don't frequent our lands, so our militia upholds order." This king was building his meager empire within a corner of the Defiant Empire, emulating the First Servant's societal structure with a limited understanding of the First Servant's true power. Rumors suggested the First Servant transformed his most loyal subjects into maramors, but Estril's king offered no similar reward. True or not, no one aside from the First Servant could create maramors, so Estril's king used the tournament to build his elite fighting force.

"It is you who will help me support my lands," the king said. "You and the rest of my Ring, the greatest fighters in all the Empire. Or at least they will be after a lesson from you, eh?" The king elbowed Grey in the ribs, and Grey forced a smile. "But that is enough idle talk. I have other matters to which I must attend. Statehood is a never-ending burden and one that I'm afraid is mine to bear." The king released an exasperated sigh. "My aide will guide you to your new home."

Grey nodded. The king left atop the bondman, and Grey allowed himself to be led back onto the fighting platform. The crowd continued to cheer as the platform jolted, sinking through the arena floor. Bondmen lowered the stone slab with metal chains, allowing a swift descent below Estril's waters.

As they descended, he noticed mosaics lining the walls. These were not the beautiful works of marble depicting the First Servant's heroics but painted stone telling the story of Estril's history. Grey spotted an image of the chimney's construction, followed by other landmark events. The only visible marble was a yellow pipe that transported ril to the surface.

"These chambers house the winners and their families," the aide explained when the platform stopped. They'd reached an open space the width of the entire chimney dotted with houses. Bondmen hung from the high ceiling to offer light, which shone over the grassy field. The verdant landscape reminded Grey of Leigh's idyllic cavern within Arndak. "You may select a vacant house, and I will return to escort you to your orientation." Grey looked down at his bloody clothing and sweat-drenched skin, imagining he must stink as badly as the day he met Emerson.

A gathering of past victors met him by the platform. "Winner in year 893," said a man. Another woman stepped in behind him. "Winner of 890. Congratulations, Bradley, and welcome." Their ritual continued until none remained.

"Hey, Grey," someone whispered behind him. Grey spun around, startled to hear his actual name.

"Leigh?" Grey asked, with confusion and relief in equal measure.

"Grey, that is you, right?" He let his facial twist slip. "Isn't it wonderful here? I never expected you to win the tournament! I guess the shifters… I mean, Callan… did a great job training you."

"How did you come to be here?" Grey asked. He strolled towards the Chimney's outer wall, and Leigh followed.

"Remember I told you I was going to Estril to find my mother? Well, it turns out she is one of the previous champions. Pretty remarkable. And she invited me to live with her in the Chimney when I found her! I've been here ever since, safe from that maramor, thank goodness. It reminds me of my home in Arndak…" Leigh trailed off, narrowing her eyes at Grey. "Why are you here?"

Grey stopped near the outer wall separating them from the deep ocean, and he imagined the vastness that lay just beyond the stone. His claustrophobia flared, and he forced a deep breath. The blasting rocks strapped to his thighs grew quite heavy.

"Grey, you're up to something," Leigh said.

The centered ahl wore off, leaving him with the lesser effects of diluted ahl. Still, he kept enough emotional awareness to know killing Leigh would be wrong. Yet he had also sworn to Bow, Callan, and Arlo that he would blow up the Chimney, which he'd known would lead to the deaths of everyone inside. He just didn't expect to recognize his victims.

"Can you leave the Chimney?" Grey asked, knowing he shouldn't even speak with Leigh. I should go ahead with my mission. He stood mere feet from the outer wall. No one had noticed the vum he carried. It'd take only seconds for him to destroy Estril's mining operation. If there's a chance I can save Leigh, I need to take it, he decided. Bow will understand.

"Why?"

"Just—can you? Please answer me."

"No, I can't. Not easily. The victors may only leave on a mission, and I'm not a victor. Life is wonderful here, but the king keeps us under his control by isolating us from the rest of his kingdom."

"I see." Grey reached down and lowered his pants.

"Grey, what are you doing?"

"I'm destroying the Chimney, Leigh." He pulled the vum and marble slabs from their holsters.

"Like you destroyed the mines in Arndak," Leigh whispered with sudden realization.

"I didn't do that."

"Not directly, but you caused their destruction."

"Didn't you do that by leaving? Anyway, aren't you going to call for the guards?" I could help Leigh escape, Grey thought. But I might not return. I have to act before I lose my opportunity. It's now or never.

"What would be the point? They'd never get here in time. Besides, palace guards wouldn't stand a chance against you."

Grey nodded, wishing he could flush the diluted ahl from his system. He didn't want to feel guilt, but ridding himself of ahl would summon the Gentleman. I could just leave. But then the First Servant will continue his silent war, and Bow will die.

"Breath this in," Grey said, offering Leigh the concoction Arlo had given him. "It'll help you survive if you swim to the surface." Leigh said nothing, but she accepted the vial. "Remember, don't swallow. Inhale." She shot him a grim look, neither sad nor afraid, then took off sprinting.

Grey turned from Leigh and slapped the sticky marble against the Chimney's outer wall. He then inhaled the pure vum, along with pure dak. Marble shone, and he took a deep breath before detonating the glowing white stone.

A blast bulged the wall outwards in a semi-sphere that protruded into the ocean. The continued explosive force prevented water from entering for one surreal moment as a roar racketed through the enclosed space. Then the immense ocean pressure sent water rushing into the Chimney with terrifying speed.

Grey dug his hands into the ground with his dak-enhanced

muscles while the ocean filled the Chimney. With a mighty push, he thrust himself out into the open, deep sea. I don't know which way is up, he realized, and true claustrophobic panic gripped his heart. He thrashed about, pulling himself through the water, but his lungs sucked in water.

A shape emerged from the darkness and wrapped its arms around Grey's torso, pulling him away from the crumbling Chimney. Light grew, and the pressure lessened until the creature threw him from the water and onto a gritty beach. Then Arlo loomed over him, pushing down on his chest until he sputtered up a lungful of water. Grey lay for a minute, coughing up more mouthfuls of water until his breathing slowed to a more manageable rate.

"Well done," Callan said after Grey sat. He stood next to Arlo, his arms folded and his face grim. "The Chimney collapsed, and ril production ceased."

"You don't look thrilled."

"Grey, we have something to tell you," Arlo said.

"What is it?"

"You must promise not to overreact. The ahl is still in your system…"

"What is it?" Grey asked again. Nerves shook Grey's spine when Callan still didn't speak. "Just tell me! Bow taught me how to handle my emotions."

"The maramor followed us to Estril," Callan said.

"The one Ezra buried?"

"Yes, it freed itself."

"So?" Grey asked, breathing a small sigh of relief. They figured the maramor would escape, after all. "We'll run again."

"I'm afraid it's not that simple. The maramor took Bow."

"Took Bow?"

"Yes."

"Took him where?"

"I tracked the maramor to Harkk using one of my flying forms," Callan answered. "The maramor carried him into the First Servant's palace."

The pit of Grey's stomach dropped, and he grew dizzy, furious, and so worried that it made him queasy. His heart sped until it felt like it might explode from his chest.

"You must be calm," Arlo urged.

"I'm going after Bow," Grey said, grabbing Agony's Joy from Callan's side.

"You mustn't," Callan said. He reached for Agony's Joy, but Grey yanked it away, strapping the sword to his back. "The First Servant will kill you."

"Try to stop me," Grey said.

"Your death will end our hope of defeating the First Servant."

"I fought in Estril's tournament to save Bow, yet you're telling me he's in mortal peril. Well… I'll rescue him."

"The First Servant kidnapped him to lure you to Harkk. Please, Grey, don't take the bait."

"Take this," Arlo interjected, handing Grey a contraption he'd not seen before, along with several vials of dak. Callan shot Arlo a look, but Arlo ignored him, for he accepted Grey's unstoppable determination. "This canister holds all four gases in their purest forms. It's good for one use, so spend it well. The other dak canisters should give you enough energy to make it to Harkk before sunrise."

Grey grabbed the canisters and took off towards Harkk without further word.

Chapter 23

Grey ran as he'd never run before, as centered dak allowed each step to carry him a dozen feet. The wind whipped sand into his face, drawing thin lines of blood across his cheeks. He ignored the pain and pushed himself even harder. Thoughts raced through his mind faster than he ran, exploding like overheated gunpowder until all that remained were emotional sensations. Bow might already be dead. No, they won't kill Bow if the First Servant uses him to draw me out. The thought set his mouth into a sunken line of grim determination.

An hour before sunrise, as Echore set and the horizon glowed a pale, deep red, Harkk's eastern mountain appeared as a dot in the distance. Grey sped across the open plain, reaching the dense forest and pushing through to Harkk's wall. His breath tore from his lungs in ragged gasps, his joints ached, and his arms bled from a thousand scrapes. Yet his need to rescue Bow shoved all discomfort into the background.

A bondman carried him up the wall, and he headed straight for the closest gondola. Pillar soldiers rested after their drunken nights, and the scattered guards paid him no attention. He vaulted into an approaching car, and it carried him up the mountain, sweeping over Keep Devum. Grey wondered if Emerson sat below, enveloped in whatever trivial intrigue enraptured the aristocrats these days. News of the Chimney's destruction would tear through Harkk and dominate palace gossip for a month, though to Grey, his trip into the Chimney had already faded into the distant past.

The gondola jolted to a halt at Harkk's uppermost ring, and Grey exited. The First Servant's palace towered above, its four arches forming a majestic cube around the top of the mountain. He barged through the same door Emerson showed him during his first trip to Harkk. No one stopped him. The chambers were empty, and the First Servant's door was ajar. Grey hesitated at the doorframe, but his anger pushed him forward. He stepped into the familiar space, a cavernous room lined with bright mosaics surrounding a raised platform.

"Thank you for coming," the First Servant said, startling Grey. He hadn't noticed the First Servant, for his mirrored cloak blended with the mosaic. By his feet lay Bow, unconscious or dead, and Grey paused by the door, unsure if he should retreat or continue. I knew coming here meant I would face him. This is my only chance to rescue Bow. So Grey pulled Agony's Joy from its sheath and stood his ground.

"Give me Bow," Grey demanded, leveling Agony's Joy at the First Servant's chest. The dak had already extracted a heavy toll from his body, but he forced his arm to keep still.

"My rule has endured ten thousand years," The First Servant said, ignoring Grey's demand while strolling around the room. "Every hundred years, a rebel arises to challenge me. It's like clockwork, a natural order to history that I don't pretend to understand."

"I don't want to rebel. Give me Bow, and I'll leave. You'll never see me again."

"My challengers must die, though their deaths bring little

joy." The First Servant stopped and regarded Grey with a curious stare. "I actually admire these insurgents, for their bravery reminds me of my youth. A few hundred years ago, Marg almost destroyed Estril's chimney, failing where you succeeded. I respected her courage, and killing her brought a sadness that itself was a precious gift. I'll mourn your death as well, Grey, because you share Marg's determination. Because you have four times now evaded my maramor, I revised my strategy and lured you here myself."

Grey feared his strength would fail, so he inhaled Arlo's four-canister aerostatic charger. Pure dak, vum, ril, and ahl surged through his body, lending him two minutes in which he might defeat the First Servant. Grey bolted across the marble tile with every ounce of speed he could muster, pointing Agony's Joy at the center of the ancient ruler's chest.

The First Servant moved faster. Much, much faster. He grabbed Grey's wrist, twisting hard. Bone snapped, and Agony's Joy dropped to the ground blade-first. It sunk into the marble floor like it wasn't there while the First Servant stooped to examine the weapon.

"Ezra crafted this blade..."

Grey sprang ten feet in the air and landed behind the First Servant while kicking with his left leg. The First Servant caught Grey's foot and pushed him back, sending him skittering across the ground. He lifted Agony's Joy and came to stand over Grey.

"You are quick," the First Servant admitted. "But experience trumps youth when an elder's feebleness isn't a factor."

"If you kill me, at least release Bow," Grey pleaded. "He served his purpose by bringing me here."

"No."

The pure aerostatic gases left Grey's system, taking all hope as they went, and the First Servant raised Agony's Joy.

Then footsteps sounded in the hall, and the First Servant's fingers convulsed. As the sword fell, Grey darted between the First Servant's legs and used every ounce of strength to strike the First Servant below his neck, catching Agony's Joy by its hilt. To Grey's surprise, the blow landed, and the First Servant fell to his knees, gasping. Grey thrust the blade through the First Servant's back, and he moaned. The footsteps stopped, and Grey raised his head to see the Gentleman. He stood with his back to the mosaics, and he cocked his head with amused satisfaction.

Both Grey and the First Servant spoke at the same time. "Not you," Grey said while the First Servant looked right at the Gentleman and shouted, "Arndak!"

Holy Echore, Grey thought in wonder, pulling Agony's Joy from the First Servant's body. The Defiant Empire's ruler had just shouted at the Gentleman.

"You can see him?" Grey asked, stunned.

The First Servant's eyes clouded with confusion, and for the first time, Grey detected indecision within the ancient ruler. Then his brow furrowed, introducing a series of wrinkles to his flawless skin, and he stood. Though Agony's Joy had torn his shirt, Grey saw with dismay that the flesh below appeared untouched, as though Grey had never stabbed him.

Before the Gentleman could wrest control of Grey, he inhaled his last canister of diluted ahl, using the aerostatic gas to enhance his Attention. The Gentleman faded from existence, and the First Servant's face returned to its usual calm.

"You've served the Defiant Empire well," the First Servant said, turning towards Grey. "I would celebrate your contribution, but first, you must die."

A potent calm descended over Grey's tumultuous worries to soothe his mind and keep him docile as the First Servant lifted him. He smelled sweat—an unexpected odor from an immortal god, and Grey wondered what secrets lay behind the ruler's ancient eyes.

Then marble exploded high above, and a figure hurtled into the hall, grappling with the First Servant until he tore the intruder clean in half. Callan's torso spun across the floor, stopping at Grey's feet.

Grey scampered towards Bow as three more shifters flew at the First Servant. Soon, dozens of shapes streamed into the palace, and though the First Servant destroyed them with ruthless precision, the distraction gave Grey time to drag Bow from the room. He pulled Bow from the palace and onto the mountainside to see hundreds, if not thousands, of shifters swarming the sky. One of Callan's flying forms stopped by Grey.

"Get on," the shifter said, using vocal cords not meant for human speech. It slurred its words, but Grey understood it well enough. He hopped on behind Bow, checking his neck for a pulse. He found one, weak though it was.

The shifter took a running leap off the mountain's edge, flapping its mighty wings to lift Grey and Bow high into the air. A field of blood expanded from the palace as the First Servant tore into Callan's many forms. Then they passed through a cloud, and Harkk faded from view.

They flew in silence for several minutes before the shifter lost strength, falling from the air. Just before they hit the ground, the shifter flapped its wings one last time, and they collapsed into a heap on a soft patch of tall grass. The shifter tried to stand while Grey rushed to Bow's side. Still unconscious, he hadn't suffered any more injuries from the fall.

"We have come many miles. Arlo waits for you a few miles to the north with his wagon," the shifter said.

"Why?" Grey asked.

"So he may heal Bow."

"I mean, why did you save me?" The shifter seemed unable to lift its head.

"I had to save you so you may destroy the First Servant." The shifter—Callan—slurred his words even more.

"What's happening to you? Why are you talking like that?"

"The First Servant is killing me. I sent every one of my bodies to the palace tonight, and I can't hold on to consciousness with only this single shape."

"But you told me your purpose was survival. You're the only one of your species. If you die, that's it."

"Defeat the First Servant, Grey. If you can do that, you may bring me back. If not me, then perhaps create another of my kind."

"I don't know how. I don't know how to do any of this." Grey knelt over Bow's prone form. He'd rushed to the palace to save Bow, not expecting to sacrifice Callan in the process. And the First Servant had shown a sliver of his true power, which eclipsed anything Grey had imagined. Pure dak paled compared to the energy at the First Servant's fingertips.

"Go with Arlo to Devum. He knows how to find Dilan, Kip, and Jeanne. They're in a house run by a member of my resistance. You must destroy vum production next. Please, Grey, promise me you will continue down this path."

"I promise…"

"Now, Grey, I leave you with a gift."

"Wait—"

But it was too late. Callan's shifter form lay its head down, and its body dissolved. Grey bent down to examine Callan's remains, lifting a coiled snake and inspecting its length until he understood its purpose.

Grey removed Agony's Joy from his back and checked its hilt. The hollow end matched one side of Callan's final form, so Grey held it against Agony's Joy. The creature snapped into place with a satisfying click and uncoiled. Its body wound around Grey's wrist, and he gave a small yelp when it punctured his flesh, adding another injury on top of his broken wrist. Then the pain vanished, replaced by a unique sensation.

"I feel you," Grey said, looking down at Agony's Joy. Agony's Joy spoke in his mind as if it merged with his body. He sensed the wind against its blade as subtle air currents pushed at its shiny surface, and he perceived his own hand around its hilt. I'll figure this out later, Grey thought, looking back down at Bow.

"I'll have to carry you, won't I?" he asked. Of course, Bow did not respond. "You've saved my life many times, but this just might make us even." Grey picked Bow up, wincing at the pain in his wrist, and began his weary march north in search of Arlo.

Chapter 24

Bow woke with a tremendous burst of energy, shooting out of bed like a coiled spring. Grey startled from the chair he'd been sitting in for the past three days, but Dilan had already rushed to Bow's side and pushed him back. Bow resisted, his eyes darting as beads of sweat flew from his brow.

"Whoa," Dilan said. "You're okay. Everything is okay now."

"Where…" Bow croaked, his arms tense against the bedsheets.

"You're in Devum," Dilan said, offering Bow a small cup of cool water, which he ignored.

"How? What happened? I remember the maramor and… nothing."

"Arlo saved your life," Grey said, walking to the bed and helping Bow sit. He relaxed a bit when he recognized Grey, accepting the water Dilan still held. "Callan saved both of us in Harkk, and I carried you to Arlo, who stabilized your condition."

"Yeah," Dilan said, "We gathered in Devum after Kip's breakdown to carry out Westing's mission. Not much luck there, I'm afraid, but at least I healed you. Arlo worked marvels without ril, but you needed a Knitter to repair your internal injuries."

"What about Estril's Chimney? Is it gone?"

"Yes," Grey answered. "I destroyed it." Along with Leigh, he thought.

"So only Devum and Ventrahl still stand."

"And the maramors and the First Servant," Jeanne added, entering the room. The corners of her eyes had sprouted a series of wrinkles over the past six months, adding ten years to her appearance, and her shoulders drooped as if weighed down by an invisible pack.

"Where's Kip?" Bow asked.

"She's outside, keeping watch. Even though we're hiding in Callan's safehouse, one can never be too careful."

"Alright, everyone out," Dilan ordered. "Bow needs to rest."

"But I'm better now that I've sipped water."

"If you sleep, you'll recover within a day or two. But push yourself too hard, and it'll be weeks before you heal."

"Alright, alright," Bow said, lying in his bed. Before he closed his eyes, he looked at Grey and asked, "You'll visit soon, won't you?"

"Very soon," Grey promised, struggling to force the words past a lump in his throat.

His trek to Devum had been arduous, with little time for reflection. A week of hard travel brought Arlo, Grey, and an unconscious Bow to Devum in record time, where they'd followed Callan's instructions to find Dilan. Three tense days of watching Dilan's healing sessions kept Grey in a state of constant stress, but now that it seemed Bow would recover, he relaxed.

Unfortunately, relaxation surfaced an unexpected emotion. Bow's weakened body brought tears to Grey's eyes. Why am I crying? Grey wondered. I rescued Bow. He's going to be okay. I should be happy. But Grey wasn't sad—relieved, maybe? He'd never heard of crying from relief. I'll ask Bow about it when he awakens.

Jeanne, Arlo, and Dilan headed to the kitchen to prepare supper, but Grey wasn't hungry, so he climbed to the roof. Much of Devum nestled amidst a broad geothermal vent system surrounding a frigid volcano-shaped mountain. Unlike wood, Devum's metal buildings resisted the intense geothermal heat, while their walls held insulating foam to help the interiors stay cool.

Kip perched atop a water tower on the roof, her eyes glued to the horizon. Like Jeanne, she looked like she'd aged years in months. Her legs had lost all color, and she hugged them against her sunken chest with pale, slim arms. Her back twisted into a tense curve of knotted muscle. She must have heard Grey, but she didn't acknowledge him.

Grey watched the icy volcano, where workers toiled in puffy, white suits to mine the aerostatic gas vum, which came from melted chunks of ice. The surrounding lands shimmered in a constant heat, but the volcano remained so cold that water would freeze mid-air if poured from a thermos. A hundred feet from the mountain's base, a boiling moat of scalding water released vapor into Devum, limiting visibility on the ground. Only the tops of the tallest buildings rose from the everlasting mist.

"You're still angry with me," Grey said, turning to Kip. She blinked several times as if she hadn't noticed his arrival.

"Huh?" Kip looked at Grey without seeming to see him, her brow furrowed and her eyes cloudy.

"For my involvement in Westing's death. You still blame me for it."

"I do." Her burning anger had evaporated, leaving a deep pool of sadness in its place.

"Why are you helping me?"

"Do you appreciate Westing, Grey?"

"We didn't spend much time together, but I sympathize

with his wish to ruin the Defiant Empire. Despite his insanity, his goals were worthy."

"That is all true. He was also my father."

"Oh..."

"If I no longer have him or my mother, all I have is his mission to defeat the First Servant. You're our best chance, so that's why I'm helping." Kip's tone was flat, and she refused to look Grey in the eyes.

"What motivated your father?" Grey asked, wondering whether someone like the Gentleman also haunted Westing. Kip said nothing, and they listened to the hiss of steam escaping beneath Devum's sewage system for several minutes. Grey almost headed downstairs before Kip spoke. Her words spilled forth like water down a raging river as though she might not talk unless she relayed her thoughts all at once.

"Westing was to become part of the First Servant's Circle, the ultimate reward for those loyal to the Empire. Those in the Circle hold more power than the heads of the four cities, the Array leaders, Pillar generals, or anyone else aside from the First Servant himself because they control the aerostatic distribution. My father passed all the First Servants tests, succeeding where others failed, and we anticipated our family's elevation. We were to become among the most powerful families in the Defiant Empire—until dad learned of his final test. To join the Circle, he had to contribute the soul of the one he loved most." Kip's voice broke with her last sentence.

"Everyone in the Circle has killed their greatest love?" Grey asked. He wasn't surprised.

"The sacrifice binds one's soul to the First Servant. I often wonder how many obey and how many refuse... and whether my father's decision to spare mom was unusual."

"The First Servant killed her anyway," Grey guessed.

"Of course he did," Kip said. Her effort to hide the emotion in her voice failed, and she moaned. "My father and I escaped when I was seven, and we returned to the Array a year later. Dad wore a new face shaped by an expert Knitter, and I pretended to be an orphan. But it wasn't the same. Something within dad broke. He wanted only to kill the First Servant. I want the same."

"That's awful," Grey said. Tears ran down Kip's gaunt cheeks, and she turned away.

"So yes, I blame you for his death, though I'm not so stupid that I don't understand why you abandoned Westing. I recognized my father's erratic behavior, but now I'm a real orphan, and I consider you somewhat responsible."

Grey said nothing. There was nothing to say. He stood in silence, reaching for empathy, but despite all his progress with ahl, he fell short. With a frustrated sigh, he climbed into the house, found a bedroom, and shut himself inside until Echore had risen and set.

Seven hours later, he emerged from a sleepless rest to join Bow, who sat in his bed.

"Are you coming?" Bow asked, giggling at Grey's nervousness.

Grey's cheeks reddened. "Yeah, of course."

"Grey," Bow said, his tone turning serious, "I'm happy to be alive, but you shouldn't have saved me. You're not ready to face the First Servant. Not yet."

"I had to save you." Bow shifted his hips to make room for Grey room to sit next to him.

"When I won the tournament and destroyed the Chimney, I was excited to tell you. Callan told me the maramor kidnapped you, and I went a bit crazy. If the First Servant killed you, I'd give up on everything." Grey stopped talking, for he now understood Kip's pain; she mourned Westing as Grey would mourn Bow.

Bow wrapped his arm around Grey's shoulder, and Grey leaned in, resting his head on Bow's frail collarbone. Grey hadn't noticed before, but Bow smelled. Not bad, but different from his own scent. Grey rather liked it. Bow's cool hand stroked Grey's arm, and Grey marveled at the sudden emotion of such a simple act. He cried.

"Sh," Bow said. "It's over now. I'm here. We're back together. Everything worked out for the best."

Grey lifted his head to respond, and Bow turned towards him. Their lips touched.

"What happened?" Grey asked. His entire face tingled, and a nervous excitement swirled through his stomach.

"We like each other," Bow explained. "I realized I liked you before we met, but your understanding has developed at a different pace. You're still figuring things out."

"I… yes. You're right," Grey said. "What do I do about it?"

Bow laughed. "Do about it? You do nothing about it as we allow ourselves to enjoy this perfect moment."

"Oh," Grey said, leaning his head back on Bow's shoulder. "I guess that's good."

"Yes," Bow agreed. "It is good."

Grey lay there for a minute, getting used to this novel sensation, until he decided he needed to tell Bow something. "Bow, not everything worked out for the best."

"Oh?"

"It's about Callan. He died to save us from the First Servant."

"So? We've seen him killed. He has thousands of bodies."

"No, not anymore. He used all of his bodies to allow us to escape. The First Servant tore him apart. He left behind a creature that attaches to Agony's Joy. It's not sentient, but we might use it to revive him in the future."

Bow stiffened. "I never forgave his actions leading to my family's death. But I suppose Callan proved himself trustworthy in the end."

"Yeah, he did. And there's something else…"

"What is it?"

"When I was fighting the First Servant, he almost killed me. He would have killed me, but the Gentleman intervened."

"He took control and helped you fight the First Servant," Bow guessed.

"No. That's the thing. He didn't. The First Servant saw the Gentleman. He was about to kill me with Agony's Joy, but he dropped the blade in shock. It's the only reason I escaped. He screamed, 'Arndak,' and I stabbed his chest before Callan helped us flee."

"You injured the First Servant?"

"He didn't even acknowledge the wound. As soon as I pulled the sword free, it was as though I'd never cut him."

"This is wonderful news," Bow said, swinging his legs off the bed with eager energy.

"How?"

"The Gentleman isn't a fragment of your consciousness! If the First Servant responded to him, he must be a separate entity."

"Unless the First Servant saw him with ahl."

"Oh," Bow said, a bit disappointed. "I suppose that's possible, but from how you described his reaction, it sounded like he already recognized the Gentleman. We'll choose to believe the latter, and such good news deserves a celebration. Let's meet with the others." Grey helped Bow out of bed, and they hobbled towards the kitchen, where Jeanne sat with Dilan.

"You should still be resting," Dilan said.

"Last night's sleep did wonders. Besides, it's time we plan our next move. Where's Kip and Arlo?"

Arlo appeared in the doorway and called Kip down from

the roof. She trudged into the room a minute later, and soon, all six conspirators gathered around the kitchen counter. Grey missed Westing less than Callan, but even the cruel swordhand's advice might have proved useful. To Grey's immense surprise, though, Bow took the lead.

"Here's how I see things," Bow said, his voice quiet but steady. "We've destroyed Arndak's mines and Estril's chimney, leaving only Devum and Ventrahl running at full capacity. It'd be a mistake to sabotage the First Servant's stockpiles, so we're left with planning how to destroy Devum's mining operation."

"That's the thing," Kip said. "We tried to find a way. There isn't one."

"Why?"

"Estril's troubles prompted a lockdown, so we'd have to bring down Devum's entire mountain to keep the miners from reaching vum."

"Grey can use the vum to detonate the mountain. Devum's volcano will provide the fuel for its destruction!"

"No Blaster can spark a reaction on that scale," Jeanne said. "It'd take enough pure vum to kill anyone." She paused for a moment. "Oh, I see…"

"What?" Kip asked.

"Grey is immune to the harmful effects of aerostacy."

"Still, we'll need to breach the volcano and plant marble throughout the mountain, enough to set off a chain reaction."

"A skilled Flyer can do it… for example, you, Kip."

"Didn't you listen? They locked Devum down tighter than Echore. Blasters guard every entrance, and flying bondmen patrol the skies."

"I'll disable the guards," Grey said. Estril's tournament proved his superiority to typical soldiers, even if he lacked the skill to confront the First Servant or his maramor pets.

"And what about the Pillar soldiers garrisoned outside the

mountain?" Kip asked.

"We seal them inside," Jeanne said. "I've studied Devum's maps. The barracks lay at the volcano's foot, a perfect spot for an avalanche. If I promise to delay the soldiers, you and Grey can climb the mountain until you reach an elevation beyond the alarm bondmen. Grey will handle the guards while you fly into the volcano's mouth to distribute the explosives."

"Wait," Grey said. "How did you learn about the guards?"

"We retrained Ventrahl's dolls to spy for us, just like Westing planned. They've been gathering intelligence here and across the Empire, and our latest reports contain detailed information about aerostatic mining operations."

"Alright," Grey said. "Let's do it. Let's go blow up a mountain."

"What, now?" Kip asked.

"Why wait? We have momentum. I say we keep going, then leave for Ventrahl."

"Hang on," Bow said. "We still need to develop the plan. Dilan, go fetch the map so we can figure out timing, escape routes, and fallback procedures."

"Fine," Grey said, sitting. He itched to move, to fight. The First Servant had nearly killed him, and he yearned for revenge.

"I suppose it's decided," Jeanne said. "We'll—"

A knock at the door interrupted her, and they all jumped to their feet. Grey pulled Agony's Joy from his scabbard while Bow tiptoed and pulled it open to expose Westing standing in the doorway.

Chapter 25

"I'm back," Westing said with a cheerless grin. His eyes stuck to Grey and never left, even as Kip flung her arms around him, running her hands down Westing's sinewy arms, which bore fresh scars. Raised lines of white flesh disappeared beneath his shirt and reappeared on his thin neck to converge at a large patch of scar tissue at the top of his glistening, bald head. His hands, which he'd once held in tight fists, now hung at his sides, fingers twitching. Grey noticed only Westing's eyes, unblinking, unmoving, and alive with a ferocious anger. Westing had never been quite sane—not since Grey had known him—but Westing's wild eyes confirmed to Grey his total descent into madness.

"You survived the maramor," Jeanne said.

"Barely—and only because it had far more interest in chasing Grey." Though Westing responded to Jeanne, his eyes remained locked on Grey.

"But where have you been?" Kip asked. "We assumed you were dead. I mourned for you, dad." Westing's arm trembled, and Grey noticed his right eye twitch. Whatever Westing had experienced during the past six months may well have been worse than death.

"Grey left me for dead."

"It was a reasonable assumption," Grey said, forcing his

voice to stay calm, as one might around a wild animal for fear of it attacking.

"I will always survive, no matter what horrors the First Servant inflicts upon me."

"How?" Kip asked, stepping back. She led Westing inside so Dilan could shut the door, which interrupted Westing and Grey's staring match.

Westing leaned against a kitchen stool as he said, "When the maramor left to chase Leigh, it collapsed the entrance to her green paradise inside Arndak. First, I had to wait for my broken leg, ribs, head, and arms to heal, surviving on the vegetables from Leigh's garden. When I recovered enough to move, I dug myself out. Without dak, the process took months. It wasn't hard to track Jeanne through the Array, so it's good the First Servant hasn't connected the dots."

"If we had known…" Jeanne said.

"Yes, yes. Hindsight, right? But now I am back. Months of labor strengthened my resolve to ruin the First Servant. So let's return to the matter at hand, shall we?"

"You should rest," Kip said.

"I'll rest when the First Servant is dead."

"Westing, I'm glad you're alive," Grey said. "But our rebellion is larger than you'd been told, for our friend Callan was a shifter who organized rebel cells across the Defiant Empire. Please, listen to your daughter's advice. We've already destroyed Arndak and Estril's mining operations, so seek rest while we enact our plan in Devum."

"You've changed," Westing said, not seeming to have heard Grey's words about Callan's true nature.

"Yes."

"You're no longer a weapon I can aim at the First Servant, so you serve no purpose," Westing said, turning to the others. "I've returned from certain death at your time of need. Forget Devum. We'll leave for Harkk, where we will dismantle the

Array's aerostatic reserves. Without the Array's support, the Pillar will collapse."

"Harkk is not our next target," Grey said. "The First Servant will kill us all if we step one foot in his capital."

"Coward!" Westing shouted.

"Fool," Grey said, anger rising through his chest, turning his cheeks bright red. Bow grabbed Grey's arm, and Grey's anger evaporated. I must be rational, Grey thought. I need the others on my side.

Taking a deep, calming breath, Grey spoke to Jeanne, Dilan, and Kip. "You love and trust Westing, but he's wrong; we must stay in Devum to destroy its volcano before turning our attention to Ventrahl. Harkk is unassailable."

"Please listen to Grey," Bow said. "We must commit to his plan, for he's the only person who might defeat the First Servant. Westing said so himself, before—"

"Before what?" Westing asked. "Never mind. I've known you for years, and I have not led you astray. Why would now be any different?" But Westing was different, and they all sensed it. The anger that once lived below his calm exterior had broken through the surface. Westing's eyes were those of a wild animal darting about the room, searching for prey.

"I'm sorry," Dilan said. "I'm with Bow and Grey. We need to destroy the vum mining operation. Callan is dead, but he left us an amazing gift we should use to prepare for our final confrontation with the First Servant."

"I agree," Jeanne said, reaching out to touch Westing's arm. He pulled back.

"Father, please," Kip begged, seeing the dangerous look in Westing's eyes. "Grey has a point. You've missed a lot while you were gone, so sit while I explain what has happened. I'm sure you'll understand."

"Nothing you say will change my mind, Kip. Nothing, not even from you. You were an infant when the First Servant killed your mother, but to me… to me, it was yesterday. We must strike the Array. Time is not on our side."

"Destroying the Array's stockpiles would be great, but they will resupply if we do not end all aerostatic production first," Bow said.

"We won't give them a chance because we'll topple the Pillar and the First Servant himself." Westing drew his sword and pointed it at Grey. "You've poisoned their minds, and they cannot see the truth in your presence. Because I am still an honorable man, I will give you a choice: leave now, and I won't kill you. Stay, and I will run my sword through your heart."

"No, Westing," Grey said. "I'm not going anywhere." He turned to Bow, and his expression softened. "Bow, I choose to stay and help you and the others topple the Defiant Empire." He turned back to Westing. "If you insist on fighting, we'll fight." Grey lifted Agony's Joy, and Callan twitched against his arm as if eager for battle.

"You're going to challenge me in swordplay?" Westing scoffed.

"I won't hurt him," Grey said, looking at Kip, for he hoped she wouldn't intervene. She managed a curt nod as tears flooded her eyes.

"Don't condescend to me, boy!" Westing shouted. He feigned a direct strike Grey knew would never come. Grey brought Agony's Joy up, already rotating to deflect Westing's true target, Grey's arm. Westing's sword came within an inch of Agony's Joy before he realized Grey's blade would slice his sword in half. He pulled away, his elbow hinging backward before extending to push the tip of his sword forward. Grey hopped aside, then slammed his sword against Westing's pommel, forcing his arm wide. Westing backed away to avoid Grey's low kick, which he'd aimed to topple the wiry swordhand.

As they fought, Grey realized that although Westing moved as quickly as he remembered, Grey had become faster still. He followed Westing, move for move through the kitchen, deflecting each of Westing's strikes to wait for an opening large enough to incapacitate Westing without injuring him. Many times, Grey spotted an opportunity to end Westing's life, but still, he waited. The clang of metal smashing against metal echoed in the enclosed space, and Kip, Dilan, Jeanne, Arlo, and Bow backed into the far corner to avoid getting hit.

Finally, Grey found his chance. When one of Westing's parries went wide, Grey rotated into a roundhouse kick into Westing's sword hand. Westing's blade flew across the room and stuck, vibrating, deep in the wooden countertop.

Westing tried to catch Grey off balance, aiming a perfectly timed punch at Grey's left shoulder to tip him over, but despite Westing's considerable speed, Grey dodged faster. He ducked under Westing's arm and landed a punch at the very top of Westing's abdomen. Westing's lungs deflated as his paralyzed diaphragm fluttered in his chest. A final stomp against the back of Westing's knees dropped the swordhand to the floor.

Westing landed hard on his stomach, with Grey's knee pressed against his shoulders. Before Westing could move, Grey secured his hands with a twine Arlo tossed him. The entire fight had taken a minute, and when Grey looked around the room, especially at Kip's trembling body, he thought further violence might ensue. Though they'd all agreed Grey's plan was better, seeing him fight Westing had shifted the mood.

Bow said, "Listen, all of you! Grey is our best chance at defeating the First Servant. Westing knew this. We all knew this. It's why we searched for someone like Grey for so many years."

"I'm doing the best I can," Grey said, struggling for words to convince the others to trust him. But why should they trust me? he wondered. He'd do anything to keep Bow safe, but that didn't give the others a reason to believe in him. They worked to save the Empire's citizens from the First Servant because they knew the First Servant's actions were wrong and immoral. No, that's not right, Grey thought, considering the others' true motivations. They're selfish, too.

Westing cared only about avenging his dead wife. Kip clung to Westing because he was her only family. Bow lost his parents in the shifter War, which the First Servant started. Callan had sought self-preservation. Even Arlo fought for the transeel's right to continue living their natural lives. Everyone fought because something in their lives pushed them to resist.

"I'm with you," Bow said to Grey. "Always."

I fight for Bow, Grey realized, and that's okay. The confusion that had prevented Grey from empathizing with Kip dissolved. Everyone else has something that they will fight for just as hard as I will fight for Bow. Grey looked at Kip, her eyes red from crying as she squatted by her mad father's side, stroking his glistening head. Grey understood her pain because he'd endured a similar discomfort when he'd almost lost Bow. Empathy settled across his understanding, adding a layer of clarity to his budding emotions. He looked back to Bow, who held his gaze with a smile.

"You get it now, don't you?" Bow asked, and Grey nodded. Arlo, though he was not even human, had withstood as much loss as anyone. He'd lost ten thousand Bows, all those he'd ever cared about or loved. Arlo looked into Grey's eyes, and a tear streamed down his cheek.

"I will follow you, Grey," Arlo said. "Heck, I've been following you around for years anyway." Grey smiled.

"I believe we walk the correct path," Jeanne said.

"I'll fight," Kip said in a choked voice. Then she added, "Whatever it takes."

"Me too," Dilan said.

"Then it's agreed," Grey said, amazed that the others now looked to him to speak. I'm no leader, he thought, but he said aloud, "Let's put Westing somewhere comfortable and get back to planning how we're going to blow up this mountain."

Chapter 26

Grey struggled up the mountain in an insulated suit to protect vum miners against the bitter cold radiating from the icy volcano. Folds of excess insulation bent into deep creases, stiffening Grey's limbs so that hopping became more efficient than walking. Despite diluted dak lending a much-needed boost, hopping in the hundred-pound suit tired Grey after only a couple minutes. It didn't help that Agony's Joy, which was pressed to his back beneath the suit, forced his torso into an unbending line. Still, he was having an easier time than Kip, who had neither dak nor muscular legs to counteract the pounds of marble strapped to her suit. Kip used ril for flying, and they hadn't yet reached a point high enough to avoid being spotted by the bondmen scouts surrounding the mountain.

Kip shouted, but only muffled words seeped through her protective visor, so Grey stopped for a minute to allow her to catch up. "We're not moving fast enough," she said through the foggy visor. Grey pulled Jeanne's map from one of the suit's many pockets, unfolding it with mitten-covered hands. He looked at the map, trying to match the neat elevation lines with their surroundings. Kip snatched the paper, spun it around, and handed it back to him.

"Oh," he said. The square shape on the map now lined up

with Castle Devum, a larger version of its sibling, Keep Devum in Harkk. Opposite the Castle, the volcano's rim loomed, marked on the map as a circle. It seemed they hadn't inched from ground level, for they stood on a ridge just before the mountainside grew much steeper.

"In sixty minutes, Jeanne will trigger the avalanche," Kip said, jabbing the map with her gloved hand. "We have to gain five thousand feet in elevation first."

The wormlike bondman on Grey's wrist lit the four o'clock ridge. Jeanne intended to trigger the avalanche further down the mountain at five, so they needed to take flight within twenty minutes to give themselves enough time to set the explosive marble and escape.

"Walk faster," Grey said.

"I can't. I'm no good on the ground. We won't make it!"

A cursory glance at the map confirmed Kip's words. They wouldn't make it in time. Not unless I carry her, he thought, pulling a canister from his suit and shoving it beneath his visor. A blast of mountain air froze a thin layer of ice to his lips as he inhaled the centered dak. New strength flowed through his limbs, and he grabbed Kip by the arms, pulling her onto his back.

"Hey!" she shouted, but Grey had already started moving, using his increased strength to take larger and larger steps until he built up enough momentum to hop, twelve feet at a time, across the mountain. For fifteen minutes, he continued upwards, taking smaller and smaller jumps as the mountainside grew steeper. Even his dak-strengthened joints weakened, and his knees buckled. He fell flat on his face with Kip on his back. The frozen ground leeched heat from his body, even through the thick insulation, so Grey pushed himself to his feet and helped Kip stand.

"Have we come far enough now?" he asked, handing Kip the map.

"I think so…"

"Alright. Now what?"

"Now, it's my turn to carry you." Kip inhaled centered ril, and she leaped into the air. She hovered above Grey, who tried to grab onto her legs, but that proved impossible in the bulky suit. Instead, she bent her knees and shoved her feet between Grey's arms to lift him from his armpits. Grey figured she'd struggle with the extra weight, but Kip soared into the air, lifting Grey as effortlessly as if he were a feather.

Wind buffeted them, for the bulky suits caught every shift of the perilous mountain air. Still, Grey was impressed with Kip's uncanny ability to use the wind's unpredictable changes to her advantage. She soon had them flying towards the top of the volcano, skimming only feet above the mountain's rocky surface with little help from her maneuvering jets. The ground whipped by in a blur until it disappeared as they crested the volcano's frozen rim.

Though Grey knew at least twelve Blasters dotted the rim, he spotted only one through the thick, cold mist. Kip lowered Grey until they hung about a dozen feet above the guard before releasing him. He dropped like a stone, shouldering the guard over the volcano's rim and dropping to his knees. The guard had no time to shout before he tumbled into the dark interior, disappearing from view.

Kip inhaled pure ril and soared down after him to distribute the marble through the volcano's frozen interior.

Grey inhaled centered vum, and Kip lit up like a lantern. Though invisible to his natural eyes, the sheer amount of explosive marble she carried allowed his vum-powered senses to follow her as she dove. She deposited the largest chunk of marble at the bottom of the deep cave, where it lay like a tiny, blinding sun, then rose to plant every other piece.

Ten minutes passed before Kip soared from the mountain and hovered next to Grey, who peered down into the glowing network of explosive marble. Jeanne insisted that a detonation of that hefty bottom chunk of marble would trigger a cascade if Grey directed the explosion.

I can do this, Grey thought, inhaling a canister of pure vum. The aerostatic gas exploded through his body, sending sparks of electricity to his fingertips, which begged to be released. He paused for the barest moment to consider the hundreds of miners below. I've made my decision, he thought as he released vum's sparks. Grey directed the marble to shatter outwards, ensuring each shard hit another spot of marble. The explosion spread faster than Grey would have been able to track had he also not inhaled centered ahl. Even with the ahl, he lost track of the detonations, so he picked random patches of marble to ignite at will.

The ground shook beneath his feet, throwing him backward from the rim to tumble down the steep mountainside. Kip swooped down and plucked him as he fell, continuing to glide along the slope until the ril left her body, and they both fell near the base of the mountain. By now, the alarm bondmen had screamed their alerts across Devum, and the guard bells clanged. Grey noticed Jeanne had done her job well, for a hill of rocks and dirt covered much of Castle Devum. She'd trapped the militia inside, for only the Castle's towers remained visible above the landslide.

"The explosion must be over," Grey said, disappointed. The ground no longer shook, and all fell silent for a few seconds as the alarm bondmen stopped their squawking. Then something deep below the earth shook, sending an ominous rumble up through Grey's legs. A moment later, another explosion boomed from within the mountain, eclipsing the detonation Grey had himself caused. Burning flames, hundreds of feet high, shot straight out of the cracked mountaintop. An intense heat rushed down the mountain, blowing away all hints of the cold that had lingered until moments ago.

Jeanne came sprinting across the hillside, waving and shouting, "The volcano is erupting. Oh, Echore, it's erupting!"

"Yeah!" Kip yelled back. "I bloody well noticed." She and Grey stripped off their suits. The air had warmed, but Grey still shivered, for the bone-chilling cold lingered in his core. He welcomed the heat, though he knew he wouldn't find it so comforting when the lava spewing from the volcano's rim reached his ankles.

"Let's run," Grey said. "Bow and Arlo await us in the market district, and Dilan should be outside the city limits with Westing."

"We can't abandon the trapped soldiers in Castle Devum," Jeanne said.

"You trapped them there yourself. Plus, we just killed hundreds of miners."

"Those were unavoidable casualties. These are not."

"Don't sacrifice your life for these fools," Kip said.

"We're not murderers. We kill guards when we must, but we do not slaughter an entire regiment. The First Servant won't get any more vum, so let's do the right thing." Grey never expected Jeanne to speak with such conviction. Until now, she'd always seemed to live in the background, thinking and observing.

"I'll help," Grey said. He still carried a canister of dak, plus three injectors with all four gases in their purest forms. Neither Jeanne nor Kip could clear a path, and he didn't want to tell Bow he'd abandoned Jeanne.

"Fine, you two go get yourselves killed. I'm outta here." Kip puffed more ril and soared into the sky, flying away from the erupting volcano. Grey inhaled his last canister of centered dak and shot towards the mountain, with Jeanne following.

Castle Devum rose from the foot of the volcano, and it now spanned a river of boiling water. Its boxy towers glowed red from encroaching lava, and the wall nearest the volcano melted. Grey leapt atop the building, making for the nearest exposed tower. Up close, the soldiers' banging rang in his ears through solid steel.

"Stand back!" Grey shouted. He unsheathed Agony's Joy and stabbed the solid metal, applying gentle force to cut a wide opening. With a dak-enhanced kick, he sent the breached wall toppling inward. A man climbed through the hole and stood, his eyes widening in recognition.

"You again!" Emerson shouted, reaching for something at his belt. Grey had last seen Emerson at Keep Devum in Harkk the night he'd stolen a supply of vum with Westing.

"Don't," Grey said, reaching for Emerson's hand, but it was already too late. Emerson had grabbed a bondman from his belt, a creature Grey had once seen Leigh use in Arndak, and squeezed its torso. A whistle pierced the air, and Grey turned and ran, grabbing Jeanne by the wrist and tugging her.

"What was that?" she asked.

"A maramor's call."

Devum's streets swarmed with people in various states of undress, having risen from their beds in the middle of the night by the alarm bondmen. Since they all fled the erupting volcano, Grey and Jeanne joined the crowd's flow. Ash soon rained down in heavy flakes that stuck to every surface, coating Devum in dark soot. Grey wiped his brow with his sleeve, but that smudged more grime across his face and burned his eyes.

As they neared the market district where Bow and Arlo were supposed to meet them, the crowd slowed, then stopped. Still enjoying dak's increased strength, Grey pushed his way through, emerging into Devum's market square.

Devum's residents lined the perimeter, leaving a wide berth for the maramor that stood in the clearing.

Bow stood across the square and mouthed words, which Grey didn't decipher, while Jeanne pushed up behind Grey and said, "We need to run. Now."

Grey ignored her, for Ezra's words now reverberated in his mind. When Grey had asked Ezra to teach him a trick that might help him defeat Callan, Ezra had replied, "There is no trick to winning a fight. You must outfight your opponent. There is nothing else." Now, faced with the maramor and with Callan's final gift trembling in excitement against his arm, Grey knew what he had to do. Grey stepped into the empty square, and the maramor welcomed him, opening its powerful arms.

A hush fell over the frightened crowd, and though they might only have minutes left until the lava buried them alive, everyone stood transfixed. The only sound now was the deep rumble from the volcano reverberating against Devum's metal buildings. Bow stepped forward into the silence, held his hands outstretched overhead, and pulled his fists apart, breaking the invisible chains as First Servant did so long ago. Grey nodded his understanding.

"People of Devum," Grey said, "the First Servant has ruled the Defiant Empire for ten thousand years. He claims to have freed humanity, breaking the chains that bound us to the old gods, who now lay forever imprisoned in Echore." Echore had risen above the horizon, hanging low in the sky opposite the spreading cloud of ash. Grey extended his arm, and Agony's Joy flew to his hand, pulled up by Callan. He held Agony's Joy aloft, and it picked up the light from the volcano, glowing red against the black sky.

"But we are not free," Grey said. "We mine aerostatic gases in the First Servant's name, and the First Servant kills his people in thanks." A murmur permeated the crowd at this.

"You don't believe me? There are whispers of plague throughout the Empire, of those dropping dead from unknown causes. Entire towns are missing, wiped from the Defiant Empire's maps as if they'd never existed. Faycliff, Arnshu, Shallow Canyon. The list continues."

"Monsters killed my entire family in Faycliff," shouted a woman from the crowd. Grey sent her a silent thanks, though he imagined she likely belonged to Callan's resistance. No one else would dare speak out against the First Servant with a live maramor present.

"The First Servant murdered everyone I've ever loved!" Grey recognized this voice, for Arlo had appeared next to Bow across the square.

"The First Servant also killed the shifters," Grey said. "They died protecting the only hope the Defiant Empire has of survival."

"And what's that?" asked an elderly man.

"Me," Grey said. The old man opened his mouth but shut it when he caught the dangerous look etched into Grey's face. "The First Servant's crimes have touched all of your lives. You all know he has killed many of his citizens. So I say, we must rise. Like the First Servant before us, we must break our bonds and reshape the Defiant Empire in our image. What is stopping us?"

"The obstacle stands before you," Kip said, and Grey raised his head to see her perched atop a nearby building. "The maramors watch our every move. They are unstoppable, invincible, and absolute. None may defy their power." She couldn't have set up Grey more perfectly if he'd put the words in her mouth.

"The maramors can be killed!" Grey screamed as he sprinted towards his foe, which held its arms open, ready to embrace him in its deadly grip. Echore hung over the foul creature as if taunting Grey with its inscrutable, mirrored surface.

Grey inhaled one of his three pure aerostatic injectors, tossing the weighty canister aside as he neared the maramor. With only two more injectors, he'd need to end this fight within the next seven minutes, or he'd be powerless against the deadly fighting machine.

The maramor waited until the last possible moment to move, but when it did, it danced aside with incredible speed, faster even than Ezra. Its claw swiped down towards Grey's back, but he avoided the blow by throwing himself headfirst into the maramor's body. The impact didn't shake the solid beast, but that wasn't Grey's intention. He brought Agony's joy down against the maramor's leg, and the blade struck.

Grey flipped back to see what damage he'd done, but the maramor's thigh remained unscathed. Within a second, the maramor had moved to strike again, and Grey retreated across the square, using Agony's Joy to deflect the maramor's blows until one landed against Grey's upper chest. Though he skidded back, the pure dak protected his body, while the ahl allowed him to keep his balance.

After another minute of defensive fighting, Grey used the second of his three aerostatics injectors, and he took the offensive with renewed determination. He let Agony's Joy slip from his hand so that Callan could swing it in a wide arc. The sword struck the maramor's marble flesh again and again, but it didn't leave a mark because the creature retreated in time with every blow. Its incredible speed negated the blade's impact.

Grey inhaled the last of his aerostatic injectors and fought desperately, trying to discover any way to hit the maramor with all the force his dak-fueled muscles could supply. But no matter how hard he fought or how he altered his attack patterns, the maramor pulled away in the nick of time.

Then the maramor's claw scraped a bloody line across his

chest, followed by a strike to the abdomen. Grey soared across the square, landing near Bow's feet, and though his vision clouded, ahl kept him conscious as Bow inhaled a canister of pure ahl.

A mirrored sphere appeared over Bow's head and floated towards Grey, merging with his soul. Then Bow retreated, and the maramor loomed overhead.

Grey rolled to the side as the maramor's foot shattered the dense stone where Grey had been lying. He sprang to his feet, and Agony's Joy snapped into his palm. The maramor began its next series of attacks, but Grey deflected them easily. He understood the maramor's movements, almost as if he predicted its attacks.

Agony's Joy slid into position to block the maramor's strike, and sure enough, the monster's fist hit the blade. It's like I can see into the future, Grey thought, and he recalled something Bow had explained, how an advanced ahl user could predict the near future. Grey allowed his eyes to flick over to Bow, who stared in unblinking focus.

With less than a minute of dak left, Grey swung Agony's Joy with all his might into the middle of the air where he expected the maramor's next attack. A bang rang through the square after the blow connected with the maramor's shin.

The maramor jumped away, and blue aerostatic gas hissed from a minuscule crack where Agony's Joy had struck. I hurt it, Grey realized, and with the realization came a new confidence. With only seconds left, Grey pounced, gripping Agony's Joy. He swung three times, smashing three more cracks in the maramor's marble flesh. Gas hissed from every opening.

The maramor now let out a continuous, deafening wail as it fell to its knees. During his last moment of strength, Grey jumped high into the air. At the zenith of his arc, he felt something push against his back, and he glanced sideways to see Kip flying in the opposite direction, having lent him considerable momentum. Grey shot from the sky like a vision from his bloody nightmares, with Agony's Joy gleaming a terrible red. Except this time, he was in control, not the Gentleman.

Grey thrust Agony's Joy into the maramor's chest, and the blade penetrated the solid marble. He then lifted Agony's Joy along with the impaled maramor, tossing the creature across the square with tremendous force. When the maramor struck the ground, its body shattered. Blue dak exploded outwards, mushrooming into the air like the volcano's ashy cloud.

An explosion rattled Devum, but the detonation didn't originate from the maramor or the volcano. It echoed from behind Grey, who spun around in time to watch a single crack run down the surface of Echore, dividing the flawless, mirrored exterior he'd known his whole life into two equal halves. The pure aerostatic gases left Grey's system, and he collapsed. Dilan appeared at his side, running his tiny hands over Grey's body to bring Grey back to his senses with ril.

If the volcano's eruption had caused panic, the crack in Echore brought utter animalistic terror. The crowd transformed into a mob, clawing and trampling one another to escape. Grey, Bow, Dilan, and Arlo ran with them, exiting Devum with Kip flying overhead.

"Dilan, I thought you were with Westing," Grey said when they'd pulled away from the mob.

"I was. But Kip came to get me after we secured Westing." They'd arrived at a small ravine where Arlo's carriage lay hidden between two boulders.

"Climb aboard," Arlo said, and they all jumped inside. Arlo's two mule bondmen tugged at their reins, building speed until they galloped across the ground. After an hour of bouncing, they reached the western road from Devum well ahead of the crowd.

"We're safe," Arlo said, pointing to the volcano, which faded in the distance.

"We're going to have to stop," Jeanne replied, then shouted, "Stop!"

Arlo pulled the bondmen's reins hard, and the carriage slowed to a stop just in time to avoid a hooded figure that stood in the center of the road. Grey moved to the front of the carriage and called, "Out of our way!"

The figure lifted its head and pulled back its hood, and Grey gasped, for the First Servant stared back at him.

Chapter 27

"So you've slain a maramor," the First Servant said. His voice was raw, as though he'd aged fifty years, and his skin sagged from his skull in a cascade of wrinkles. Grey remembered him as a vital teenager, but even his crooked stance suggested he wore the body of a much older man. His dark eyes, which hinted at a deep and unstable power, still shone with dangerous intent.

"You can build another maramor," Grey said, standing up and drawing Agony's Joy. If the First Servant intended to kill him, Grey decided he'd rather fight than surrender.

"Statues of my fearsome creatures litter the Defiant Empire, but only four maramors exist. Now it's three."

"Explain yourself," Grey said, gripping Agony's Joy tighter.

"If you insist. I have enough energy to tell you how foolish you are before I go."

"Go?" Arlo asked, his voice trembling with a potent mixture of hope and fear. Arlo no doubt wondered whether the First Servant might end his life, as he had slaughtered almost all transeel. But when the First Servant spoke, he ignored Arlo and addressed Grey alone.

"I've protected the Defiant Empire for the past ten thousand years, and I am tired. Exhaustion has seeped into every bone such that I cannot gain vitality, no matter how I rest. Still… you deserve to understand the terror you've unleashed, Grey."

Grey lowered Agony's Joy. "Fine. Say what you have to say." He dropped from Arlo's carriage and stood facing the First Servant. Based on their past meeting, he figured no amount of dak would stop the First Servant from snapping his neck should the mood strike—but that was true whether he stood his ground or cowered twenty paces away.

"The old gods will return," The first Servant said, raising his head towards Echore. The crack that ran down its center added to its eeriness by splitting the world's reflection into equal halves.

"So you didn't defeat the gods and lock them in Echore, as you claim."

"Oh, I defeated them. For the past ten thousand years, I have suppressed and controlled their wills, but their bodies cannot cease to exist, for they are part of the fabric of our world."

"The aerostatic gases," Grey said, guessing the meaning behind the First Servant's words.

"Estril. Devum. Ventrahl. Arndak. You recognize these as my four great cities, but I named them after the four gods. Isn't it fitting that humanity should abuse the gods' bodies, just as our former masters once sacrificed us to fuel their power?"

"When I shattered the maramor, a tremendous amount of dak exploded into the air. Are you suggesting that I set free one of the four gods?"

"At least you're not stupid, Grey—only unwise. I built the maramors from the flesh of the gods, out of a substance you call marble. It gives their aerostatic bodies physical form. Without it, they become ephemeral gases that we inhale to grant ourselves a sliver of their power."

"There's a price to pay for their power. Aerosticians die young."

"Every gift demands a sacrifice. By inhaling the aerostatic gases, you accept the gods' gifts in exchange for a piece of your soul until you die. Well, not you, Grey. You don't die."

"Why not?"

"At first, I mistook you for a common rebel, but your daring escapes from my maramor proved you were inhaling multiple gases without ill effect. Ten thousand years of experience offered no obvious explanation for your unprecedented ability, at least… not one I would accept. The truth was too obvious to grasp: Grey, you and I are alike."

"I'm nothing like you," Grey said, spitting at the First Servant's feet. He killed only under the Gentleman's command, not because he sought death, while the First Servant slaughtered millions.

"Not in actions, but in body, for we share a creator. I should have realized that Sir Arndak designed you as his servant, just as Lady Estril conjured me ten thousand years ago."

"Arndak didn't create me," Grey said. "My father died in Shallow Canyon in the dak fields when I was a child."

"Don't be daft. That man was no more your father than I am your mother. Why do you suppose Shallow Canyon held dak, only for its fields to dry up upon your departure? I locked much of the god Arndak within the body of the maramor you just destroyed, but he must have regained enough of his soul to direct part of himself elsewhere, to form you."

"I'm not made of aerostatic gas."

"Are you sure, Grey? Must your flesh match that of any other human?" The First Servant's skin hardened, and he looked like a maramor. Grey's hand shot to Agony's Joy, but the First Servant's flesh softened while his face relaxed. "Sir

Arndak meant for you to destroy Echore, Grey, so that the gods would be free to wreak havoc on humanity once again. Why you didn't destroy it long ago is the only mystery left. I'd have figured Sir Arndak would compel you to do so."

"The Gentleman is Sir Arndak," Grey said, shaking his head in disbelief as the puzzle pieces slid into place. Now the First Servant's shock at seeing Sir Arndak made sense.

"The Gentleman? Is that what you call him? Sir Arndak always wore the finest suits because he appreciated how much his gentlemanly appearance contrasted with his unquenchable bloodlust."

"How did he create me?" The world spun around Grey, and he grew dizzy. Bow appeared at his side, helping him to stand.

"He shaped you as Lady Estril built me. It was the gods' constant struggle for supremacy that brought about my existence. Lady Estril grew me from a piece of yellow marble, her physical form, thinking I would tip the gods' unending struggle in her favor after a millennia-long stalemate. The gods had many bondmen from which they drew their power, but no servants with free will."

"Each of the gods consumes the consciousness, or souls, of their subjects. Lady Estril fed upon human souls. Lady Ventrahl drained transeel souls. Sir Devum used the shifter soul. Sir Arndak, though… I never discovered Sir Arndak's source of power. Without taming his fuel, he eventually broke free.

"I was Lady Estril's first servant, able to work on her behalf without direction—unlike her human subjects, whom she tied to her will. We shared the power to feed upon human consciousness, giving us a crucial edge over her three rivals, and she intended to solidify her rule by creating others like me.

"Lady Estril is wise, but she is also proud. Her hubris

blinded her to how my desires differed from her own. She built me to serve her, yet my flexible biology enabled me to consume the other gods' powers as well. Not only was ril at my command, but also dak, vum, and ahl."

"So you took their powers to steal control of humanity from Lady Estril."

"No, I took pity on humanity. Call it youthful fancy, but I did not have the same callous attitude towards life the other gods developed over their eternal lives. I saw the suffering that Lady Estril's people endured. I watched the endless killings, the families ripped apart. So I planned to free humanity from the gods, and to do so, I knew I needed power unlike any the gods possessed."

The First Servant looked towards Echore, and Grey followed his gaze. The mirrored sphere now hung overhead, and Grey almost thought he found his reflection on its polished surface.

"Unsatisfied with her tenuous advantage, Lady Estril built Echore from the cavern below Harkk's western peak. She transformed a part of herself into the purest expression of the human soul, a silver sphere mimicking the invisible halos atop her subjects' heads. Her plan was simple. She would wield Echore like a magnifying glass to focus a beam of full human consciousness into Harkk's palace. Whomever controlled the palace would swell with awesome power… so long as they never left its marble walls."

"That's why you didn't come after me yourself," Grey said. "You sent the maramor because your strength falters outside Harkk." Grey lifted Agony's Joy, readying the blade to strike the First Servant.

"Yes, but contemplate your next move with care. My mind holds information you'll need for the dark centuries to follow."

"Fine," Grey said after a long pause. He would listen to the

First Servant and then kill him.

"Very good. Once Lady Estril finished building half of Echore, I dropped hints that exposed its location to Sir Arndak, Sir Devum, and Lady Ventrahl. They formed an unprecedented alliance, uniting the shifters with the transeel to assault humanity. The ensuing war raged for centuries, so long that the will to fight one another became ingrained within each of the gods' respective societies.

"Lady Estril defended Harkk while I finished creating Echore from her body as she intended. It left a massive cavern within Harkk's western mountain, which Fizzers have taken. When I was young, it was a holy place, the home of the god Lady Estril. Echore was to be her super weapon, and I was to aim this mighty canon at her enemies, using it to divide the other gods' souls into so many pieces that they'd lose themselves. They'd become aimless bits of aerostatic gas with no will.

"After I launched Echore into the heavens, I did as Lady Estril asked. Well, almost. I also included Lady Estril in my sights, along with the other gods. A million humans perished in a day, lending me enough power to blast the gods into diffuse collections of aerostatic gas."

"So the gods were merely vast sums of pure aerostatic gas," Grey said.

"Don't say 'merely.' If you gather enough pure ril in one area, you will wind up allowing Lady Estril to regain control over herself. She would have her willpower again, and her wrath would be unthinkable.

"Even my dilution of the four gases didn't prevent the gods from gathering. Their souls attracted aerostatic gases, so I built four shells to imprison their bodies."

"The maramors."

"Yes. I trapped the gods' souls within the maramors, and I controlled them with Echore's power."

"You didn't store all the aerostatic gases within the maramors, though."

"Just enough to silence their wills. I spread the remaining gas across four separate locations, where I built the Defiant Empire's great cities."

"The aerostatic gases did not stay locked beneath the ground," Grey said.

"Leakage was inevitable, and I planned for it by teaching humanity to harness the gods' power, ensuring the gases would never become too concentrated."

"While poisoning your people…"

"Yes, aerostacy shortens their lifespans, but I calculated that if I grew my population, there's always be enough humans to control the gods. Hundreds of thousands of people would die from natural causes each year, gifting me the power of their souls through Echore, an ability I wielded to keep an iron grip on the gods.

"And it worked for ten thousand years. I sacrificed a small percentage of humanity each year, just enough to keep the gods' wills suppressed, and their bodies contained. I eliminated most transeel and shifters to prevent Lady Ventrahl and Sir Devum from sapping energy from their souls… but I never discovered the source of Sir Arndak's power. As centuries passed, his strength demanded I spend more fuel to fend off his persistent attacks."

"Fuel? You're talking about humanity, about killing the people you had saved from the gods!"

"Ironic, isn't it?" the First Servant asked, his tone deadpan.

"You're growing people to slaughter them," Bow said, speaking for the first time.

"My system evolved in concert with Sir Arndak's shifting tactics. You discovered my farm in the north, where ril speeds up human growth and produces humans ripe for the slaughter. Their deaths empower me, via Echore, to restrain

Sir Arndak."

"That's terrible."

"The alternative is worse, as you will soon discover. Would you choose to destroy humanity, or would you prefer millions of free humans to continue flourishing within the Defiant Empire?"

"I'm not sure," Grey answered.

"Consider the bitter taste of Sir Arndak's personality, his pure malice. His peers are no better. Like I said, you'll see for yourself soon enough. Now that Sir Arndak is free, I have lost control. There aren't enough humans alive today to give me the power to suppress his will. The other three gods will follow. My ten-thousand-year reign has ended."

"Why not help us fight?" Grey asked. "Work with us to discover a different method that doesn't involve mass murder."

"There's no other way."

"Then help us fight. We have a better chance of defeating the gods together than apart."

"Fill your lungs with their bodies, and you'll forever be a leech. Grey, please understand that you hold no power of your own; all your skill depends on the aerostatic gases, while Sir Arndak is power incarnate."

"Then we don't fight them head-on. We'll formulate a different strategy," Grey said, desperate for another answer. He'd thought he'd experienced the worst of the Gentleman, but if Sir Arndak's unrestrained malice eclipsed what Grey had already endured, he feared all was lost.

"There is no 'we.' My plan kept the gods at bay, but you have broken them free. Just as I judged the gods unworthy and shattered their will, so too have you judged me. What follows is your problem. Grey, you are the Second Servant."

Chapter 28

"What do we do now?" Bow asked, but no one heard him. Arlo gazed into the distance where the First Servant had disappeared while Dilan and Jeanne both lowered their heads in despair. Kip bent over an unconscious Westing to wipe sweat from his face, and Grey looked up at Echore, which had begun its nightly descent towards the horizon. When he turned east, he saw the distant sky glowed a fiery red above Devum.

"We'll go to Harkk," Grey said. They'd raced ahead of the mob, but Grey figured that the fastest runners would soon catch up.

"Why Harkk?" Arlo asked, blinking to clear a lingering vision of the First Servant.

"We need evidence that the First Servant told us the truth."

"You expect to find the answers in his palace?"

"Not the palace, no. But perhaps below. Ezra told me he took Agony's Joy into the pit beneath Harkk's western mountain, where the First Servant helped Lady Estril create Echore. I must have been there while the Gentleman... I mean, while Sir Arndak was controlling me. Maybe I'll remember something from my missing two years that will help."

No one appeared convinced, but neither did anyone

suggest an alternate plan. So they climbed aboard Arlo's wagon to begin the long ride to Harkk, taking turns at the bondmen's reins to speed their journey. The bondmen maintained a moderate pace for three days until, early on the fourth morning of their trek, they arrived at Harkk. Grey expected to find the palace in ruins, but Harkk appeared untouched as its twin mountains bathed in the morning light.

"I'll stay here with my father," Kip said. Westing had awoken two days ago, though Grey had declined to untie him. He decided Kip would free Westing if left alone, but he found he didn't much care. I have more significant worries, he thought.

"As you wish," Grey said, leaving with Bow, Arlo, Dilan, and Jeanne.

Bow's Array credentials granted them access to the city, and the sleepy guard posted at Harkk's first ring didn't bother to question them, nor did anyone notice them enter the mountain and begin their descent to the Fizzer cavern. Callan's comforting form squeezed Grey's arm, stirring within him a memory from a year ago when he had followed Callan into the mountain.

The Fizzer cavern appeared as Grey remembered, with oily sludge dripping from the walls and ceilings into a deep pit at the center of the gaping space. Grey tried to envision the First Servant here, transforming Lady Estril's body into Echore, but his imagination failed him. What did the process entail? Advanced aerostacy? Or did the First Servant carve Echore with a chisel from the god's body? Grey doubted he'd ever find out.

A couple of men jeered from the edges of the rotting path, but they fell silent when Grey flashed Agony's Joy at them. Word spread, and no one else approached as they made their way through the shantytown.

"How do we get down there?" Dilan asked when they

arrived at the pit. "We don't have Kip to fly us, and even if we did, we're out of dak."

"You all wait here," Grey said. "I'm going to climb down with Bow." No one questioned him. In fact, in the three days since the First Servant named him Second Servant, they all feared him. Well, all of them except Bow. Even Westing had halted his constant struggle to escape.

"Take this," Arlo said, handing Grey a glowworm bondman. Grey passed it to Bow.

With Bow clinging to his shoulders, Grey climbed, using Agony's Joy to form handholds on the slippery wall where none existed. He descended until the opening closed overhead, and the dim light of the glowworm bondman lit only the surrounding wall. The sludge dripping from above smothered Grey's arms, making it challenging to find suitable handholds.

"There's a platform you can jump to, about five feet away," Bow said, and Grey pushed off the wall, landing on a hard surface that tilted towards the abyss. Looking down, Grey spotted another platform right below, so he and Bow dropped to the lower level.

"This is pretty gross," Bow said, holding up his arm, which was covered in black oil.

"Yeah, we should clean up a bit."

Grey and Bow stripped off their outermost layers of clothing and used their fingernails to scrape off as much dense liquid as possible. This is worse than the sewage bondman, Grey thought with disgust.

"I don't enjoy the smell," Bow said. Grey agreed, for a rotting decay saturated the air and burned his eyes.

Bow held up a glowworm, but the little light showed only more darkness overhead. He and Grey walked to the platform's edge, peeking over the side to spy the curved surface of a mirror like a second Echore. Oil dripped onto the mirror, but its reflective surface absorbed the foul substance and maintained its immaculate appearance.

"Do you remember this place?" Bow asked.

"No. Not really." But that wasn't entirely true. A vague sense of familiarity settled over Grey, but no memories surfaced.

"Allow me to help." Bow inhaled a vial of ahl and placed his cool hands on Grey's temples to send a stabbing pain spiking into Grey's skull. His knees buckled, and he spun away from Bow's outstretched arms.

"What happened?" Bow asked in alarm, helping Grey to sit. "That shouldn't have hurt."

"I've been here before," Grey said, scrambling across the platform. "Hold on to my legs." Grey crawled over the platform's edge and leaned down, using Bow's weight to anchor him. He pressed his fingertip to the mirror, which was warmer than his flesh. When he pulled himself up, he lay on his back as a confusing jumble of memories sprang into view, only to disappear beneath the seething tide of his subconscious.

"I remember trying to break this sphere," Grey said. He pressed his fists into his eye sockets, trying to piece together the images that continued flashing behind his closed lids.

"Break it how?"

"With my fists, with a silver dagger, and with aerostacy. When nothing worked, I discovered Agony's Joy embedded in the platform." Grey ran his hands over the stone, discovering a hole that matched the size of Agony's deadly blade. "I picked up Agony's Joy, and I remember striking the sphere's surface repeatedly, but the leading edge left no mark."

"What else do you remember?" Bow asked.

"Nothing. Nothing at all. But I understand why I'm claustrophobic, at least. Sir Arndak built me from his flesh, a body that the First Servant trapped underground for ten thousand years. Enclosed spaces surface my buried fear of returning to that prison."

"But that doesn't explain why Sir Arndak brought you here to shatter the mirror."

"I guess it's part of the mechanism that gave the First Servant his incredible power. When Sir Arndak failed to disrupt the power source, he sent me to kill the shifters."

"Why them? Better to eliminate humans since their lives give the First Servant his power."

"Their deaths also give him power..."

"True."

"I'm just guessing, Bow. No matter how I focus, I can't remember more. Sorry."

"Don't be sorry," Bow said. "It might take years of our joint work to remember the rest."

"Years?"

"Yeah. Ahl is tricky. You see..." Bow continued speaking, but Grey wasn't listening. He smiled because Bow envisioned them together for years to come, and that brought him a joy so pure he almost choked.

"What're you grinning at?" Bow asked.

"You want to continue helping me." Grey wanted nothing more than Bow's continued company, though he still struggled to understand the emotions driving his wish. Just as perplexing was Bow's intention to stay with someone as confused and broken as Grey.

"We've been through a lot, and I don't intend to give up now," Bow said.

"I've killed people. I've done terrible things."

"So have I."

"Sir Arndak might control me now that he's free. What if I can't stop him, even with ahl?"

"He'll be fighting me, too. Together, we'll defeat him like

we did the maramor."

"I could hurt you, Bow."

"Stop trying to come up with excuses to push me away, Grey. I'm not going anywhere. I…" Bow's cheeks reddened, and he looked down at his feet. Grey had never expected Bow to shy away from his emotions, but now he seemed unwilling to speak.

"What is it?" Grey asked, baffled. Bow's cheeks had lost their intense redness but still glowed in the dim light.

"I love you, Grey." Bow said the words with deliberate care as if trying to savor each syllable.

Grey opened his mouth but found his throat had gone dry. He wanted to say the words back, but something stopped him, a deep fear that prevented him from uttering the simple phrase. He would choose to battle the First Servant again rather than give voice to his feelings, even if he shared them.

Bow took Grey's hand, and Grey blurted, "I love you, too." Now that he'd spoken, a sinking dread dragged at the pit of his stomach. Insane thoughts pounded through his head, irrational questions that he tried to ignore. What if Bow had professed a false love to trick Grey into obedience? Perhaps Bow intended to use him as Westing and the others wished? Grey lowered his head in consternation.

Bow touched Grey's chin, lifting his face. He stepped close and placed a hand on Grey's shoulder for stability before standing on his tiptoes. He leaned in, and his breath touched Grey's lips the moment before they connected. They'd kissed in Devum, but that had been of an accident. This kiss was intentional. When Bow's lips locked with Grey's, Grey accepted the truth of Bow's emotions. All his doubts faded, and he trusted Bow's feelings towards him and his towards Bow. When they pulled apart, tears ran down Grey's cheeks, where he left them to dry.

"What do we do now?" Bow asked again, repeating his

question from three days ago.

"Well," Grey said, thinking, "we set out to overthrow the First Servant, and we've accomplished that goal. Now, we must ready ourselves for a fight against the gods."

"How? The gods are even more powerful than the First Servant."

"We'll discover a way," Grey said, and he believed his own words. He held Bow's hand with firm determination and thought, We'll win because I have you.

Other Books by Alexander Jacobs

Did you enjoy *The First Servant*? Visit AJWriting.com for a selection of Alexander Jacobs' other books!

The Void

An obsessive Riverwalker priest convinces Birch, a dying man, that he is a reincarnated mythical icon destined to restore magic to a world in decay - but nothing is as it seems. Is the void's promise of immortality a blessing, or is it another Riverwalker lie? Birch spends his dying days on a journey that will transform the Riverwalkier religion forever.

The Other Side of Gold

First book in *The Ethereal Kingdom* Trilogy

Cayden's golden eye cast him as a dangerous outcast amongst the other children in his isolated village, and he spends his time daydreaming about a massive tree towering above a diamond city. Little does he know, the city is real. On a quest to discover the secrets of his past, he encounters men made of glittering metal, trees that float through the sky like blimps, and new friends who will help him bring balance to a world thrown into water.

The Ethereal Hand
Second book in *The Ethereal Kingdom* Trilogy

Cayden and Leyna race to unite the witches Perianths, and Sky People before a malevolent entity names Sevron consumes their world. Centuries of fighting and mistrust won't be easy to overcome. Meanwhile, the answers Cayden seeks may be held inside the mind of a young (yet very, very old) boy named Dakota.

His Ethereal Kingdom
Third book in *The Ethereal Kingdom* Trilogy

Years have passed. Leyna never forgave Cayden for his decision to follow Dakota's plan, and she seeks another solution on Earth. As Sevron's unassailable power demonstrates the futility of even the best-laid plans, Cayden searches for answers that may exist beyond their reality.

www.ingramcontent.com/pod-product-compliance
Lightning Source LLC
La Vergne TN
LVHW010541160826
845677LV00013B/2948

* 9 7 9 8 3 6 6 2 2 0 1 5 6 *